MW00795313

STOLEN IN PARADISE

PARADISE SERIES

BOOK 31

DEBORAH BROWN

STOLEN IN PARADISE
All Rights Reserved
Copyright © 2024 Deborah Brown

ISBN: 979-8-9859189-9-1

Cover: Natasha Brown

PRINTED IN THE UNITED STATES OF AMERICA

STOLEN IN PARADISE

Chapter One

The four of us were having breakfast at our favorite restaurant—the Bakery Café. As more rain threatened, we'd bypassed our usual table on the sidewalk and settled on the next best thing: one under the covered patio. If mayhem should break out, it wouldn't escape our notice, as we'd be able to watch everything unfold.

This was our weekly meeting to update the husbands on details that might've gotten left out of the retelling when we got home from one of Fab's PI jobs. To say she rarely said no to a client would be an understatement. Her husband, Didier, was already happy with her, as just yesterday, she'd gotten a call from a new client to investigate a break-in at one of his properties in a questionable area. She'd come to her senses as she headed out the door and shuffled the case off on Toady, a private investigator friend who lived up to his reputation as an ass-kicker extraordinaire.

"Since you're so much better at details than me..." I pointed to my bestie, Fabiana Merceau. What I should've said was that she'd skimp on the details to the point Creole and Didier wouldn't care what happened. Lately, we'd arrived back home in one piece, and that was what they cared about the most. "Make sure their teeth are grinding by the time you're done."

"You're damn annoying," Fab hissed, her eyes shooting sparks.

"Everyone knows that."

The guys laughed.

"You're just worried that Frenchie will cut off the monkey sex." I winked at Didier. Fab and Didier were the perfect couple—both born in France, dark-haired and blue-eyed—and he really understood her. He also didn't try to tame her or hold her back, as long as she brought him along for the ride.

"See what I have to put up with?" Fab nudged her husband's shoulder with her head.

Didier winked at her.

"Okay. Fine. I'll give the update. Then I expect my bestie status back." I grinned at Fab. "This whole week, we were angels; we didn't even think about stepping into the middle of trouble." I waited for our husbands to stop laughing. "Questionable jobs got shuffled off on a-kickers, and that happened more than once." An exaggeration, but it sounded good.

Creole pulled me to his side and brushed my cheek with a kiss. "I sort of believe you."

"Sort of..." Didier humphed. "I'd go with somewhat."

"Same thing," I said, which garnered a chuckle.

"Before Madison launches into wherever she's

going with her retell, what she's said is mostly true." Fab grinned at me: *Payback*. "I'm going to jinx it by saying that this week, my calendar is open—you know that'll start my phone ringing, and as to what kind of jobs will roll in, who knows."

"I've got a surprise for you." Creole brushed my cheek with another kiss.

I made a face. "I don't like surprises and neither do you."

"You're going to like this one." Didier laughed, continuing to grin.

"I suppose you're in on said surprise, and not one hint tossed my way." I stared down Fab, who didn't flinch.

"It's the first I'm hearing of it. I'll be going over the marital rules with my hub later."

Judging by Didier's smile, he was clearly looking forward to whatever Fab had planned.

"I hate to break up this cozy chat we've got going here, but your Porsche just backed out of its parking space, and I know you're not behind the wheel." I shifted in my chair and watched as it took off.

Without a moment's hesitation, Fab jumped up and sprinted out of the restaurant to stand on the curb as her sportscar disappeared out of sight. Didier joined her. She stepped into the street and stood there until a horn honked. He pulled her back to his side and hooked his arm around her as the two came back inside.

"You've got a tracker on it, so it shouldn't take you long to find." I raised my brows.

"What I want to know is how whoever was behind the wheel got past my alarm system." Fab grabbed her phone from her pocket and brought up the app. "We've got to go." She nudged Didier.

"Do you mind —"

Creole cut Didier off by tossing his keys at the man. "Try not to get my truck jacked."

"Not helpful, hon." I nudged him. "Keep us updated," I called to Fab's and Didier's retreating backs. Turning to Creole, I added, "When Fab catches up with the car thief, and she will, she most likely won't kill the person, but they might wish they were dead. I know she's loath to involve the police, but she needs to make that call."

Creole nodded and settled the check. "Are you making me walk?" he asked on our way out of the restaurant.

"Catch," I said, tossing him the keys to my black Escalade. "You haven't gotten to drive the replacement coach." My beloved Hummer had been blown not quite to bits, and as much as I'd hoped, there hadn't been enough left to glue back together.

He held open the door, and I slid inside. When he got behind the wheel, though I already knew the answer, I asked, "Do you have the surprise in your pocket?"

"Five minutes and you'll get the unveiling." He enveloped my hand in his and squeezed.

Whatever it is must be something at the office, I thought as he turned onto a side road that ran along an inlet of murky water. Any chance of catching a glimpse of it was blocked by warehouses and other businesses.

Creole turned onto a deteriorating dirt and cement patch that could loosely be labeled a driveway and stopped at the front gate. He got out, pulled a key out of his pocket, unlocked the gate, pushed one side back, and got back behind the wheel, then drove inside and parked in front of the roll-up door of the warehouse.

I scooted up and peered out the window at the big, rundown building. Some work here and there, and it wouldn't fall down, at least not anytime soon. "Sooo…" I asked after Creole and I got out and continued to stare at the building.

"Patience." He hooked his arm around me and led me to a small door off to the side, then pulled out a key with a green ribbon tied in a bow on it and handed it to me. "Our latest acquisition. And you'll be the one to decide what we do with it."

"Now *this* is a good surprise." I jumped up and laid a big kiss on him. Then I whirled around and surveyed the large lot, taking note of the half-dozen cars caked in grime parked along the back of the property. "So many questions." I unlocked the door and pushed it open, and we stepped inside. The small empty room, which had probably been an office, reeked of mold and mildew, but that was an easy fix. "What's the story?"

"Logger Jensen, who owned this warehouse for thirty years, died recently. His daughter, Troll, inherited the property and wanted to unload it, and fast, as-is. So I made her a cash offer, and she signed on the dotted line."

"Family name?" I arched my brows.

"Didn't ask and you wouldn't either," Creole said with a chuckle.

He opened another door and ushered me into the main area of the warehouse. He hit the light switch, and nothing; the overhead florescent lights were missing. He walked over and fought with the roll-up door to get it to go up, and it creaked in annoyance all the way to the top. Along both side walls were row after row of shelving to the ceiling, and what wasn't boxed up appeared to be an assortment of personal items. The back wall was made up of cages of various sizes, some with locks. In each one, the inventory was stacked every which way, more than a few items appearing to be similar, and the common theme was outdoor equipment.

"Before I forget, is everything that was left behind ours to dispose of? And would that include the vehicles?" The sheer volume of the little I'd seen so far would be intense to get sorted through.

"Troll gave me a set of books, which are at the

office. I casually glanced through them as she was handing them off, and it was clear that Logger had no interest in keeping a coherent set of records. As far as the cars go, unless the titles are in Logger's name, the registered owners will need to be contacted. No need for friendly, just tell them to pick their vehicle up or we're leaving it on the side of the road."

"That sounds illegal." I managed not to snort. "If it were me suggesting ditching the cars, you'd have a fit."

"You're right." He grinned at me. "One more thing you need to know… This deal was a Xander find. Before you ask why he didn't go to you first, it's because I was there when the call came in and told him not to."

Xander Huntington was our Information Specialist and first-rate at digging up anything we needed. He shared office space with Fab and me.

"When I mentioned, more than once, that I wanted to own the whole block, Xander put it out there that he was the man to call with a good deal. I know that in the process, he's made a number of friends that keep him up on what's going on in Tarpon Cove." I made my way down one row of shelves, checking them out. "What kind of business was Logger running? Rent-a-shelf?" I quirked my brow. "In the paperwork that Troll dropped off, was there contact info and that sort of pesky information for all these items?"

"Logger ran this as a self-storage place," Creole

said. "A major factor in Troll's desire to sell is that she knew nothing about the business and had no clue how her father ran it. But knowing you, you can get this organized in a blink."

"Now I know what you're up to. You're hoping this new project will keep me too busy for my other job as Fab's sidekick."

Creole laughed. "My first thought was that my wife wants to own the block, and when this opportunity came up, I thought this transaction would put you one building closer."

I walked over for a closer look at the shelves, making sure not to touch anything, as everything was covered in inches of dirt. It was hard to determine how long this stuff had been stored here, but judging by the filth, a damn long time.

"Does this business have a name? Is it still attracting customers?"

"I've been calling it Logger's, but since there's no signage..." Creole shrugged.

"I'll get with my street peeps and see what I can find out about Logger. Also thinking we may need some legal advice as to how to proceed, just to keep us out of trouble," I said. "Have you given any thought to what we're going to turn this place into?"

"I'm leaving that completely up to you. As we've found out, there's always someone who wants to rent warehouse space. It'll be spelled out in the lease agreement that it damn well better be legal or they can count on getting their butt booted out to the highway."

"Pretty sure it's not legal to put anything about butt-kicking in the lease, but since we'll be meeting face-to-face, it can be made clear then that we're not joking." I air-boxed. We'd leave it out of the lease, but the butt-kicking promise would be made very clear. "After some legal advice, I'll get my crew scheduled so they can get to work cleaning this place out."

"I know the people on your *crew*, and they're always happy to get a call from you, as it means it's going to be *fun*."

"Ixnay on the fun part," I groaned. "That's code for dead something, and I'm not talking bugs." I sniffed the air. "Think we might've lucked out, as I haven't caught a hint of that special smell. To be on the safe side, once the warehouse is cleaned out, I'll give the crime scene cleaner dude a call, and he can rid the warehouse of any and all smells."

"Where did you meet that guy anyway?"

"You know… friend of a friend."

Creole snorted. "Another thing: until we're certain that there aren't going to be any issues with this property, you're not to come here by yourself."

"I can always hire Fab for guard duty, though I'll have to trick her, and when she finds out I lied, I'll have to make her feel bad so she doesn't kill me."

Creole laughed.

I took my phone out of my pocket and walked around taking pictures. It was clear, what with the non-existent lighting, that not all of them were going to be good shots. When I was done with that, I opened an app and made some notes.

"I'm going to have to rethink hating surprises, as this one was great." I pocketed my phone and stood on tiptoes to give Creole a long kiss.

Chapter Two

Back in the car, Creole made a call and found out that Didier was at home, so instead of heading to the office, he drove back to the compound. That was the name given to the block when Fab's father bought it for her and Didier as a wedding present, and it was where we all lived.

Once back home, Creole hit the button for the security gate, drove through, and waited for it to close, done by mutual agreement to keep out trespassers. He cruised slowly down the block. We had one neighbor — Casio, a retired Miami police detective who now worked as a private detective, and his brood of four. There wasn't a car in the driveway, so he wasn't home. Fab and Didier lived at the far end.

Creole pulled into our driveway. Once out of the car, he pulled me into his arms and kissed me. He cupped my cheeks in his hands. "Are you going to behave?"

"It's not on my agenda." I made a face. His tough-guy scowl was a ruse, as I'd seen the flash of humor in his eyes. "If I get the opportunity to go shoot something up, I'll give you a call. How's that?"

11

"If that's the case, and you call before you leave the house, you'll have a happy husband."

"Yeah, okay." Warding off more of the *behave* speech, I laid a big kiss on him, then turned him around and smacked his butt. "You don't want to keep Didier waiting."

Just then, Didier pulled up in the truck and waved out the window. I waved back.

"Don't forget…" Creole made a phone gesture and made his way over to the truck.

Once in the house, I dumped my purse on the bench in the entry and eyed the clock in the kitchen, making a mental bet with myself that it wouldn't be long before Fab was picking the lock and making herself comfortable. I grabbed a cold water, my laptop, and phone. On my way to the couch, I opened the sliders to let in the slight breeze blowing in off the water, then settled back and kicked my feet up. I picked up my phone, knowing I needed a crew to clean out the warehouse, and made a call. Cootie Shine was at the top of my list. He technically worked for The Boardwalk, a company owned by family and friends and run by Creole, Didier, and my brother, Brad. I'd gotten permission a long time ago to snag the man when I needed him. I didn't know how he did it, but he managed to keep everyone happy and had a reputation for doing stellar work.

"Hey Coots," I said when he answered. "This is your fave person in the Cove." I loved the man's growly laugh.

"Bet you're up to something."

"Creole started it." I was in the middle of telling him about our latest acquisition when Fab breezed in through the sliders and threw her sexy self down in the chair opposite me, heaving out an aggrieved sigh. I put the call on speaker so I didn't have to repeat every word and then get admonished for anything I forgot. "What I need is for the two of us to do a walk-through of the warehouse, and you can tell me what to do with the stuff that's been left behind so it can be cleaned up. Dumping it on the curb isn't an option, as I don't want to get in trouble with the code department."

"I know you rent to at least one trash picker at that other property you own. Who better to ask for disposal tips than him?"

I'd inherited The Cottages, a ten-unit property on the beach, and it was filled with an eclectic bunch of guests, which included a couple of regulars. I'd often heard that *eclectic* was code for crazy and knew it to be true.

"I'd rather not involve the professor, as I'd like to get everything disposed of as efficiently as possible. Since he's a major hoarder, it would be difficult for him to part with anything, and then it would end up at The Cottages."

"Okay then. Mum's the word about you having junk galore to get rid of." Cootie growl-laughed. "How about we walk the property first thing in the morning? We'll meet there, and you can tell me what you want done." We agreed on a time and hung up.

"I'm not allowed to go to the property without a bodyguard, and you're it." I flashed a deranged smile at Fab. "You get zilch—in other words, no exchange of favors—just gotta do it out of the goodness of your heart. Now that we've agreed, what's up with your car?"

"Wrecked! Whoever was driving smashed into a pole and took off." Fab's blue eyes snapped with frustration. "The front end sustained all the damage; the front bumper pushed all the way up to the windshield. Didier and I saw what looked like a teenager cut across the road and disappear. We assume he was the thief, as we didn't see anyone else making a quick getaway. Kind of hard to believe he had anything to do with what down… but not discounting him just because he appeared to be so young. Stealing and wrecking the car! I get the latter, but you'd think it'd have to be someone very familiar with electronics to be able to boost my car."

"Where is it now?" I asked.

"The cop that got called to scene had it towed. My insurance company will be dealing with it now. Once the adjuster sees it, I have no doubt that it'll be totaled."

"You're awfully calm. I can't imagine you letting someone get away with jacking your car. You're going to want to know every detail about how they did it so it doesn't happen again."

"That's why I called Xander and asked him to hack into the street cameras and ID the thief. And no, I didn't ask him to farm it out to one of his dicey connections. You have to know that he tells you he does that and then does it himself."

"He goes to jail, I'm kicking his butt. If it's one of your jobs, then know that you'll be the one to suffer my 'tudiness." I eyed her. "If anyone would know if car theft is becoming a problem in the Cove, it would be Spoon." Besides being married to my mother, he owned a body shop—appointment only.

"Tomorrow, I have a bodyguarding job, so I'm thinking I'll have Madeline and Spoon over for dinner, along with everyone else, and have the guys cook. I'll put your mother in charge, because as you know, she enjoys planning big dinners. Another bonus for her is that she loves to tell us all what to do. By then, I should have a picture of the thief, and I can show it to Spoon and everyone else and see if anyone can ID him."

"I vote we sit out on the patio at your house so we can enjoy the amazing view of the water."

Chapter Three

Awake early the next morning, I eased my feet out from under my oldster cats, Jazz and Snow, and slid out of bed, leaving Creole sleeping. I crept out of the bedroom, started the coffee, and took a shower. By the time Creole opened his eyes, I was dressed in jeans paired with a long-sleeved tee. I tucked my Glock into the back of my waistband and tied a sweatshirt around my waist, which I didn't need because the weather was sweltering but which made a good cover for my gun. I stuffed a pair of flip-flops into my bag and slid into a pair of tennis shoes — I didn't expect to be running for my life, but experience had taught me to be prepared.

Creole made his way out to the kitchen and slid onto a stool at the island. I put a cup of coffee in front of him. "Thanks for bringing me coffee in bed." He gave me a once-over... more like checked me out three times.

"I don't have time for antics this morning."

"What are your plans for the day?" he grumbled.

I would have so enjoyed waffling, mumbling a bunch of nothing and watching his frustration grow, that I almost laughed.

"Fine." He slapped his hand down on the island top. "I'll cancel my meeting so I can see what you're up to for myself."

"I'm fetching my bodyguard, meeting Cootie at the present you bought me for a walkaround, and planning to come away with a to-do list." I stopped short of grinning. "Before you start, you know that I was given the go-ahead a long time ago to call Cootie anytime. You also know that no matter what else he's got going on, he'd never let a Boardwalk tenant wait on anything, which is why he's a favorite."

Our family and friends had partnered in a joint real estate venture, and the biggest project to date was The Boardwalk, which consisted of attractions, shops, restaurants, a collection of rides, and a hundred-slip marina. Creole, Didier, and Brad kept busy with The Boardwalk itself and several offshoot projects. Separately, Creole and I had expanded into other real estate projects.

"You could have said all that instead of getting me worked up."

I walked over and put my arms around him. "That would've been no fun at all." I kissed him. "Just know that if I have to behave, then so do you."

"So noted. I'll be interested to hear Cootie's plans for brooming out the property."

"We're expected at the neighbors' for dinner, and it wasn't clear whether that was tonight or tomorrow, as it depends on Mother and Spoon, so you should check with Didier."

"Anything new on Fab's Porsche?"

I shook my head. "She wants to track down the culprit, and her plan is to get info from Spoon."

"Didier wants her to let law enforcement do their job while she picks out a new car."

"Good luck to him."

Creole pulled me up against him. "Don't volunteer to go chasing after a car thief."

"You can't suck the fun out of life."

"I can try."

He was laying a kiss on me when we heard honking out front. He grabbed his mug and rinsed it as he looked out the garden window. "It's Didier and Fab. I'm sure she'll get behind the wheel of your car when she's done making out with her husband."

"Well, at least she'll be in a good mood." I grabbed our briefcases off the entry bench and handed his to him, and we walked out together.

Fab always drove because my driving made her sick. Who knew sticking to the speed limit could do that to a person? I'd admit in a hot second that if we were being chased, I'd rather she were behind the wheel. In a tight spot, she could hold her own and make sure that we got out in one piece.

"Behave, you two." I shook my finger at Creole and Didier and laughed as I slid into the passenger seat of the car. "Head out like you're going to the office, and I'll tell you where to turn."

"Your mother and stepdaddy are coming for dinner tonight. When I told Madeline I was cooking, she made a barfing noise." Fab followed the guys out of the compound and cut across the main highway.

I choked back a laugh. "Did you send her to her room? That's what she would've done to Brad and me, as rude noise-making wasn't allowed."

"I bet you did it anyway."

"Pretty much. Brad and I learned to time it right to stay out of trouble."

"I told Madeline that she was in charge of dinner and let her think it was her idea, since it was clear that she wanted to be the one to plan everything." Fab turned off the main highway and onto the two-lane road that wrapped around the far side of Tarpon Cove.

"Ah Mother… sometimes she's such a sneaky one that she ends up giving us exactly what we want. Knowing you, you got what you wanted, as I know you two agree on almost everything when it comes to these dinners." I jabbed my finger to the left. "Turn onto the concrete patch." It didn't surprise me to see Cootie's truck waiting on us. He'd climbed out and was leaned up against the front bumper.

Fab and I had met the man in the murky waters of Card Sound, and he hadn't hesitated to help us out of a tight situation. Ever since, he'd told us not to hesitate to call when one or the other of us needed anything at all.

"Can't wait to see this place." Fab didn't sound the least bit sincere.

I fished the keys to the gate out of my pocket, hopped out, waved to Cootie, and unlocked the padlock. He shoved one side open, and after some resistance, it started moving, creaking and groaning with every inch. The other side didn't budge, even when he gave it a couple of good kicks. Cootie motioned us inside. Fab pulled in, parked in front of the warehouse, and got out. Cootie went back for his truck and parked next to her. I pushed the gate closed, not wanting to invite anyone to stop for whatever reason.

Cootie got out of his truck, a big grin on his face. "Asked around about this place and found out that old man Logger would store anything for a few bucks, no questions asked. Heard some stories on that score—it'll be interesting to see if they're true. Also heard that most of the people didn't show back up to collect their goods. Don't get paying a storage fee for something you're never going to reclaim."

Instead of inquiring what *interesting* meant, I opted for ignorance. "We need to keep an eye out for any paperwork left behind that will make this cleanup job easier."

"It would probably be faster if me and your bar manager spread the word around town that anyone who ever stored stuff here better come and pick it up, and pronto," Cootie suggested.

I owned Jake's, a dive bar in the middle of town, and the manager, Doodad, could spread news faster than anyone I knew. "That's a great idea. If they don't have paperwork, they'll need a good description of what was stored, as we can't let people just come in and grab whatever catches their eye." Once it got around that the warehouse had re-opened, it would also bring those wanting to pull a con out of the woodwork.

"The downside is the junk pickers looking to make a buck will also show up, offering pennies," Cootie warned. "Depending on what we're working with, I may call in one I know to take whatever's left off our hands."

"Does she have her phone out?" I nodded to Fab, who was walking the perimeter of the property.

"Sure does."

"Take pictures of the license plates or some way to ID the cars," I yelled after her. She turned and shook her phone, indicating she was doing just that. "Whatever we do here, it has to be legal, as jail doesn't appeal to me."

"Hear hear, sister."

"You can have the honors." I tossed him the keys.

Cootie went in through the office and into the warehouse. He pushed up the rollup door, which screeched in annoyance at being bothered.

I stood in the doorway as he walked around and inspected everything.

Fab joined me. "What's going on in here?"

"Another reason you're here is so you can answer that question. The good news is that I didn't smell death-stink the first time I was here and I'm not sniffing it now."

"There's one car over there that I'm betting is worth something, even in its current sad shape. There's always someone wanting an old fixer-upper. Spoon will know what your options are," Fab suggested. "What are you going to do with this place?"

"I'll have to wait and see how it cleans up."

The two of us watched as Cootie removed a small box from one of the shelves, produced a knife, and cut it open. After a quick look, he closed it back up and brought it over to us.

"This is what I heard whispered about." Cootie held out the box for me to take.

I pointed to Fab and stepped back.

She took the box without hesitation, set it on the ground, and opened it.

"You're lucky nothing hopped out or you'd be a dead man," I told Cootie, who was eyeing Fab with amusement.

"Is this what I think it is?" She pulled out an ornamental vase with a cover; it had a narrowed neck above a rounded body. "Appears to be an urn, and..." She twisted off the cover. "Yep, a dead person... the ashes anyway. If you didn't know, you don't get a smell when it's done this way."

"Do we know who the dead person is?" I asked and got a *Why are you asking me?* look in return. "Rumored, huh?" I quickly scanned the shelves. "Does that mean there's more... boxes?"

"I saw several boxes that looked the same... so I'm thinking there's more," Cootie said with a slight smile. "It got to be a joke around town, the number of boxes of ashes that were dropped off here, and it appears some were never picked up. The talk is that most took their sweet time picking up their loved ones. No one had an answer as to what happened if they didn't bother."

Not often speechless, I eyed the box as Fab handed it back to Cootie and he relocated it to one of the shelves.

"The upside..." Fab grinned. "You have an in with a funeral home in town, and you know the guys would love to be part of the solution."

Really. I shook my head at Fab.

"To make this easy, as I'm going through everything, I'll make a list, so you know how to proceed. Then I'll stack the dead people along one wall." Cootie chuckled, then whipped out his camera and walked around, taking pictures.

Fab did the same thing, heading in the opposite direction.

What I needed was some legal advice before I did anything and before getting anyone else involved. I pulled out my phone and made a couple of notes. I'd taken a few steps inside and now moved back under the rollup door to survey both the inside and out, realizing what a major job it was going to be to get the property cleaned up.

I was done and getting bored when Fab came back, pocketing her camera. "Didier told me it was a great deal."

Cootie returned. "There are at least a dozen more boxes."

Swell.

"What I'll do is make a list of what needs to be done, and then we'll talk again and decide how to move forward," he suggested.

"I like the idea of a list," I told him. "But before we touch anything, there are a few legal issues that I'm going to need the answers to, and what to do with the ashes will be at the top of the list. There's also the question of the personal belongings and the cars."

"The good news on the ashes, if you could call it that... on a couple of them, there's a sticker with a name and date," Cootie said.

"Are we done here?"

I turned to Fab, shooting her a look that said, *Be nicer.*

"You two can go on ahead," Cootie said. "I thought I'd stick around and take a few more pictures. When I'm done, I'll lock up. If word hasn't begun to spread already that Logger's warehouse has changed hands, it will, and we don't want any unwanted visitors."

"Agreed there." I handed him the keys. "If you're going by the office..." He nodded. "You can leave them with Lark." The Boardwalk office manager, who was always on top of everything.

Cootie took his phone back out and headed back to the shelves, inspecting them one by one.

"Is it too early for a drink?" I asked as we got back in the car.

"You can't be getting your drunk on, since you're coming for dinner tonight. Besides, you're going to want to be sober when you make an announcement about all the dead bodies that were found. The reactions will be fun."

"It's been a while since one of us has had shocking news at a dinner. Speaking of... I wonder who else Mother invited, as you know how she subscribes to 'the more the merrier.'"

"It wouldn't surprise me if I had a house full. It doesn't bother me in the slightest when I know someone else is seeing to every detail. Madeline has never done a slack job, which is another reason I'm fine with whatever she does."

"Since you're depriving me of the opportunity to get my drunk on, you need to turn left, as I'm going to at least need coffee." As she turned into the drive-through, I reminded her, "Extra whipped cream."

Fab placed the order and got us both an extra-large, putting both cups in the holder.

"Not one word about our findings at the warehouse." I put my index finger across my lips.

"You don't even have to tell me what you're up to—that way, I can be as shocked as everyone else." Fab smirked. "You'll need to arrive early so you can set the table."

"You know I love to do it." And she didn't, so it worked out perfectly.

Chapter Four

Once home, I took a nap, then grabbed a shower, chose a colorful dress, and pulled my red mane into a ponytail. I left a note for Creole and hiked down the beach to Fab's house. I knew Creole would have a hundred questions for me about the warehouse and had decided to make a dramatic show when announcing the day's events. If I had to, I'd remind him of his own words: *We're a perfect couple.* There'd been a few times when no one would've thought anything of his changing his mind about the marriage... but no, he'd stuck it out.

I walked up the steps from the sand to Fab's patio, kicked off one of my slides, and ran my foot through the pool water—the perfect temperature. It didn't surprise me that, looking around, you wouldn't have a clue that guests were arriving in a couple of hours. Maybe sooner, as Mother liked to be early. Probably where I got the same trait. I walked over to the bar refrigerator and grabbed a water; it would do until a pitcher of margaritas magically showed up. I sank into a chair, pulled out my phone, and texted Mother: *How many guests for dinner?* When I didn't get an answer, I

27

called, and it went to voicemail. Based on what I knew of Mother, I tallied up the possible guest count on my fingers.

"What are you doing?" Fab had slipped out of the house and sidled up to me without making a sound. She flopped into a chair across from me.

"Deciding how many tables we're going to need. I'm going to need your brawn to help cart one of the tables out of your storage closet."

Fab flashed six fingers at me. "So that's what you were doing—guest counting." She smirked. "The one that's out all the time is going to be fine, unless you're going to tell me someone's got cooties and we need to spread out."

"How about a favor wager?"

Amongst family and friends, we traded favors like cash, even better than money in most cases. The one caveat—no griping or dancing around when asked to put out.

"Someone who doesn't know you would jump on that, but not me. I can see it in those shifty brown eyes of yours that you're thinking you've got a sure bet. So no thanks." Fab flashed a phony smile.

"Okay, Ms. No Fun. I'm thinking ten to fifteen guests. And I can verify with one call if it's going to be the latter."

"Madeline said—"

I cut her off. "When have you ever known Mother not to invite more people? When you put her in charge, your house is her house."

Exuding frustration, Fab started counting on her fingers, which had me laughing. "I have a family count of ten."

"You're forgetting..." I jerked my thumb over my head in the direction of Casio's house.

"I forgot that Casio and his brood have been adopted into the fold. I suppose he's the one you're going to call?"

"Yeppers." I got back on my phone and called his cell, knowing he'd pick up unless he was running after a lawbreaker. He'd retired from the Miami PD and was now a private detective. He was also a single dad, as his wife had passed away, and picky about the kinds of jobs he'd take, and those with any chance of getting shot at were a big no. "It's Fab and me," I said when he answered, putting the call on speaker.

"Both of you? Can't wait to hear what this is about." Casio's tone said otherwise.

"Are you coming to dinner at Fab's and bringing the kiddos?"

"Why?"

"Do you want a place to sit your butt or are you going to be comfy on the concrete?"

"What if I said I wasn't invited?"

"See you next time then."

"You're invited," Fab yelled, giving me a shake of her head.

"Good thing. Madeline called and talked to Alex. Like all teenagers, he thinks he makes the decisions for the household. They got it worked out, and he informed me that we didn't have to bring anything."

"Bring your party manners, big guy." We hung up. "Now if you could help me cart out one of the tables, I can get started."

We hauled a table out and pushed it up against the one already there.

"We'll leave the chairs for the guys to fetch. If you want to be helpful, I'll take a drink." I flashed Fab a shifty smile.

"You're going to have to wait. We're not getting our drunk on early; we don't want to miss out on anything."

"Yes, ma'am." I walked over to one of her outside cupboards and started taking out the dishes.

* * *

Creole and Didier were the first two through the front door. On their heels were Mother and Spoon, who was loaded down with bags from the Bakery Café, which meant an array of desserts. Once I had a peek at the choices, I'd be sneaking something back to my house. I hugged Mother, and when Spoon had set everything down on the kitchen counter, I enveloped him in a hug. "Be prepared to have your brain picked," I whispered.

He laughed. "The box with your name on it is the only one you better be hiding to hoard for yourself."

"I'm betting that everyone has a box with their name on it, and all of the choices are different."

The front door opened again, and Brad's brood preceded him and Emerson inside, their kids, Mila and Logan, came running over and wrapped us all in hugs. Seconds later, Casio and his bunch came through the patio doors. Alex and the twins, 1 and 2, stood back, because they were cool. The twins had names, but since you couldn't tell one from the other, 1 and 2 worked. Besides, if you did call them by their names, they loved to answer to either. Lili, who was the youngest, came running and lavished us all with hugs.

I met my brother and Emerson as they followed after their kids and hugged them both. "You know how you're always crabbing about being the last to know? Well, you'll be getting a major update tonight." Brad rolled his eyes.

"Looking forward to it," Emerson said.

"How's business? I'd ask if you've taken on any criminals of late, but I don't suppose that happens in family law," I teased.

"Lately, my clients have all been well-behaved."

"The guys are tending bar out on the patio," Fab told Emerson and Brad.

"I don't suppose you have that pitcher you promised me?" I eyed Fab.

"That sounds yum. I want one too." Emerson laughed.

"I'll fix you up, babe." Brad winked at her.

31

Creole came through the door with a pitcher and a glass in his hand, poured me a drink, and handed it to me.

"You're the best." I toasted him. Mother groaned from behind me; I'd recognize the sound anywhere.

"You're going to behave, aren't you?" She gave me the stare that told me I'd better do so whether I wanted to or not.

"What is it you like to say? Oh yes, 'You can't suck the fun out of everything.'" I leaned in and kissed her cheek. "I apologize in advance, how's that?"

Mother hooked her arm in mine. "Let's take this party out to the patio."

We ended up taking our drinks down to the beach so the kids could chase one another around in a game of tag. Casio kept one eye on the kids, staying close enough that he could hear if any of them needed his immediate attention. Someone had had the foresight to line up beach chairs.

"Good to see all of you," Spoon toasted. "I thought we'd get the brain-picking over with now — before we eat and while the kids are out of earshot, since I'm not sure where the conversation is going."

"As you know, my Porsche got stolen," Fab told everyone. "It was wrecked, and I want to know whether car theft is on the rise here in the Cove or I just got lucky. I did get a picture of who I think might've been the thief — a teenager — and if so, it appears that he used a key."

"Using teenagers to commit crimes is quite common now. The adults involved think they won't end up doing jail time if they're caught. They'd be wrong," Spoon said in disgust. "As for the key, if the group is sophisticated enough, they're always coming up with new tricks, and one of them is a small fob that will get the engine started. Forward me the picture, and I'll spread it around and see if anyone recognizes him."

"Are you going to share our good news?" Creole grinned at me.

"You mean the surprise gift you gave me?" I made a shocked face.

Didier winked at me, and it wouldn't have surprised me if Fab had shared every tidbit, as it was too juicy to not do so.

"Why don't you share the news?" I waved at Creole.

He proceeded to tell everyone about the warehouse acquisition. Mother's eyes went up to her brow line. She didn't like the side ventures, as some had come with more than a few problems. She'd have liked me to be involved in anything other than real estate, but she hadn't been explicit with her suggestions as to what else I should be doing.

"I want to thank my bodyguard for her patience and eagle eyes." I toasted Fab. "But most of all my husband for the gift... which included twelve dead bodies."

You could hear a pin drop, even in the sand, and everyone's face had the same look of shock... except for Fab and Didier, who didn't bother to cover their grins.

"You signed off on the building as being smell-free," Creole reminded me.

"I'm not saying they were fresh and just dumped. The condition that they're in, it's not possible to say how long they've been there, as the only one who'd know, the old owner, is dead." I got a couple of head-shakes for that one. "I'll let Fab relay the deets, as she had a closer view of the remains than I did — her and Cootie both."

Fab stood and curtsied, enjoying every minute as she sauced up the details. "Surprised me that not one was stashed in a cardboard box, but in all cases, tasteful urns were chosen."

I refilled my glass from the pitcher that I'd remembered to bring along. I wasn't the only one, as Fab and Emerson also had theirs sitting in the sand next to their chairs. You can't let good alcohol go to waste.

"Word spread, and quickly, that Logger would do anything for a buck, and we're not talking a lot of money either," Spoon told us.

"I'm thinking that before anything in the warehouse gets touched, I'm going to need legal advice. I'll be calling my lawyer tomorrow, unless you'd like to take on dead bodies and maybe stolen cars," I said to Emerson, who didn't look averse to the idea. I didn't know the latter to be a fact, but nothing would surprise me.

"Emerson isn't interested," Brad said emphatically.

"Actually, I think it would be fun, but I couldn't give you good advice. I do want you to keep me updated, as I enjoy hearing about some of the cases that you find yourself in the middle of." Emerson patted Brad's hand so he'd stop his hissy fit.

"I'll take over the warehouse, and once it's cleaned out, we'll figure out what we're going to do with it," Creole said with a shake of his head. It was clear that none of what he'd been told was something he'd expected to hear.

I'd let him off the hook later, telling him I had a few ideas about how to proceed. Once he heard Fab's and my funeral friends mentioned, he'd be relieved.

My phone rang, and I pulled it out of my pocket.

"Really, Madison. You should turn that off," Mother said, barely managing to cover her grin.

I flashed the screen at her, knowing she couldn't see it. But Fab could, and her brows went up. "I have to answer because if I don't, the next time you get arrested, Mother, Cruz won't show up." That had everyone laughing. I shushed them and answered. "Counselor, to what do I owe this honor? Can I put you on speaker, since the family is gathered and they're dying to know what you want? Can't be chit-chat, since you've never once called to do that."

"That speaker business is an odd habit of yours," he half-chuckled, clearly not amused.

Even though that wasn't an answer, I took it as a no.

"I called to thank you for inviting my kids for the week—they're damn excited. I wanted to make sure we're on the same page, and that you have everything covered and nothing is going to go off the rails."

"What are you talking about?"

"Oh no you don't. You better not be backing out by claiming ignorance. Do I need to remind you that I've kept that ass of yours out of the slammer a few times?"

"Calm your shorts, Counselor."

All eyes were on me before, but now they were hanging on every word. Fab got up and jerked on my hand so I'd share the phone.

It was dead silence on the other end.

"When I asked what you were talking about, I wasn't asking so I could come up with a con I could run, having changed my mind. I just need to know a few details. More than one person has lauded my ability to come up with solutions—most of them legal—so I'm sure I can do the same for you."

"You make my head hurt," Cruz grouched. "You're telling me that you don't know that school is out for the week and that underwear-wearing professor is entertaining ten kids in what he's calling Crum's Camp at those cottages of yours?" After a pause, he grouched, "You're awfully silent."

"I thought you loathed him?" No answer to that one. To my knowledge, he hadn't gotten over the prof banging boots with his granny. "Crum has kid rapport, and I've yet to meet one that doesn't like him. So you can bet they'll have a great time." I was shaking my head the whole time, telling myself I couldn't off Crum until Camping Week, whatever that was, was over.

"I wanted to give you an incentive to make sure my kids have a great time. If they do, then the next time you call the office, I'll take the call."

"You know what happens when you ignore me."

"You track my ass down, much to the disgust of my assistant." His laugh sounded rusty.

"Can't wait to meet your kiddos."

"Just making sure we're on the same page." He unleashed another rusty chuckle and hung up.

"What was that about?" Mother asked. "You should've put Cruz on speaker, no matter what he thought of the idea."

"Before you get started, I'm not available for… whatever." Fab flashed me a sneaky smile.

"That's what you think." I jumped to my feet.

Creole grabbed the back of my dress and pulled me down on his lap. "No brawling where the kids can see. Maybe later, when they've gone to bed."

I glared at my husband, who winked. He also hooked his arm around me to make sure I wouldn't start trouble. I repeated the conversation.

Casio unleashed a shrill whistle, loud enough to make everyone flinch. He cupped his hands over his mouth and yelled, "Alex," then jerked his thumb: *Get over here.*

Alex came strutting over, reminding me of his dad. Casio leaned in, and whatever he said, the kid answered quickly, nodding.

"Let me guess—you know what's going on and you're going to fill me on the details?" I directed at Alex.

"We're off school for a week, and the six of us were going to hang with Crum for a couple of those days. Then I heard that some kids he mentors up north got invited. They say the more the merrier." Alex bared his teeth in what was meant to be a smile, another carbon copy of his dad. "When that happened, Crum upped his game, and now all of us are sleeping at The Cottages. Our group is looking forward to it, and probably the others, unless they're stupid. I doubt that, as Crum doesn't have patience for stupidity."

"When is this happening?" Creole asked.

"Everyone's coming to our house this weekend, and then we move to The Cottages on Monday for the week," Alex told him.

"When did all the planning for this go down?" I asked.

"Just a few days ago."

I got a flinty look from Alex, and it was clear he was trying to figure out how to give me the most evasive answers he could. Another trick from his dear old dad. "As you've probably already guessed, I'm the last to know about what's going on. In the spirit of neighborly relations, if anything goes south, I want you to call me." I shot him my own assessing stare.

"And do I get one of those favors that everyone around here is always wanting?"

"With the stipulation that it can't be used for anything illegal."

Alex grinned and nodded. "Deal." He held out his knuckles, and I bumped them with mine. Then he ran back to where the kids were hunting for something that'd just crawled out of the water onto the shore.

"You're a big pussy, having your kid tell me," I said to Casio, who just grinned.

"You asked him." He shrugged.

"Madison Westin," Mother tsked.

"Raise your right hand and tell me you don't agree." Instead of an answer, I got the *behave* stare. "I assume your kids will be partaking in the camping experience?" I eyed my brother.

He held up his hands in surrender.

"I forgot to tell him." Emerson made a face. "But yes, they're very excited."

"Now that Brad knows—and he hates being the last to know—" That got a couple of chuckles. "—be aware that he thinks Crum's a nutjob, so don't be surprised if he whisks you and the kids out of town."

Everyone threw out ideas as to where ten kids were going to be camping at The Cottages.

I was happy when the phone rang, alerting us that the food had arrived.

Chapter Five

The next morning, Creole handed me a cup of coffee and two aspirin as soon as I opened my eyes. I inched my way backward and leaned up against the headboard. "I thought I was pretty well behaved, considering I sucked down every last drop of the margaritas Fab made for me."

With his own coffee in hand, he sank down beside me. "Lots of news last night, and most of it would fall into the not-good category. One bit of good news though: I'm going to take over the warehouse and deal with the remains and whatever else is found."

"If you say it that way, then for sure a raft of bodies will fall out of the ceiling." I groaned as I conjured up the image, which made Creole laugh, so score one for me. "I'm no pussy, and I'm not bailing. I've already got my to-do list started. Thus far, it's only in my head, but I'll soon get it down on paper." The cats were stretched out at my feet, and I rubbed their backs with my toes.

"I don't want you remembering this as the suckiest surprise gift of all time."

"That'll never happen." I leaned into him. "I'm more stressed about the camping adventure and the five kids I've never met. With Cruz's kids involved, no one can be allowed to have a bad time or I'll never get him on the phone again. It's already hard enough. And he might follow through on his threat to have me arrested if I track him through the courthouse again to get his attention."

"Just know that you can shuffle the warehouse project off on me at any time."

"I've got a few calls to make and questions that need answering, and then I'm going to get the cleanup started. But first on my agenda, since time is running out before the kids arrive, is getting over to The Cottages and asking, 'What the hell?' of various people that I should've already heard from."

I'd finished my coffee, and Creole set the mug on the bedside table, scooped me up, and carried me into the bathroom.

After a warm shower, I almost felt like a new person… less hungover anyway. Since I wasn't sure where my day was going to take me, I decided on one of my favorite colorful beach dresses and slid into a pair of slides. I twirled in front of Creole, who'd paired jeans with a button-down shirt. He whistled.

We were halfway down the hall when we both paused at the pounding on the front door. It sounded like a couple of cops.

"Fab knows you're home. That's why she didn't use her lockpick." I chuckled.

"More likely it's because Didier's out there and threatening mayhem if she doesn't wait for one of us to answer." Creole stomped over to the door and threw it open. Fab had her fist back, ready to give it another pounding. "Oh look, it's the neighbor. The dude behind her is the husband that can't control her." Both he and Didier laughed. "Come in." He motioned. "You're in luck; there's leftover coffee."

Both their noses went up simultaneously, as they were coffee snobs and preferred the blends that could grow hair on your chest.

"We're not getting comfortable, as Madison and I need to hit the road." Fab led the way to the island, where we all took seats. "Showing you what an amazing friend I am, I got you an appointment with Tank at the office at noon. Yes, I did promise lunch, and I've already farmed making that happen out to Lark. Thank goodness she knows what everyone likes. Xander's also going to be at the meeting to update us both on any information he's dug up."

"Lunchtime? But you're here now, so what do you need?" I eyed her.

"This is a good one." Didier laughed.

"A client from the old days called..." She ignored my and Creole's groans. Anyone that knew her knew this could be going anywhere. "If you're both done with the noise-making..." Her eyes traveled around the island. "All I need to do is check out an address, and then I'll know if I need to farm out the job."

"What's the job about?" Creole grouched.

"Client confidentiality." Fab smiled at him like he was a stupe for not knowing.

"What's your wife up to?" Creole demanded of Didier.

"You had to know you weren't going to get out of here without some kind of explanation," Didier told his wife, who was fuming. "I'll do the honors. Fab needs to case a building to see if she can get in and out and retrieve the information the client needs without ending up hurt, in jail, or dead. And neither she nor the client even knows if it's there or not."

Annoyed, Creole called out Didier: "This job screams illegal, and you're calmly sitting there with that smirk?"

"I've been assured that this is a drive-by. I also stipulated that I wouldn't handcuff her to my wrist if Madison agreed to go along." Didier turned his smirk on me.

"Here's my offer." I ignored Fab's growl. "I accompany you and make sure you behave, and in return, not a crabby word out of you about stopping at The Cottages, which we can do before or after our lunch appointment. The timing would depend on whether this job is out Miami way, as you know how I love the drive up there." Not.

"Deal."

That was too easy. I eyed Fab suspiciously.

"Just know that your husband's life depends on

you keeping your word," Creole said as he and Fab traded glares.

"And you try to remember, you have my life in your hands." Didier pulled Fab to his side.

The four of us walked out, Fab and I getting in the Escalade and the guys in the truck. Once at the main highway, they turned off and we continued north.

"Where are we going? What's this job really about?"

"The daughter of my client, Austin Raynes, has carved out a lucrative career as a social media star, and her ex is blackmailing her with a sex tape. She doesn't want it out there to follow her the rest of her life, and I can't say that I blame her."

"And since Mr. Raynes knew about your sneaking-around talents from your previous life, he hired you to find it and get it back." She'd be the one I'd call for such a job.

"If I hadn't heard the desperation in his voice, I'd have turned him down." Fab sighed and hit the gas as she shot up Highway One. "You'll be happy to know we're only going as far as Florida City. Xander ran a check, and the ex is living in a rented townhouse there."

"It's been a while since you've done any breaking and entering; are you sure, even if you think it's an in-and-out job, that it's something you want to do?"

"I promised Didier this was just a drive-by, and

I'm keeping my promise." Speeding up the highway, it didn't take long before she turned off and wound her way through a residential area, pulling up to six townhomes in a row—clearly new construction. "Just great, he lives in the middle unit." She parked at the end of the parking lot, got out, and put on her tennis shoes, then handed me an earpiece. "I'm going to walk around the back and check it out. You should get behind the wheel, in case I come running." She didn't wait for a response.

I put on the earpiece and climbed into the driver's seat. "Testing."

"Yeah, I hear you."

"If you run into anyone, you're a real estate agent, checking the place out before you bring your client."

"Good one. Personally, I wouldn't like this place, as there's no security." Fab had rounded the building and was now out of sight. "There's a grassy strip back here and easy access to all the units through their sliding glass patio door."

"What are you doing?" It was taking her too long to round the other end of the building.

"Hold on a second." I heard her rustling around, and she finally made an appearance and cut across the driveway.

I hopped out and got back in the passenger seat, happy not to be a getaway driver. "Does whatshisname live here by himself?" I asked when she got back in the car.

"Tech Harris," Fab said in a tone of voice that implied she'd told me before. "Despite my promise, if the television hadn't been on, I'd probably have gone inside. Getting in would be a piece of cake."

"You could send a couple of Toady's men over here to threaten the USB drive, video, whatever it is he has out of him. Or tie him up and ransack the place. Threaten to dump his remains if he doesn't cough it up."

Nothing scared Toady. He wrestled alligators and then befriended them. Now that he'd started a private security company, Thugs, he only hired like-minded men, who always got the job done, no matter how messy.

"I'm in need of a good adrenaline rush, and this job excites me." Fab was already back on US-1 and headed back toward the Cove. "Didier will like your idea better."

"You could accompany whoever Toady assigns. But I can tell you he won't like that idea, as you're his favorite and he wouldn't risk anything happening to you. I can also tell you that Didier isn't going to want to hear about you tagging along."

"That's two good points for you."

"When you get my bill, you won't think you're so funny." That didn't stop her laughing. "We've got time to go to The Cottages and, with a looming lunch appointment, an incentive to make it quick."

"What are you going to do to about the camping whatever?"

"I'm hoping that everything has all been planned out and all I have to do is crab about being the last to know. But also—and don't laugh or tell anyone—I have a couple good ideas of my own."

"Of course you do." Fab smirked.

Chapter Six

With no traffic and by virtue of not paying attention to the speed limit, Fab flew back to Tarpon Cove in record time. She turned off the Overseas, rounded the first corner, and backed into Macklin Lane's driveway. My manager liked living across the street from where she worked because she hated being the last one to know when something went down. To aid her in that endeavor, she'd had Fab install security cameras. So on the off-chance she did miss something, she could play back the footage.

"How about I toss out a suggestion?" Fab said. "Don't look surprised — it's not like it's my first time doing it." Without waiting for an answer, she continued, "Start with asking, 'What's new?'"

I stared across the street at the ten-unit property that faced the beach. It was made up of individual brightly painted cottages situated around a u-shaped driveway. I also owned the apartment building next door. I eyed both properties, and all appeared to be quiet. From past experience, I knew that could be misleading.

"Why don't I continue my backup role and you

figure out what's going on?" I suggested when we were on our way across the street. Before I could get an answer, the office door opened and out trooped Mac and Rude. Rude had once managed the building next door but had since taken over management of a storage unit that Creole and I had added to our portfolio. She'd hooked up with Cootie years ago, and they were quite the match. Neither said no to anything, and the dicier the better.

"Hi ladies." I only remembered to smile after Fab poked me in the back. My attention went to their feet. Who had on the ugliest shoes? I wouldn't voice that question. I think the women tried to outdo each other in their shoe choices, though neither would admit to it. "Isn't it a little hot—" I mean, it was ninety degrees. "—for fur-lined flip-flops?" Another question I wouldn't ask: *Aren't your feet dripping in sweat?*

"Aren't they the cutest?" Mac picked up her foot and shook it at me. "I'm trying these out before winter hits."

And the temps drop to seventy? "You certainly bring your A-game when it comes to shoes."

She preened.

"They'd make my feet sweat," Fab whispered.

"What about mine?" Rude grouched, shaking her foot. She wore… I squinted. Slides with lacy pink women's underwear across the top. *Okay.* "Those are also quite something. You two been out scouting for shoe finds?"

"We got these bargains at the flea market in Homestead," Mac told me.

"Even better if you got a good deal." I turned to Fab. "What do you think?" The death stare I got almost had me laughing.

"You both are always ahead of the game on footwear." Fab shot me a sideways glance: *So there.*

The two grinned.

"Let's sit in the barbecue area, and you can update me on the latest." We were steps away from that area, where there were cement benches. Its best feature was the unobstructed view of the driveway.

"I've got to get to work. Don't want Boss Lady finding out I was late." Rude blew kisses and ran to her car.

"One thing about Rude — if anything out of the ordinary happens, even a dumpster fire, she gets hot on the phone." I got another poke from Fab. So much for subtlety.

Mac fiddled with her voluminous palm tree-patterned skirt. Appearing frustrated, she balled it up and shoved the material between her thighs, her lower legs now able to catch a little sun. She pulled her phone out of her bra and made a call. "Get your ass out here and explain yourself. You-know-who is here. If you're not here in two minutes, I'll find you and put a bullet in your ass." She shoved the phone back where she found it. "Two minutes, and you'll have your answer."

She tapped her wrist, forgetting she didn't have a watch on.

"How about a tidbit as a thank you to me for not putting a bullet in *your* ass?" Fab told her with a flinty stare.

Mac grinned. No matter what Fab served up, the woman fan-girled.

Less than a minute later, Crum came running through the trees in mismatched ratty tennis shoes and no shirt, his tighty-whities just barely covered with a grass skirt.

"Seriously, you need to have a talk with the man about his undies being *completely* covered. Absolutely no peepshows," I said to Mac, whose glare let me know she didn't want to be the bearer of the news.

"Hello, ladies. Here I am and time to spare."

"Have a seat." Fab said in a fierce tone, pointing to a chair. "If you change your mind and decide to go on the run, I'll find you."

Crum glared at her, letting her know she was a moron. The retired college professor prided himself on his off-the-charts IQ, though given most of his antics, you'd never know that to be the case.

"What in the hell have you gotten us into?" I said, cutting off the stare-down between Crum and Fab. "No pussy-footing around, just straight out."

Crum held up his hands in protective mode. "Upfront, I want you to know I've got this covered. It was one of those situations that started out innocently enough, and then one thing led to another... and now there's eleven kids coming next week."

"I'll take the condensed version, unless it makes my head spin trying to figure out what the hell you're talking about. Then you'll have to start over with the essay version."

"I was tutoring my regulars via Zoom, as they live up in Ft. Lauderdale, when one of Casio's kids raced into the room, and when he saw more kids on the screen, he wanted to know if they were coming to camping week. Then one of them ran off camera and got their mother, and so, of course I invited them. I've got to say it didn't start out as camping anything. Just that the kids had a week off school and they needed someone to make sure they weren't getting in any trouble. Who better than me?" Crum preened.

"You also tutor Cruz's kids?" Fab asked, laughter in her tone.

"I've been called in a couple of times when the kids have major projects they want to ace." Crum's nose was pointed straight in the air as he stared Fab down. "They weren't part of the original invites, but somehow, they found out— word of whatever—and wanted to know why they didn't get an invitation. I went with, 'Slipped my mind.'"

"When were you going to break the news to me that we were being invaded by ten kids?"

"Eleven. I had to get my ducks lined up and be certain that they wouldn't be running amuck. I'm going to need access to the bus." Crum wiggled his brows at me. "I've made a list of field trips, which we're going to vote on when the kids get here, and then go from there."

The old yellow short bus had turned out to be a good buy, as it had gotten more use than I'd have thought when first approached about purchasing it.

"Where are they going to sleep? You better not tell me the beach."

"Maybe one night," Crum threw out.

"Musical beds," Mac chimed in with a knowing nod.

"Just know that I expect you to make sure that there are no hiccups of any kind. And that every kid has a damn fun time."

"We're striving for that." Mac gritted her teeth. "Me and Crum have been brainstorming ways to make it easy on the two of us."

"Wait," Fab said. "I want to hear about musical beds."

"We have one cottage open, plus the one we never rent out, which isn't enough room, so we had to come up with other options, since we're thinking they won't be amenable to sleeping on the floor." Mac's eyeroll told me fat chance that they'd agree to that. "If we can't make it work here, we'll load them up and haul them to the compound. Plenty of beds at your houses."

"If you need absolutely anything at all… call Fab." I pointed at her, in case they'd lost their minds for a moment and didn't know who I was talking about. "She'll also be making regular checks to make sure nothing has gone awry that would subject us to hysterical calls from the parents."

Instead of throwing a fit, Fab grinned at the two: *Gotcha now.*

"Seriously, you better bring your damn A-game," I directed at Crum. "And instead of giving you the 'what not to wear' speech, I'll cut it short: your underwear or lack thereof is not to show. Period."

"The ladies like this look." Crum gyrated his hips.

"That's nice," I said, sounding like it was anything but.

I heard a loud cackling and then singing… off-key. Miss January, an inherited tenant, wobbled down the driveway. Her boyfriend, Captain, had her firmly anchored to his side, or she'd have already been face down. The forty-something looked eighty — besides a hard life, health issues were also a factor.

"Isn't it a little early to be sauced?" Fab eyed the two.

Miss January noticed our attention on her and waved. "Helllooo," she screeched. "We're going on an adventure." More screeching.

"Do you have your phone on you?" Mac

barked at Captain.

He glared and pulled it out of his pocket, holding it up.

"Don't hesitate to call… if…" Mac eyed the man.

Captain nodded, albeit reluctantly, steered Miss January away from us, and the two headed to the sidewalk. We watched until they disappeared from sight.

"Where's the other resident drunk?" Fab asked Mac, who gave her an exaggerated eyeroll.

"Joseph has somewhat dried up, as he claims Svetlana doesn't like it when he drinks too much."

"I'm sure he and his blow-up babe have interesting conversations, and he's sober for all of it," Fab said with a shake of her head.

Joseph was the other of the two inherited tenants, and he plugged along, doing whatever he damn well pleased despite his health issues. Thankfully, he'd stopped ending up in jail every other week. The promise (or threat) that I'd made to stop bailing him out, and no more middle-of-the-night pickups, had gotten him to clean up his act.

"If you're done with the interrogation, I need to get back to planning." Crum stepped backwards a few steps. "Since you didn't object to me using the bus, I'm getting it out of storage and booking the driver." In his typical style, he didn't wait for an answer and just jetted over to the palm trees and disappeared.

"This wasn't as painful as I imagined it would be." I made a face, hoping the entire week was uneventful.

"I'm going to need a vacation after this week is over." Mac held up her foot, admiring her toes. "Still trying to figure out who I'd get to fill in."

"Good luck." Having played office manager a few times, I knew it wasn't an easy gig, as a day could start off quiet and turn into chaos. "You know who to call." I started to point my finger at Fab, and she knocked it down.

The three of us laughed.

Chapter Seven

"I'm thinking, since we're talking about kids, that they won't have high expectations and will have a great time no matter what they do." Fab pulled out of Mac's driveway, staying off the main highway, and took a couple of shortcuts, turning into things that appeared to be people's driveways but got us over to the street where we both owned property. For once, I didn't have to ask her to slow down so we could make sure everything was quiet as we coasted past.

Fab owned two warehouses that she kept rented out. Creole and I owned four, and all would be rented once we got rid of the dead people.

"You've been out cruising the streets in the middle of the night again. Do you take Didier along for these jaunts?"

"He grouches when I sneak out without him, so I give him a heads up when I'm about to leave. He hasn't decided whether he's impressed that I'm able to find these shortcuts or just thinks I'm not playing with a full deck."

"My vote is on the former. I'd also bet that Didier likes being included and not having to hear about your antics after the fact."

"Someone just pulled onto the property next to your new one and behind the gate." Fab pointed over the steering wheel, stopping across the street. "No sign, which isn't surprising for this street. Do you know who your neighbor is and what they do?"

"I'll leave the 'get to know you' business to you." I flashed her a fake smile.

She turned into their driveway and rolled up to the fence. "There's no way to get the attention of anyone behind the gate and let them know you're out here. Why not hang a sign: 'You're not welcome—now git'?"

I scooted forward with a chuckle. "Promise me—since there's no lock on the gate, hence you won't be able to pick it—that you won't be climbing over. There could be dogs, or someone with a gun."

"You're no fun."

"Heard that one before."

Fab scoped out every inch of the property she could see before backing out and making the short drive to the Boardwalk offices. I breathed a sigh of relief that she hadn't jumped out and vaulted over the fence with the 'Hi neighbor' speech, but I wagered that she'd soon be back and poking around.

Just like at the compound, we waited inside the gates for them to close. Fab parked in her space, marked with a 'Tow Zone' sign that she'd had delivered, laughing when she got more than a few questions as to where it came from.

I got out, and Arlo, Lark's Golden Retriever, came bounding over, as he knew I was good for treats, which I tossed to him and he caught. He'd be back for a head scratch once he was done wolfing down the dog biscuits. What caught me by surprise was that Clive, the office manager shared by the second and third floors, had been playing frisbee with the dog.

"Since you've got time to romp around with Arlo, guess we don't keep you busy enough." I eyed him.

"It's my morning break."

Fab turned to me and asked, "Are breaks specified in your contract?"

"You two are hilarious today," Clive said, and we could hear his eyeroll.

"Everyone's inside waiting on you." He flourished his hand. "I'm going to help Lark unload her car." He and Arlo went over to where she'd just parked.

The Boardwalk offices were on the first floor. Two lawyers—Tank, aka Patrick Canon, and Emerson—along with a couple of private investigators—Toady, Casio, and a few guys that worked for them—had taken over the second floor. Fab, Xander, and myself were on the third. Lark, the office manager, handled everything for the Boardwalk office.

Creole, Didier, and Brad were at the conference

table, along with Tank, Toady, and Casio. Word must've gone out that there would be food and plenty of it. I kissed Creole and sat between him and Tank, Fab next to Didier.

"You know you could've called me to help out with that new client of yours," Toady grouched.

"I don't recall telling you what I was doing." Fab glared at the man.

"No secrets around here," he grumped. "Anytime you need something and it doesn't need to be by the book, you call me, and it's done."

"I may take you up on your offer. We'll talk later," Fab assured him, then went on to relay that she'd done a drive-by. She skipped the part where she'd gotten out of the car and cruised the property on foot. "I was surprised that there was such easy access."

"Did Fab tell you about the dead bodies?" I asked Tank, getting everyone's attention. He smirked, and I took that as a yes.

Xander got off the elevator and sat across from me. He tapped the cover of his laptop, which I deciphered as meaning he had information for me.

"Where's Emerson?" I asked Brad. "You may like being the last to know, but she doesn't."

"You know that's a lie. Name one person in the family that likes to be the last to know anything. Just one. Keeping up with you is exhausting." Brad grinned at me.

At that moment, Emerson blew through the door. "I better not have missed anything."

"You're right on time," Fab told her. "Food just got here." She nodded to Lark and Clive, who were coming through the door carrying a mountain of boxes.

"I sent you an email about what steps you should take with regards to your ashes cache," Tank told me, clicking away on his laptop. "Just know that if you're arrested, I'm on call."

"The thought of going to jail isn't humorous." I made a face.

"I suggest that you have Cootie round up all the boxes," Tank added. "Hopefully they're all marked in some way. Once you've done that, give your friend, Sheriff's Deputy Kevin Cory, a call."

Everyone laughed at Fab's loud groan.

Kevin lived at The Cottages, but despite that, our relationship was strained. He thought Fab and I took too many legal shortcuts, and in truth, he was right. But neither of us would admit that to him.

"Thanks to the sheriff, we've got a connection to take our calls. I'll call Officer Cooper, and he can tell his buddy Kevin."

"I know," Fab said, "have Clive make the call."

Having heard her, Clive loudly mimicked the sound of brakes squealing, showing how he felt about being thrown under the bus.

"Before you make that call..." Xander said. "Of the car license plate numbers you sent over, two were reported stolen."

"Of course they were," I said in disgust.

"For both of them, it was right around the same time more than three years ago."

"The cops will have them hauled to impound and then track down the registered owners," Tank informed me.

"Can you find out who owns the properties on either side of our new one and, if they're businesses, what they do?" I asked Xander.

"Already working on that." He winked. A lot of the time, he was one step ahead of our requests, and it appeared this was one of those times.

Lark unleashed a shrill whistle and waved us over — time for food.

Although they clearly wanted to hang back and eavesdrop, Fab, Didier, and Toady made their way to where Lark had laid out everything she'd ordered.

Creole had other ideas and pulled me into a hug. "If you decide you've had enough of your surprise, you can toss it back at any time."

"You know I'm not going to do that."

"What's with wanting to know who the neighbors are?" he asked.

"It's a good idea, don't you think?" His intense stare told me that my response wasn't an answer as far as he was concerned. "Fab saw a truck pull up to the gate to the north, and of course, she wanted to know who the heck it was and was frustrated at finding no bell or any other way to get someone to come running and open the damn thing."

"The people that own property along this street mind their own business and expect others to do the same. You don't have to pass that along to Fab; I'll have Didier do it." Creole grinned.

"When you disappear, never to be seen again, it'll be whispered that I offed you and fed you to alligators as a snack."

He laughed and swept me up into a kiss.

Chapter Eight

So Creole couldn't complain about not being kept up-to-date, I pulled out my phone and called Cootie right then, flashing the screen at my husband. He arched his brows.

"Hey dude," I said when he answered. "How are our dead friends doing?"

Cootie barked a laugh. "They've got their own shelf. I'm happy to move them to wherever you need."

"Based on Tank's advice..." I went on to relay what Tank had said. "I'll report the find to the cops."

"Only two of the boxes weren't labeled. Let's hope the information on the labels turns out to be helpful."

I agreed. We hung up, and I called Deputy Cooper, Kevin's partner.

"Uh-huh," he answered.

"That's not friendly."

"How can I help you, Ms. Westin?"

"Creole and I acquired another warehouse and found some ashes that I assume to be human remains. My lawyer suggested that I call it in."

There was a long silence, and then he asked, "Where is this place?"

I gave him the address.

"I'll be there within the hour." We hung up.

"How did that go?" Creole nudged me. "I should've pulled a Fab and put my ear to yours."

"Cooper kept it professional. He was probably wishing for the umpteenth time that he wasn't our go-to guy."

"You need me to go as front man?" He air-boxed.

"Thinking this is going to be pretty straightforward. But I will make note of that offer and cash in at another time." I eyed Fab and Didier, who'd sat down across the table but also shoved their chairs back, giving me zero chance of eavesdropping on their conversation. "They're up to something."

Creole nodded. "Aren't they always?"

"Hey, you two," I interrupted Fab and Didier. "Your wife has that cagey look on her face—don't let her talk you into getting in trouble," I warned Didier, who grinned. "I'm going to stop at the new property on the way home, and before your nose goes in the air about how you're going to get home, I'm certain Didier will give you a ride."

"You can forget it; I'm going with you."

"Hold up your right hand and swear not to complain." I demonstrated.

Fab rolled her eyes.

At Creole's laugh, I leaned in and kissed him. "Don't forget to behave."

"Same goes for you."

I grabbed my briefcase and crossed the room to Lark's desk. "You're amazing, the way you feed us all, and everyone loves every bite."

"You know, if I started buying leftover sandwiches from the gas station, that could cut down on the lunch crowd."

The two of us laughed.

Lark reached behind her into a bag, pulling out a smaller bag and handing it to me.

I peeked inside and found three cookies. "You're the best." I knew that everyone would leave with their own bag.

In her typical style, Fab showed up at my side and peered at the bag I was shoving into my briefcase. "You could buy your own cookies."

Lark laughed. The two of us waved and walked out to the car.

"Please, you think I'm passing up cookies that I know are good?" I made a face, letting her know that wasn't going to happen.

Fab got behind the wheel and gave the property one last scan before heading to the gate. "What did Cooper say when you called?"

"I figured he'd have a few questions, but not a one; just said that he'd be there within the hour. Pretty sure I heard him grumble something about being certain it'd be a good one before he hung up."

Fab made the short drive down the street, where the gates were open. She pulled inside and parked next to Cootie's truck.

We got out and crossed the driveway.

Cootie met us at the warehouse door. "Hello, ladies." He walked us over to one wall and pointed out a stack of boxes of various sizes.

Right then, two patrol cars turned into the property and parked opposite the rollup door.

"You coming?" I asked Fab, who shook her head in response and slipped outside, going the opposite way. "Hey guys." I waved as I met the two in the middle of the driveway. "It's been a while. Hope you haven't missed the frantic calls."

Cooper laughed. Kevin shook his head.

"Here's the deal…" I told them about Creole buying the warehouse. "There are a dozen boxes inside, of which two aren't labeled, and all have urns inside. Cootie opened one, and it had ashes in it."

"I knew about Logger's 'I'll store anything' business, but ashes?" Kevin scrunched up his nose. "To my knowledge, there was never a 911 call regarding this property or pertaining to the business. Let's hope it stays that way with the new owners."

"One can hope," I said, failing to dial back the sarcasm.

The two officers exchanged raised eyebrows, and Cooper said, "Let's see what you're talking about."

I led the way into the warehouse, and the two traded hellos with Cootie, who led them around, explaining what he'd done. Kevin and Cooper both checked out the boxes.

Fab was back and motioned me to come outside, where we stood at the rollup door. "You'd better be listening. We're not taking a single one of those boxes with us. The Escalade is new, in case you've forgotten, and if the ashes were to spill everywhere, it would be an impossible cleanup. You're not going to get every bit of ash with a vacuum, and then—"

"Would you stop? You've got my promise that we're not transporting those boxes."

"Once they're done checking everything out, I'm going to ask Cooper if they've arrested anyone in connection with my stolen car. I'd ask Kevin, but he won't tell me anything. If it *was* the teen who got access to my car, I've got a couple questions I'd like answered."

"Didn't you have Xander put an alert out? If there'd been an arrest, he'd have found out and passed the info along," I reminded her. "Until you decide on your new purchase, how about I make you a deal on one of the vehicles out in the back of the lot?"

"There's two out there with possible fixer-upper potential, but not interested. You should have Spoon give you his assessment—he'd know whether to fix or junk."

"I already dropped the hint, and he told me

that he'd arrange a time with Cootie to check them all out. But first he reminded me that I need to contact the registered owners. I assured him that I was working on who owned what. He thought it would be easy enough for him to find someone to take all of them off my hands and said that, depending on what we're dealing with, he'd know who to call."

Cooper walked past us, his phone pressed to his ear.

"Why don't you go eavesdrop?" I wiggled my brows at Fab.

"I would if I thought I wouldn't get caught." She clearly thought it over, then followed the man.

Kevin finished laughing it up with Cootie and ambled over. "Unless we have reports of stolen dead people, this may be your issue to deal with—as in something respectful and not the trash."

"I expect you to be in the front row at the group send-off ceremony."

He rolled his eyes. "Your digger friends would probably know if someone had misplaced a loved one."

"They're at the top of my list to call. In the meantime, I haven't gotten around to mentioning that two of the cars in the parking lot were reported stolen a few years back."

"You're not kidding, are you?" he said, his words dripping with sarcasm.

"I wish. As for the rest of the vehicles, all except for three of them were signed over to Logger. The ones that weren't, the registered owner will be contacted."

"Don't be surprised if you don't hear back from them, because if they were interested, they'd have picked them up already. Then you'll have to take it to court."

"In the meantime, I'll let them collect more dirt and grime."

"Do I dare ask what you're going to do with this place?" Kevin asked.

"Make certain to rent it out to someone doing something illegal." I grinned.

"I know you think you're funny, but you're not."

"In all honesty, we haven't decided yet. But I can assure you that Creole and I want someone drama-free." I saw his surprise. "Do you happen to know what the businesses on either side of this one are?"

"That way, the guy restores classic cars." Kevin pointed toward where Fab had seen the car drive in. "The other guy inherited the property from his grandfather, and it's rumored that he lives there. I've heard that he does odd jobs that no one else will touch, or won't do without charging too much money, and he'll do them dirt cheap. Both men are loners and keep to themselves." He gave me a pointed stare.

"What you're saying is skip the meet-and-greet?"

"Pretty much."

I saluted him.

"Point out which cars are stolen, and — not that I don't believe you — I'll call them in before I call out the tow truck." Kevin led the way to where the cars were parked.

I checked my phone for the information Xander had sent and pointed the stolen cars out. All of them were completely covered in a thick layer of dirt. "So what happens once the cars reach impound?"

"The owners get contacted, and if the cars aren't picked up, they get sold or junked." Kevin checked them all out. "What are you doing with the rest of these?"

"Tried to interest Fab in one, since she's rideless, but her nose went straight in the air."

"There hasn't been an arrest on her Porsche. The Cove has been experiencing an uptick in vehicle theft — all high-end, so we're on the lookout."

"The male that Fab saw running from her wrecked car… If it was him, he had to have had some kind of device." I was hoping he'd expound on that.

"Some of these people are smart enough to come up with an illegal alternative. You'd think they could come up with a legal way to make a living." Kevin's phone rang, and he stepped away to answer it.

Cooper made his way over. Fab had disappeared once again, but my car was still here, so I wouldn't be walking.

"There haven't been any reports of missing or stolen ashes, so they're all yours. I'm certain whatever you do will be respectful." He gave me a flat smile.

"What is it with you two? Kevin basically said the same thing. Not sure why either of you would think I'd junk them or some such alternative."

Kevin got off the phone. "Flatbed is on the way." He told Cooper about the two stolen cars. "Be interesting to know if Logger knew. The only reason I think he didn't know is we never got any calls to come out here or anything else associated with the man."

The flatbed made record time and backed onto the property. While Cooper and Kevin went to talk to the driver, I went to find Fab. Cootie was talking her ear off.

"How long are you going to be here?" I asked him.

"Until the cops leave."

"That means we can slip out of here," Fab said, letting me know she didn't want to waste time.

"As for the ashes," I told Cootie, "I'll let you know what we're going to do with them once we've decided."

"If you decide on a funeral, make it raucous." He slapped his knee. "The last one I went to, a brawl damn near broke out, and the only reason it didn't was because this one—" He stared at Fab. "—threatened to shoot whoever threw the first punch. There went the fun. Everyone quieted down and quickly found their seat."

"If I go with some sort of sendoff, I'll take raucous into consideration. Just know that there's no turning down my invite to the final soiree."

Fab jerked on my arm, and I waved as the two of us got in the car.

Chapter Nine

It surprised me when Fab parked at our favorite taco truck. The place was short on looks but they turned out the best food, and thus far, neither of us had gotten sick.

"Something's wrong with me; I'm craving one of their canned drinks." A margarita in a can wasn't my first choice but still tasty.

"Must be the same thing that's ailing me, as it sounds good."

After grabbing our drinks and food at the window, we easily snagged one of the two tables they parked on the dirt. If you squinted, you might see a smidge of water in the distance.

"This will be a quick call," I said, taking out my phone. I called Raul, flashing the screen at Fab, and briefly told him about the remains and that I wanted to find them a final resting place. We agreed on a meeting time in the morning. "Raul wasn't the least bit repulsed when I told him about the find—unless I read him wrong, he sounded excited," I told Fab when I hung up.

"Knowing Raul, his excitement level shot up when he heard the number of remains he'd be getting at one time, and you can bet he'll turn it into a business opp."

I laughed at Fab but knew she was right.

Fab's phone rang, and she took it out of her pocket, glanced at the screen, and made a face. When she answered, did she put it on speaker? No.

I was left to decipher who she was talking to. Since she barely got a word in and her answers were clipped, I assumed a difficult client, and one that was trying her patience before they even got started.

"I'll get right on it." She hung up and pocketed her phone.

"I wouldn't have to ask 'What the heck?' if you used the speaker button."

"I'm going to need your help on this one."

"Until I hear the details, I reserve the right to tell you I'm busy." I returned her stony stare with an amused one of my own.

"That was Gunz, rattling on about finding some relative… or so he thinks anyway. You know that when one of his relatives or one of their friends rings up, wanting a way out of some mess they've gotten themselves into, they always claim a DNA tie, knowing that he's not likely to say no. And they're right."

Gunz was Fab's biggest client. Unlike previous clients, he was adamant that she not put herself in any kind of danger, as he didn't want her getting hurt or putting her life on the line.

"It's a coin toss as to how dicey the request will

get, given that we're talking about one of his so-called relatives."

"Though he claimed Goff Redmond was related, he hedged when it came to where he fit in on the familial line. Even though the relationship was unclear, Gunz posted the man's bail, and the dude has skipped. Gunz wants him found before his court hearing."

"How the heck are you supposed to find this Goff person when you don't know the man and I'm betting Gunz gave you no information as to where to start looking?" I struggled not to roll my eyes. "I'm reluctant to ask, but what did Goff do that he needed bail?"

"There was a car accident, and the two drivers jumped out and got into a fight, each claiming the other was at fault. Goff then picked a fight with the cops. It was suggested that alcohol may have played a part and a blood test was taken, but Gunz hasn't heard the results yet. After he sprang Goff from jail, he also got his car out of impound but didn't give him the keys, so he's got no transportation."

"Knowing neither bail nor impound is cheap, it's swell of Gunz to pony up the cash for the maybe-relative. The longer you let the latter go without picking up your vehicle, the higher the costs skyrocket." I shook my head, having dealt with both in the past.

"All I wanted was off the phone, as he was working himself into a tizzy over Goff taking off, and I can't say that I blame him. The good news is that the guy is local, so I'm thinking you can get a lead on him faster than I can."

"Just a reminder that if this Goff person has blown the Keys, I have zero connections," I reminded her. "Have you forgotten that anyone I could call, you also have the number for?"

"He's local, as in Marathon," Fab said, making it sound like *our lucky day*, then laughed.

"Let's say we find him. Then what does Gunz want done?"

"Once again, that's where you come in. You get Goff all shined up and make sure he gets to his court date."

"Did you forget that Gunz is your client and you're his favorite? And — another reminder — that I don't work for him? He tolerates me, but only because the two of us are friends and he has to accept that we're a package deal if he wants your talents. He's not going to appreciate you shuffling the job off on me." Fab grinned, enjoying that I was irked off. "Here's my counteroffer: I accept the job, along with your help, under the condition that when I call Gunz, he takes my call, and when I hit him up for a favor, he puts out without any grumbling. Or Plan B: You make the call and get me what I want."

"Done."

"That was too easy." I cleaned up the trash and threw it in the nearby can. "Text me a pic, take me home, and I'll get on it."

Chapter Ten

The next morning, I finished off my coffee and set up shop on the kitchen island. The first person I emailed was Doodad, aka Charles Wingate III— not sure how he came up with the nickname and never asked—sending *need to find this guy*, along with a picture of Goff. Knowing he'd want more info, I saved him a reply by sending Goff's name plus, *A drunk relative of Gunz's that needs to show up for a court date.* Before clicking send, I added, *Reward if you locate and get me an address before he traipses off.* I refilled my coffee mug and downed half of it before checking my emails, but no response... yet.

My appointment with Raul and Dickie was fast approaching, so I texted Fab, *Be here in ten minutes.* I went down the hallway to the bedroom, scratched the cats, and grabbed a pair of slides to go with my casual A-line dress the color of seawater and scooped my hair into a ponytail.

It didn't surprise me at all when I walked out of the house to find Fab in the driver's seat. "When are you replacing your car?" I asked as I slid inside.

"Didier asked the same thing last night. I told

him no need, since I drive yours all the time."

"What happens when you want to impress someone by showing up in an overpriced ride?"

"Good point." She nodded.

"In case you've forgotten, first stop is the funeral home, and then I'm flexible after that," I said as Fab turned onto the highway and headed over to Tropical Slumber.

The building that housed the funeral home had undergone numerous incarnations, and you'd never know it got its start as a drive-through hot dog stand. Only the old-timers knew and still joked about the smell.

"Are you planning on one big funeral for the dozen strangers or does each one get their own send-off?"

"Thinking a group deal. Won't that be fun?" I struggled not to laugh. "You might want to un-pinch your nose. If you asked Mother, she'd tell you there are severe health issues caused by doing that."

"Speaking of... you know if you want Madeline to show up at the service, you're going to have to trick her. You better not tell her that whichever option you go with was my idea."

"Like she'd believe that." I shook my head. "Since Raul has had overnight to think about this, pretty sure he's already got an idea or two that won't involve a circus."

Fab pulled into the parking lot and parked opposite the red carpet. The front door opened, and Raul stuck his head out and waved.

The two of us trooped inside, and I took the seat just inside the door. It should have my name on it, as where I sat never varied. I smiled at Dickie, who'd claimed his usual chair on the other side of the room and wasn't looking as pale as usual. I didn't want to stare, but he might've gotten a little sun, giving a tad bit of color to his pale pallor.

"Sounds like you came into quite the find. Anyone else might have thrown the boxes out," Dickie said, his face pinched at the thought. Cremation wasn't his favorite option, as he prided himself on his dressing-the-dead skills, making them look their best for their final hurrah.

After a short conversation, Fab and Raul took seats along one wall. Fab must've gotten the word that there weren't any recently deceased in the viewing rooms or she'd have taken off for a look-see.

"I'd talked to Logger a few times over the years and, when he mentioned that he stored remains, told him that he could bring them here and we'd make sure they were handled with respect," Raul said with a huff. "He assured me that eventually all the remains got picked up. Apparently, that was a flat-out lie."

"Raul just shared a really great idea that he had with me," Fab told me.

"I knew you'd have a solution." I smiled at the man.

"Not sure if you know this, but we acquired the land that backs up to this property, and we've just finished construction on an outdoor mausoleum." Raul's smile let us know he was satisfied with how everything turned out. "As for your ashes, before we do anything, we'd need to try contacting the family members, if possible. If any of them aren't willing to step up, then those urns can go into one of the crypts, which were built to hold either a coffin or urn. If we're able to get all the names, or even some of them, we'll have a plaque made."

"Don't want to hear any argument about this being a freebie, because it's not." I gave him a stern stare. "There's good news: only two of the boxes don't have a name. As for the others, I'll have Xander try to track down a relative."

Raul smiled his thanks. "How about a tour?" He motioned for Fab and me to follow, Dickie joining us. He led us out the door, around the back, and across the perfectly green and groomed lawn to their newest addition, a mausoleum constructed in white marble.

"You did a great job," Fab told him, and I nodded.

Raul and Dickie both loved the praise.

"We're going to add some seating and a few more things, as we want it to be inviting," Raul told us.

We continued to walk around and gradually made our way across the patio and around to the front door.

"When the boxes are ready to be picked up, give us a call, and we'll arrange to have them brought here," Raul offered.

I was effusive in my thanks, and we both got back in the car.

"I can't believe how smoothly that went," Fab said, honking and waving as she cruised out of the parking lot.

I'd breathe a sigh of relief when the boxes were out of the warehouse. "Love all the additions those two keep making. They've turned it into a very swanky place. I forgot to tell them that I plan to arrange for some advertising to show my appreciation for making this so easy. All of which I'll run by them first."

"Raul's never going to object to getting a spotlight shone on their business," Fab assured me.

My phone rang, and I pulled it out of my pocket. Jake's. "Let's hope this isn't another dead body at the bar. I'm only discounting that possibility because had that been the case, the call would've come in earlier."

Before I could say anything, Doodad asked, "How much is that finder's fee for your friend Goff?"

"This is now a group call." I hit the speaker button. "Gunz is picking up the tab, so name your price."

"Hmm... I'll give it some thought, and by the

time you get here, I'll have it figured out."

"You're saying that Goff's at Jake's?" Fab demanded.

"He's here alright. But no worries about him going anywhere, as he's feeling peaked after a night of getting his drunk on." Doodad chuckled. "You on the way here or what? Know that whatever you plan to do with the man, you didn't arrange for that service in advance and I'm kind of busy right now, so..." He hung up, but not before I heard someone yelling his name.

"What *are* we doing with Goff?" I asked Fab as she hung a u-turn.

"I suppose that depends on what kind of shape we find him in. Don't forget that in addition to being shined up, he needs to be sober and whatever."

"'Whatever' is clear." I scrolled through my phone and called Shirl, who now had her own concierge nursing service. "Hey girl," I said when she answered.

"When you're all sweet-sounding, that means something's up." Shirl chuckled.

"I've got a drunk to deal with — one of Fab's clients, who's now both our problem — and it's out of our skill set." I gave her a heads up and put her on speaker, then launched into the backstory.

"There's a clinic up in Homestead where he can dry out," Shirl suggested. "But he has to want to do it. It's not one of those places that will force him to stay."

"Goff Redmond is his name. He has a court date coming up, and it's in his best interest not to show up drunk... that's if he wants to stay out of the slammer."

"My suggestion is that once he's sobered up, you hire someone to stay by his side until his court appearance. Knowing you, you can make that happen."

I heard the humor in Shirl's tone. "We're about to have our first meet-and-greet with the man. If he's amenable, would you find out if we can take him to Homestead?"

"No problem with that. Then come by here and I'll ride along with you to make sure all goes smoothly," Shirl said.

"We're taking you up on your offer," Fab said. "A while back, we had another drop-off of the same sort, and the woman jumped out of the car into traffic. It would be nice if that didn't happen again."

I winced, remembering that episode.

"I can promise I won't let that happen," Shirl assured us. "I'll call you with an update, and by then, you'll know if this Goff person is going to agree to a road trip."

Just as we hung up, Fab pulled into the parking lot of Jake's, which sat at the back of the property. She passed the lighthouse, which had been payment for one of those vague jobs she did. I wanted it to pay for the space it took up, but Fab wanted it to sit there and look regal. We turned at the far corner of Junker's, an old gas station that had been transformed into an antiques store that specialized in garden items. Junker and his wife looked down their noses at dealing with the public and preferred to deal only with store owners who bought in bulk.

Fab parked at the back entrance of Jake's, and we entered through the kitchen. Cook's door was closed, and since his car was right outside, it meant he was in a meeting. I waved to the line cook, who had on earphones and was dancing around behind the grill.

Kelpie, the bartender, was holding court and entertaining the regulars by gyrating around, showing off her dance moves in a full neon skirt that barely covered her cheeks and a top that showed off every curve. The men hung on her every word. She pointed to the deck, letting us know that we'd find Doodad at the reserved table.

Fab held up two fingers, and quick as a flash, Kelpie handed over two glasses with soda in them. We took them outside and sat across from Doodad.

"Is Goff tied up out here?" I looked around and didn't see anyone.

He snorted. "Goff got his drunk on here last night. Threw him out at closing. He made his way out to the dumpster and took a nap. Didn't want to disturb him, lest he empty what was left in his stomach on my shoes."

"Think he's still there?" I asked.

He turned his tablet around to display the screen, which showed where the man was passed out. I'd momentarily forgotten that we had cameras all over the property. The good thing was that we didn't need to use them very often.

"Are you on friendly terms with this Goff character?" Fab asked.

"I know of him, how's that? He's come in a few times. Never started any trouble," Doodad told us.

"Thinking about this, I have no clue how we're supposed to get the man sobered up unless he cooperates. If he's a habitual drunk, what are the chances?" I filled Doodad in on the details I'd left out previously.

"You can't force the man to go on the wagon," he said, as though it were a no-brainer. "If you get Goff to the place and he says, 'Not interested,' they're going to be damn annoyed that you wasted their time. Your options are: get an a-kicker over here to scare him into not fighting it or, better yet, have Gunz deal with his own family issue."

"Well?" I looked at Fab.

"Before we get Gunz involved, we need to go out to the dumpster and see if Goff is amenable. Someone could take him a cup of coffee and a couple aspirin." Fab stared at Doodad, who didn't flinch.

"I'll go out and see what kind of shape he's in." He wrinkled his nose. "Just know that my price just went up."

"If we can sluff this job off on you—meaning the less we have to do cleaning him up and transporting him north, the better—it'll mean more cash, favors... you name it." I smiled craftily.

Doodad stood, grabbing his laptop. "Not sure what the hell I'm doing, but for that kind of bribe, I'll get the job done." He disappeared back inside the bar.

I barely got my mouth open before Fab pointed at me. "You're not bailing on me." Her finger wagged. "Don't deny it's on your mind, as I can see it in your eyes. This is where I remind you that you already agreed to help me on this one."

"Wasn't thinking about bailing, per say, but I was remembering our last trek to the sober place and thought we were in agreement on never making another run."

"I recall it playing out that way. But... should this kind of situation come up again, we're going to have to remember from the start so we can refuse. For this one, we're stuck and have to just suck it up."

"With our odds, it will happen again," I grumbled and got a glare.

Fab pulled out her phone and scrolled across the screen. "Might as well watch the action."

"I'll pass on a ringside seat. The only thing I want to know is when it's a done deal." I answered my ringing phone after looking at the screen—Shirl. "Good news?"

"It could be. They're willing to take him in exchange for a donation, but he has to be agreeable. No forcing him."

"Doodad is having a talk with the man now." I updated her on our conversation.

"If Doodad's smart, and I know he is, when he confronts Goff, he'll use the threat of Gunz kicking his a— all over town. That would motivate anyone that knows the man to at least make an attempt to get their life in order rather than risk getting their you-know-what handed to them."

"Hope you're right."

"One more thing, if you manage to dump this whole mess in Doodad's lap and he ends up making the trek to Homestead, my offer is still on the table. He can stop here and pick me up."

"You're the best."

"Not so much, as you'll be getting a bill. So let me know." Shirl laughed and hung up.

"Sorry, I forgot," I said in response to Fab glaring a hole through me for not putting it on speaker. "Thinking we've lucked out here..." I repeated the conversation. "The only thing is Gunz is going to get hit with some extra charges. If he flips, then let him know that on the next job, he can damn well do it himself."

"If Gunz gets what he wants, we won't hear a single complaint about him picking up the tab. One thing I know for certain is that he doesn't crab about the cost of anything. Probably because he knows that I don't inflate the bill."

"If we pull this off without having to deal with drunk dude, in addition to the cash, you and I both are going to be tossing in some favors," I told her. "And I suspect that Doodad would also like a couple from Gunz."

"He might have to settle for getting them from the two of us," Fab said with a knowing smile. "Gunz would rather pay and never hear about it again."

Doodad came rushing back out onto the deck. "Making progress. Goff is stretched out on the couch in my office. He's not the slightest bit interested in making the trek to the sober place, thinking he can dry out on his own." He rolled his eyes. "Told him to think of the bigger picture, which is that it would keep Gunz off his back."

I told him about Shirl's offer.

"Nice of her, but I've got this handled," Doodad assured me. "Thinking we'll make the trip north, and if the place doesn't freak him out, Goff will stay."

"Let me tell you what happened when the two of us made the same jaunt you're about to go on." Fab launched into a retell of our previous trip.

"The woman jumped into traffic?" Doodad asked, making a face. "My luck, Goff would get run over, and that's all I need. I'll be calling Shirl after I check on the man and make sure that he didn't hit the exit when I turned my back."

"When you don't have a clear idea of what you're dealing with, backup is always a good idea," I told him.

"I'll give you a call when we've got his butt checked in."

Chapter Eleven

It had been a quiet couple of days, and I was enjoying what was left of my coffee, hoping for a day of doing nothing, when an alert pinged on my phone that someone was at the front gate. I looked at the security feed and stared at the cop car, an officer standing next to it. It smelled like trouble to me, and since I didn't recognize the man, I decided to pretend I was in the shower. I waited to see what Fab was going to do, as I knew she was at home. Nothing. She must have been "showering" also. After a few more attempts, the officer got back in his car and left.

I called Tank, and when he answered, he asked, "Is this about being invaded by law enforcement?"

"Fab's assessment?" Damn, the woman was fast.

"I'll tell you what I told her: 'I'll check into it and get back to you.'" We hung up.

I headed down the hallway to take that shower and change, as my neck hairs told me that the cop would be back. I chose a short-sleeved black dress with a full skirt and paired it with slides, then strapped on my Glock. I wondered where the cats had disappeared to but found them in the kitchen, being fed some delicious morsel that Fab had brought with her. It never surprised me when she made herself at home.

"Did cop dude have the wrong address?" I asked.

"Just talked to Tank and assured him I'd relay his update. The cops would like to talk to us about the job I did in Florida City — Tech Harris. Before you shoot questions at me, as I can see them coming, I don't know anything else. Except that Tank is going to arrange for said discussion to happen at his office. He's calling back with the time."

"That so-called job was nothing more than a drive-by," I reminded her. "Unless you went back and I haven't heard about that yet."

"So you know that I do listen, I hired Birch to go flex his muscles and scare the blackmail evidence out of the man. Didier didn't think much of the idea, saying I better be prepared to step up if Birch goes to jail. Before we could get into a fight, Birch called and told me that he'd have to put the job on hold for a couple of days, as he had a last-minute emergency job from Toady. He said he'd call as soon as he got back to the Cove."

"Aren't you questioning why the police are involved? And want to talk to you? But I can tell that you have something else up your sleeve. What is it?" I had a good idea what was coming next but wanted to hear it from her.

"Thinking that if Harris is included in this sit-down, it may be a good time to check out his place. If we can leave before he does, we might be able to get to his townhouse and have a look around before he gets back."

"Oh brother. You need to keep a low profile until you find out exactly what it is the cops want. Walking into something blind..." I shook my head and picked up my phone.

"Who are you calling?" Fab demanded.

"Creole. I'd like to stay married, and hiding this..." *No way.*

"He already knows. Probably anyway. Since I called Didier."

I got voicemail and left a brief message about what was going on, not wanting to rely on Fab's version. "I'll be in the office later." I hung up. "I think we need to talk to Tank before giving any kind of statement and you need to forget going by Tech's place until you know what this meeting is about."

"You're right. And no rubbing it in."

I grabbed my briefcase and purse and followed Fab out to the car. I opened the back door and dumped my stuff next to hers, then slid into the front. "Since you were hired to check this guy out, are you going to out your client? Do you have some kind of confidentiality clause?" If it were me, all bets would be off once the police got involved.

Not bothering to answer, Fab roared out of the compound and over to the office, for the most part sticking to the speed limit. Once in the parking lot, we got out and rode up to the third floor. There wasn't a soul in sight on the first floor.

I walked into my office and nodded at Xander, who was, as usual, pounding away on his keyboard. "Did you hear about Fab's latest case? The guy who was running a blackmail scheme? Now the cops are involved, and anything you can find out before we have our sit-down with them would be swell." I flicked through my phone and gave him the address, happy that I'd saved it. "I'm afraid to ask if you've got anything else for me."

He chuckled. "I'm working on a list of the dead people that were found at your new acquisition. Also know that word went out that if you've got stuff stored at Logger's, you better get over there or it's being tossed. Not sure if that last was said. It was also made clear that without a description, and a good one, people won't get squat."

Just great. I winced at the announcement going out before I was ready to deal with anyone showing up. "I have a few more questions that I need answered before I give Cootie the go-ahead to clean out the warehouse. If he hears that crazies might be showing up in an attempt to load up on freebies, he might pass on the job."

"Cootie won't be the least bit intimidated; he'll see it as fun." Xander gave a knowing nod.

Fab breezed into the office. "Tank is ready for a chat."

I stood and turned to Xander. "If we're led out of the building in cuffs, get a bondsman on the phone."

"Got you covered." He grinned.

Fab and I rode down in the elevator in silence and walked into the second-floor office. Tank, who was sitting at the conference table, waved us over, and we took seats across from him.

"The news isn't good. Tech Harris was found dead."

What? Dead?

"Contacted a friend on the force," Tank continued. "He told me that a security camera picked up the two of you at Harris's townhouse." He nodded at Fab. "You were caught creeping around the building while your friend here sat in the car."

"Natural causes or...?" I shuddered. "Was he found the same day we were there?"

"It's being investigated as homicide, and as to the discovery of the body, it was a couple of days after you were there."

Fab told Tank about her client and why she'd been hired.

"Did anyone else who didn't live there get picked up on the security cameras?" I asked.

"Not that my friend mentioned."

Fab went on to tell Tank that she'd tried to contact her client to let him know that the cops had questions for her about Harris and she was going to answer them all truthfully, but it went to voicemail. "I don't feel comfortable putting him in the line of fire without at least informing him first."

"Did your client know that you'd found a current address for Harris? If so, did you give it to him?" Tank asked.

"When I first called with an update, I told him that I'd found an address but wanted to verify it first, and yes, I gave it to him."

"What about you?" Tank looked at me.

"It was one of those jobs where my role was ride-along chick." I ignored Tank's snort. "If Fab had come running back to the car with someone chasing her, I'd have shot them." Fab grinned at me.

"No need to repeat that last part." Tank's phone rang, which he answered. "On my way down." He hung up and told us, "Don't run off," then left.

I took out my phone and texted Creole: *Cops are on the way.*

Seconds later, I got a response: *We're on our way back to the office.*

"Husbands will be here when they get here."

"That's helpful." Fab rolled her eyes.

The door opened, and a quick glance at Fab told me that we were both surprised to see Kevin and Cooper stroll in.

"I thought we were getting some unknown

officer to grill us." I smiled at the two officers. "Good to see friendly faces."

Cooper laughed.

"Nice to see you too." Kevin shot me a fake smile. The two men took a seat at the conference table.

Tank got them sodas.

"When the sheriff heard you two were involved, he reassigned us," Cooper told us.

"I'm certain you both remember the deal that was made, don't you?" Kevin eyed us.

There was no need to remind him that we didn't negotiate the deal.

"We remember." Fab returned Kevin's stare. "As I recall, the deal we made with your boss was that cooperation goes both ways. I can see that you haven't gotten over wanting to arrest the two of us, but you're going to have to wait. When was Harris offed? That way, I can begin with my alibi."

If they were surprised that we knew the man was dead, it didn't show.

"We're not here to arrest you," Cooper assured us. "We want to know why you were skulking around the property where the man lived."

Kevin sat back with a smirk.

To my surprise, Fab told the two about her client and didn't leave out anything she'd done. "If, as suggested, you have security footage from the property, it'll back up when I was there, how long I stayed—which wasn't very long—and that

I didn't leave with blood all over me."

That last wasn't helpful, but I refrained from voicing that.

"And you?" Cooper nodded at me.

"I'm sure your footage verifies that I never got out of the car." I shot Kevin a flinty smile, and he barely covered his brief grin. "If Harris was blackmailing one person, it wouldn't be a stretch to think he was doing it to someone else… or getting ready to do it again. That would give you more than one suspect to choose from."

"What are you going to tell your client?" Cooper asked Fab.

"That the dude's dead. Pretty sure there won't be any tears shed." Fab met Cooper's stare.

"I'm sure you won't mind handing over contact info for this client of yours so I can get in touch. There's still the issue of whether he did or didn't get back what Harris was using for the blackmail. Did he retrieve it himself? Have someone else do it? If so, they somehow managed to get in and out without being seen." Cooper eyed her.

"All those scenarios are illegal," Tank said with a wide grin.

"I can honestly say that I didn't set foot inside the townhouse," Fab told Cooper. "What about you? You'd know if any blackmail material was left behind, since you had the run of the place. If not you, then another officer. Surely you'd have heard if anything was found."

"That would fall under official information—

need to know," Kevin said.

"Is there anything else?" When neither officer said anything, Tank stood. "If you have any more questions, officers, don't hesitate to call me first, and I'll set up a meeting."

"If you hear anything else about Harris, I hope you let one of us know," Kevin said.

I flicked my thumb toward Fab, *her case*. I wondered if this was the end of it or if Fab had some other trick up her sleeve. I'd bet on the latter.

It didn't escape anyone's notice when Cooper motioned Fab over to the sliders and the two stepped out on the deck. From the looks of it, an intense discussion ensued, and zero chance of eavesdropping.

"What do you suppose that's all about?" I asked.

"I was about to ask the same thing," Tank said. "Thinking I should've been invited. Hope Fab knows when to stop talking."

Kevin also hadn't been invited to the chat and, after grabbing another drink, sat back down at the conference table.

Maybe now was the time to work on the relationship with Kevin... or not; we'd see how it went. "When are you going to lighten up?" I ignored Tank's snort. "Back when, there was a time when we were amicable. It wouldn't be so hard to be pleasant to one another, would it? You know Girl Wonder over there could be useful to you two." I cast a glance at the deck.

"Pleasant?" Kevin's brows went up. "I don't remember those days."

"You get the idea."

"Since I've been ordered to be *pleasant* by the boss, I'm working on it. Just know that if you push the boundaries, all bets are off."

"Got it. I'm about to ask something that could be construed as a favor—could you lighten up on the tenants at The Cottages?"

Kevin unleashed a loud snort, and I heard Tank laugh. "You should be thanking me for stepping in during some of the so-called entertainment that goes on there before someone dies."

"Thank you." I pasted on a crazy-girl smile. "While you're waiting on those two, my lawyer here suggested that I ask if anyone's reported any theft of personal belongings."

"Nothing in relation to Logger. As I told your lawyer, I double-checked, and the man was never once reported to law enforcement and didn't have a criminal record."

"When everything gets boxed up, would you like to come haul it to impound or wherever?" I asked.

Tank burst out laughing.

"You're hilarious. And no. It's your problem. Unless you find an actual dead body, and in that case—call." He eyed me, as though trying to figure out if that had already happened. "If you're paying this guy—" Kevin glanced at Tank. "—

pretty sure he's got a suggestion or two to keep you out of legal hot water. You and your friend should follow them."

We sat in silence until Fab and Cooper finished up. Cooper headed to the door, and Fab came back and sat down.

"Guess it's my turn to find out what's going on." Kevin shoved his chair back and joined Cooper, and the two officers left.

Chapter Twelve

"Tank and I are eager to hear what you and Cooper talked about," I said to Fab. "Kevin even more so. Think his feathers were ruffled at being excluded."

"Cooper wanted to be assured that I hadn't done an inside walkaround. He was interested in finding any evidence of blackmail and whether my client was the only target. He'd checked out all the usual places and wanted to know if he missed any spots," Fab told us. "I ran down a couple of places I was sure he'd already checked out, and he had. Raynes isn't going to be happy that I gave up his name, but I wasn't going to let Kevin and Cooper think I had anything to hide. I did tell Cooper that I'd be telling my client to expect a call. I shouldn't have taken this case. Not because of the murder, but because of what I was going to have to do to retrieve the blackmail material, if it was even possible."

"If you'd had unfettered access to the townhome, do you think you could have found Harris's hiding place?" Tank asked her.

"I'd have stood a good chance, as I'm damn good at finding hiding places where most wouldn't think to look. The interesting tidbit I got was that Harris didn't have a safe, or not one they found anyway. I suspect that the cops will be going back for another look around. I asked whether, if evidence of blackmail was found, the cops would eventually make it public, as I'm certain that'll be Raynes' first concern and I'd like to be able to tell him something... more like reassure him."

"And?" I asked.

"I got a 'depends' answer."

"They bag it, put it into evidence, and hold it until it's no longer needed to make a case. After that, if it's a sex video, then they'd probably destroy it," Tank told us.

"You might want to make it clear to your client, before he goes off his spool, that there was nothing you could do once the police got involved," I suggested.

"Called a couple more times this morning and left a couple of messages; not sure if one set off a red flag, but the phone's now been shut off. It's likely that's the last I'll hear of that client. And in a lot of ways, that's a good thing."

That would be a first — one of her clients gave up and went away? "What have you got for me on my warehouse finds?" I asked Tank.

"Speaking of phones that no longer work, I tried to contact Logger's daughter, and hers has been shut off. Asked Xander to follow up, and he got back to me. According to neighbors, after the money from the sale of the warehouse cleared her bank account, she skipped town and didn't leave a forwarding." Tank blew out a frustrated breath. "My advice is to post a legal notice online. I'd say a newspaper, but who reads those anymore? Not anyone around here. But do it anyway. The type of people that Logger catered to, you'd have better luck getting the word out through your sources. And to cover your... box everything up and hold onto it for at least six months."

"And the cars?"

"Xander got me the contact information for the registered owners, and I've been making calls to inquire if they're going to pick up their vehicle or sign it over. So far, I've gotten zero cooperation. The ones I've talked to thus far wanted off the phone without committing one way or the other. I suspect they thought it was a scam." Tank unleashed a disgruntled sigh. "Hopefully, they'll make a couple calls and find out that I'm not full of it and that Logger's does have a new owner. Even if they make the effort to check up on me, I don't expect to hear back, since none of the cars run, and in their current condition, it would take a considerable amount of money to get them running again."

"If I don't hear back from the owners about recovering their vehicles, I'm going to have them towed to an impound lot where I have an in, as they'll know what to do, it won't be my problem anymore, and I won't be treated like someone trying to pull a con."

"I knew Spoon would come through." Fab grinned.

"As for the dead people—"

I cut Tank off. "Delegated that to our funeral friends. In the meantime, Xander has Clive contacting the next of kin, letting them know it's time to get on the ball and pick up their dearly beloved. If they don't, then the deceased will have a final resting spot at Tropical Slumber."

"Surprised Clive didn't tell Xander to take a hike."

"He thinks it was my suggestion, and I'm good with that. I also expect that no one will enlighten him." I stared at Fab.

"If any of the people contacted know about the Tropical Slumber option and that it won't cost them anything, fat chance that they'll step up." Fab turned to Tank. "Raul and Dickie recently finished construction on an outdoor mausoleum, and they're eager for residents. Gives them more cred if there's a couple of plaques... saying whatever they say."

"I've heard that they never say no to anything."

"If one of your clients is looking for a flamboyant sendoff, Dickie and Raul will deliver," I told Tank. "Just know that they like to keep the fights to a minimum."

"I'd heard that they never say no to any funeral request that can be conjured up," Tank said with a shake of his head.

"Pretty much." Fab nodded. "Madison and I can attest to the truth of that, as we've been guests at some interesting ones."

"What she meant to say was that we were in attendance as guards—to keep the peace—of sorts."

The door flew open, and in walked Creole and Didier.

"About time," Fab snarked.

"We ran into Kevin and Cooper on their way out and got an update. Cooper assured us that neither of you were a suspect." Didier winked at his wife and sat down next to her. "Should you two get taken to jail, be sure to make us your first call, and we'll get you bailed out and give you a ride."

"You're hilarious today," I said.

No, he isn't. Fab shook her head.

Creole dropped down next to me and pressed a kiss on my cheek. "Happy to see that the getaway driver isn't in cuffs."

"You two are quite the comedy team."

Fab jumped up, whipped through her version of the replay in a couple of sentences, took a bow, and sat down.

Our husbands rolled their eyes.

"Never a dull moment." Tank laughed. "What you left out is the stellar legal advice I gave for how to resolve your warehouse issues."

I nodded at Creole, letting him know I'd fill him in later and everything was under control.

"On the way over, we talked about taking our wives to lunch." Didier smiled at us.

"Sounds good," Fab said after a glance at me.

Chapter Thirteen

A girl could get spoiled with two whole drama-free days. The phone didn't ring incessantly, and nothing required my immediate attention. I took advantage of the quiet, kicking back outside on the deck, my feet on the railing, enjoying the light breeze blowing across the water. The view never got old. I downed a cup of coffee and began making progress on my to-do list.

An annoying sound had me looking down at the sand. Fab was running along the shoreline, singing into a bull horn and ramping it up to be as obnoxious as possible. She waved as she crossed the sand and ran up the stairs and onto my deck. I stuck my fingers in my ears. She set down the bullhorn—one of her prized possessions—and flounced into a chair.

"No coffee for you," I said, a finger-shake in my tone.

"No squashing my fun." She picked up my notepad and scanned the sheet. "You've been busy."

"I green-lighted Cootie's crew to clean out the warehouse and store everything at Cove. And I turned over making sure all the required legal notices got published to Clive."

"After it's cleaned out, what are you going to do with the place?"

"No clue. What I do know is that whoever rents it is undergoing a background check to try to minimize illegal activity," I said. "I'd prefer to know the person—friend of a friend or something like that."

"All this tells me…" Fab smirked and circled the paperwork with her finger, "you're free for a ride-along."

"My answer depends on how you answer, 'To do what?'"

"Goff—you remember the drunk? — well… he walked away from the sober house last night, and I need to go pick him up."

"We're going to drive up US-1 looking for someone out for a stroll? It probably won't be difficult, as hardly anyone walks on that road. That's if he hasn't already stuck out his thumb and gotten a ride."

"Xander tracked his phone and reported that Goff took a sand nap last night on a miniscule strip of beach on the side of US-1. So…" Fab said with raised eyebrows, "he shouldn't be hard to locate."

"Then what?"

"That's where you come in."

I unleashed the eyeroll I'd been holding back and made it a dramatic one. "A reminder here:

you have the same connections I do. But in the spirit of friendship and all, I'll throw out a couple of suggestions. Call the no-name motel and book our room, then hire someone to hand-hold. And try for someone with a personality."

"There's a slight glitch. Already talked to Gunz, and he hinted around that he wanted me to take Goff home and keep an eye on him myself."

I laughed so hard, I had to bend over and take a breath. "Gunz's lost his mind."

"Here's my hot idea: you arrange everything and keep my name out of it, and when Gunz finds out, I'll tell him it was a done deal and I couldn't hurt your feelings."

I laughed again. Fab glared. "The only person who'd believe that cockamamie story, or anything else you feed him, would be Gunz." I picked up my phone. "How many days until Goff makes his court appearance?"

"A week from today."

I called Birch, and when answered with a grumpy hello, I asked, "You have the skills to deal with a maybe-drunk that needs to dry out or stay dry, not sure which yet?"

"Yeah sorry, I'm still working the other job." It was clear he was relieved not to be available.

"Maybe next time."

After he grunted, the two of us hung up.

"Rollo probably knows someone," Fab said. "Once we've picked Goff up and see what kind of condition he's in, I'll give him a call. With any luck, there will be someone at the Dump that can be hired to keep an eye on the man."

"Don't you think No Name sounds better than the Dump? The motel has been spit-shined, and the last thing you want is for Gunz to overhear you calling it that." I scrolled across my screen and called Rollo. He didn't answer, but his nephew/cousin/whatever did, and he remembered me and reserved a room. "Now you owe me," I told her when I hung up. "Tomorrow, camping week starts, and I need to put in an appearance. You can come along, and between the two of us, we can make sure that everything is going smoothly and no one's going to get hurt."

"What would make us a favorite is to teach them some sneaky trick." Fab grinned.

"Their parents might not find it so amusing if we get them into any kind of trouble, as in if the cops show up," I said, and the two of us laughed. "I'm thinking the day after tomorrow, I'm going to throw a welcome breakfast at Jake's. There's plenty of fun to be had, and they can party it up until we open at our regular time. By then, they'll be back on the bus to... Crum will have it figured out."

"Jake's is a *bar*."

"Just think of the stories they can tell their parents about getting their drink on. For breakfast no less." I struggled not to laugh.

"You need a reminder that in that group of kids, there are at least two parents that are lawyers." Fab clearly thought I'd lost my mind, and it showed on her face.

"Got it." I saluted.

"Ten minutes." She tapped her wrist, jumped up, and motioned me to do the same. "I expect you out front in tennis shoes and your gunslinger pants." She grabbed her bullhorn and ran down the steps to the sand. When she started singing again, I was happy to get back inside the house.

Nine minutes, and I was back out front, having tucked my handgun into the side pocket of my workout pants. I slid into the passenger seat and asked, "Anything new on the dead guy? How about your client?"

"Nothing on the *dead guy*. The good thing is that there have been no more visits from the cops. As for my sort-of client—and I refer to Raynes as that only because we never really came to an agreement—his phone is off. Probably junked. Calling his office would be a waste of time and would really set him off."

"If Raynes had nothing to do with Harris's death, why is he making sure you can't reach him? The cops, if they want a chat, will show up at his home or office regardless. I doubt that he'd put them off, as it would make them suspicious." My phone rang, and I pulled it out of my pocket. It took me a minute to recognize the name, and when I did, I smiled. This should be interesting. "You in jail? Need bail?" I asked when I answered.

Fern Wallace's growly laugh came across the line. "I've never been to the hoosegow, and I'm too old to be committing felonies. Thinking it wouldn't be fun to be locked up with one of those Bertha chicks you see on TV."

Fern was Gunz's Aunt Somebody or Other, both had been vague on the relationship tie. She'd been the one to give Gunz the moniker of King amongst family members.

"What can I do for you?" I asked. Fern had called before, and it was never to say, *Hello, how are you?* I put it on speaker so Fab could get the details in real time. If this call was going to be anything like the time the guy fell out of her ceiling, it would take both of us.

"I need a favor, and not a freebie — you can bill Gunz. He did say once that if I ever needed anything to give you or the sexy one a call. It was a long damn time ago, but I'll be sure and remind him."

Fab nudged my arm at *sexy* and grinned as she gunned it out of the compound.

"We'll both do what we can."

"My neighbor, who's an old goat, thinks someone is trying to steal his house out from under him, and I believe him, since he's not prone to making things up and he's not senile. I was thinking that you could have a sit-down with him at my house. The sooner the better."

"It can't be today, as we're working on another case. So how about tomorrow morning? You still living in the same house?" I asked.

"You betcha."

"Me and Sexy will be there."

Fern hung up, laughing.

"Is Gunz going to be irked off that one of his relatives called us without going through him first?" I asked.

"All he cares about is being kept updated and getting credit for whatever happy ending we can manage." Fab took the curve to US-1 and hit the gas.

"If we find Goff and he's all sandy and soggy, are you going to let him in the car?" I asked, knowing the woman had exacting standards for how pristine any car needed to be, and that included mine. She didn't tolerate driving one with a speck of dirt inside or out. Thankfully, she'd taken getting it detailed on as her responsibility.

"That's why we keep beach towels in the back." When I turned to look, she added, "I replaced all the supplies the day after this baby got delivered."

Fab cruised up the highway, and it wasn't long before we both spotted the lone figure walking south on the side of the highway. She hung a u-turn and pulled up alongside Goff, who looked like a dried-up drowned rat. He stared back, surprise on his face. She rolled down the window, yelled, "Get the hell in the back," and hit the unlock button.

He opened the door and stuck his head inside. "You're wasting your time; not going back to the sober house. Too many rules." He slammed the door and took off running.

"Were you giving him a hair-raising glare, and that's why he took off?" I got a growl, so maybe. "Guess Goff doesn't realize that his only option for a getaway is to go for a swim, and I wouldn't recommend it out here. Supposedly an alligator or two have been spotted." When he appeared to slow, I said, "If you're expecting me to chase him down and haul his butt in the car — not doing it."

Goff had stopped running and was bent over, hands on his knees. To my relief, he didn't barf.

"Guessing he doesn't have it in him to run the rest of the way." Fab had been coasting along the highway, and when Goff stuck out his thumb, she parked and jumped out. Before closing the door, she yelled, "You drive. I'll do the hauling." She took off running, and when Goff noticed, he started running again. It didn't take her long to catch up to the man and jerk him around by his shirt.

He wrestled out of her grip and had plenty to say as he backed up. Fab matched him step for step, staying up in his face, the two in an intense discussion, with Goff wagging his head the whole time.

They finally came to a stop, and I rolled up alongside them and rolled down the window. Not the best position for eavesdropping but better than nothing.

"Get in," Fab ordered, emphasizing that with a flick of her finger as she opened the back door.

Goff started his backward march again, and I pulled around him, leaving him two options: the water or the middle of the road and hope not to get mowed down.

"You're going to get yourself killed." Fab leapt forward, twisting her fist in his shirt again, and gave him a shove before he could jump into traffic. "I've got a place for you to stay—"

"I don't want to go back." He threw himself on the ground, covered his face with his hands, and started to cry.

"If you'd let me freakin' finish," Fab yelled, "I was about to say I've got you a place back in the Cove."

Goff sobbed over whatever he was saying. From the look on Fab's face, she understood very little. She stood over him, not giving him an inch of room. After several minutes, when it was clear Fab was about to explode, she bent down and talked into his ear. He nodded several times and stumbled to his feet. Just as he was about to climb inside, he appeared to change his mind, but Fab was ready for him and shoved him inside. He fell face down on the back seat, and she lifted his legs and shoved them inside, climbed in, and slammed the door. I didn't hesitate to hit the gas and managed to merge into traffic without anyone honking.

"Are you going to shoot me?" Goff tearfully asked.

"Thought about it, but here you are in one piece," Fab snarked.

"Can I get some water?" he whined.

"We're out," she snapped.

I was driving with one eye on the rearview mirror and handed my unopened bottle over the seat.

"You even look at the door handle, I'll shoot you, push your body out the door, and let the cars behind us run you over," Fab threatened a wide-eyed Goff, who'd managed to sit up.

It surprised me that he didn't start sobbing again. He gulped in some air and sat stoically, barely moving an inch.

"Here's the deal," Fab barked, then made an effort to dial it back. "Gunz has set it up for you to have a place to stay in the Cove. You might want to remember that he bailed you out and you repaid him by jerking him around. If you screw up this time and get kicked out for whatever reason, don't be surprised when your bail gets revoked and you sit in the slammer until your court date."

Goff slid down until his head disappeared behind the seat.

My phone rang, Rollo's name popping up on the screen. "Wanted you to know I got your request covered. There are two others here that are in the 'need to be sober' boat, and the three of them can hang together and complain how life is unfair." Rollo snorted.

"We're headed your way." I hung up.

"Listen up, Goff," Fab growled. "We're taking you to a motel owned by Gunz. There will be plenty of people around, and hopefully, you can stay out of trouble. Know that if you screw this up, you're on your own."

I hit the gas, and for once, it was me that was flying back to the Cove. Traffic cooperated, and I made it to the motel in record time, pulled around the back, and slid into a parking space.

Fab and I got out, and we waited to see if Goff was going to get out on his own. Tired of waiting, Fab leaned in and hissed in his face, and he practically threw himself out the door.

"Once you get your legal issues taken care of, Gunz is well-known for helping family members get back on their feet," I told the man as he stumbled forward.

Fab pointed the way, and after a long look around, he hustled inside the gate. It was clear he liked what he saw, as he continued to check everything out with interest. "Hey, Spec," he acknowledged a man sitting in a chair by the pool. The man stared and finally nodded.

"Look, you have a friend already."

Fab rolled her eyes at me.

Rollo came out of the office, and she made the introductions; then the two had a short conversation out of earshot. When they were done, Rollo approached Goff and gave him a pep talk, then laid down the rules. He made it clear he was in charge and Goff better be listening. It appeared that he was, as he nodded a few times. Rollo pulled a key out of his pocket. "You'll be sharing a room." Goff followed him across the courtyard.

"Let's get out of here," Fab grouched.

"Don't you want to —" I watched as Rollo unlocked one of the doors.

Fab cut me off. "No hand-holding with Rollo. The man's got it under control. After a few words, I realized that I didn't have to worry that Goff would go off the rails again. Rollo won't tolerate it."

I handed Fab the car keys. "I'm sure you've had enough of me behind the wheel."

Chapter Fourteen

I was enjoying my cup of coffee and staring intently at my computer. It was early for guests, but I watched as a police car rolled by on the security feed and I recognized the driver. I heard Creole making his way down the hall. Horrible wife that I was, I'd forgotten to bring him coffee in bed.

He nipped at my neck and hung his head over my shoulder, attempting to get a look at my laptop screen.

I closed the lid. "Do you have your pants on?"

"Am I getting lucky?"

"Later." I swiveled around and looked down. "Good, you have your shoes on." I slipped past him, grabbed a coffee tumbler, filled it, and handed it to him. "Let's go."

"What are you up to?"

I took my car keys out of my pocket and shook them at him, then repocketed them quickly, not wanting to lose custody. "It's a short ride, and you'll find out when we get there." I flashed my simpleton smile. "You coming?" I took a couple of steps towards the door.

"Can I just get a straight answer?"

"I've got something better in mind." I got to the door and held it open for him. "Chop, chop, or you're going to miss out." I knew that another attempt to dance him around wasn't going to work out well for me, so I ran out and jerked open the passenger door, then hustled around the front and got in the driver's seat.

"Whatever this is about can't be good," Creole gritted and barely got the door closed before I began to back out. I sped the few feet to Fab's house, squealed into the driveway, and parked next to the cop car.

Before Creole could shoot more questions at me, I jumped out of the car and raced to the door. He was right behind me as I inserted my lockpick and threw open the door, yelling, "We're here."

Fab, Didier, and Cooper were seated around the island, mugs of coffee in front of them. Fab rolled her eyes, and Didier smirked.

"How the hell did you get in?" Cooper barked.

"Sorry we're late," I said, ignoring him, and took a seat. No one could miss Creole's grin as he sat next to me. "You've got some pluck, dude, drinking what these two consider coffee. We brought our own." I pointed to the two travel mugs, having remembered to grab mine the last second before jetting out the door.

"Harris's townhome burned down last night," Fab blurted.

That was the last thing I was expecting to hear. "What about the rest of the string?" I asked, remembering that he lived in the middle unit with two on each side of him.

"Everyone got out, thank goodness, and no one was hurt," Fab assured me.

"A fire is one way to make sure no incriminating evidence ever turns up… as long as Harris didn't store it somewhere else. Happy to hear no one got hurt. You got any suspects?" Creole asked Cooper.

Before he could answer, I cut him off. "You better not be here to question Fab."

"I assured Cooper my wife has an alibi." Didier smirked.

"As I was about to ask before these two arrived…" Cooper cast a glance at Creole and me. "Do you have contact information for your client, Raynes? Would you know if he's in town or not? His office says that he's out of the country."

"As soon as I heard about Tech Harris's murder, I called and updated him. Since then, I haven't been able to get ahold of him," Fab told him.

"When I showed up at his office, they said they'd pass along the message to give me a call, but I haven't heard back from the man," Cooper said, sounding exasperated.

"Do you have any leads on who murdered Harris?" Didier asked.

Cooper shook his head and stood. "If any of you hear anything at all, I'd appreciate a call." He beelined for the front door.

When it closed, I asked, "What do you know?"

"Really, Madison," Fab said in a put-out tone.

Didier nudged her. "Go ahead and tell them."

"Fine. Then I want to know how you managed to show up within minutes of Cooper," Fab huffed. "I talked my backup sidekick into going and checking out Harris's place. When we arrived, the flames were eating up the curtain in an upstairs window. I called 911."

"Your snoopiness probably saved the people on both sides of that unit." I turned to Didier. "Since you're backup to the backup, I'm not the least bit annoyed that you're taking the middle-of-the-night jobs, as I'm certain that's what this one was."

"Do you have a hard time getting Fab to listen when you throw out a good idea?" Didier asked with a smirk. "In this case, I thought sitting in the parking lot to see who showed up after she made the call would be a very bad idea."

"Good one." I shot him a thumbs up.

"Just as we got to the main highway, here came the firetrucks and cops," Didier told us. "I was about to tell Fab, 'Let's get even farther away,' when she jammed on the gas."

"Is that why Cooper was here—he found out you were in the vicinity?" I asked.

"No, thank goodness. And since he didn't ask directly, I wasn't about to volunteer 'Just happened to be in the neighborhood.' Who would believe that? No one," she answered her question.

Then pointed to me. "Cough up how you ended up here."

Tempted to make a barfing noise, I restrained myself. "Good timing. I decided to check the security feed, which I don't do very often, and saw the gate open and Cooper drive in. Feeling certain that my lack of an invitation was an oversight, I decided to remedy that, and here we are." I waved off her response. "Same thing you would've done, except you'd have trekked down the beach."

"It was good timing, as Cooper was about to board his high horse and your arrival calmed him down somewhat," Fab admitted.

"Got the impression that he'd like better info from you but is also afraid of what you'll tell him. He doesn't want to have to go to his boss and ask, 'Can I arrest her now?'" Didier chuckled at Fab's head-shake.

"This relationship with Cooper and Kevin...?" Creole lifted his brows. "It's iffy. It'll take Kevin a long time to get on board." *If ever* hung in the air. "Why were you at the property?"

"I planned to search Harris's townhouse for evidence. I'm good at finding places most wouldn't think to look," Fab told him.

"I can attest to that, as I've seen her in action." I smiled at her.

"I tried to talk Fab out of attempting to retrieve evidence for a client who's blocked her. Was she listening?" Didier eyed her with raised brows as he shook his head.

"Next time, I'll listen; how about that?"

Didier laughed and hugged her. "Don't be surprised when I remind you of your promise."

"We need to get it together for our morning appointment." I slid off my stool. "I need to change into my workout pants." I winked at Fab, as she knew I meant the ones that had room for a gun on the side of the leg. "And tennis shoes."

"Fat chance of you two going anywhere before we hear why you've got a job that requires a gun," Creole barked.

"Fernie's an old broad who's got a neighbor in need. It's doubtful that we'll be needing the firearms, but if she has another man fall out of her ceiling like the last time, we may need a bullet for him," I told our hubs, who went from annoyed to amused.

"It's *Fern*, and she's not going to like being called an old broad," Fab admonished. "She's a relative of Gunz's, and when a family member doesn't have the stomach to call him for help, they call her. I know she's vying for assistant to the fixer but hasn't pulled it off yet. Gunz knows she wants to work for him."

"You know—"

"I don't want to know and neither do our husbands," Fab said, emphasizing with finger-pointing.

"Don't be mean."

Creole and Didier laughed.

"*Fern* wants to get in good with the King, as she likes to call him — maybe we should get her to man-sit Goff… to show off her skills." Ta-da in my tone.

"It's not your worst idea," Fab conceded.

"Show of hands. Who wants to wager that my idea at least gets a tryout?"

Creole and Didier had a silent exchange, not unlike me and Fab, and shook their heads. "I'll pass," they both said.

"You're no fun." I held out my hand to Creole. "Come on, babes." I turned to Fab. "Once we're done with Fern's neighbor, hope you haven't forgotten that today is *Welcome to Camping Week*."

"Did you get your party set up?" Fab asked with a smirk.

"You bet I did." I smirked back. "I've got all the players lined up and ready to go, and I'll be issuing my invitations today."

Fab told Creole and Didier that my idea of fun was to invite the kids to Jake's. Neither man believed her. "Wait until you get the video."

"Fifteen minutes." I tapped my non-existent watch, tugged on Creole's hand, and out the door we went.

Chapter Fifteen

"I need a caffeine boost before we hit *almost* Marathon," I told Fab as she cruised down the Overseas. "And a little something to go along with it."

"I'm thinking we're going to go with something healthy today — my treat."

"Please no."

Fab pulled into the coffee joint and ordered. "Two kale smoothies."

I slugged her in the arm and hissed, "Ick."

The female clerk laughed and apologized that they didn't make them.

Thank goodness.

Fab got us each a coffee and a muffin and cruised out of the drive-through. "Before you start on dumping me as a friend, save your breath — it's not happening."

"If kale turns up in my cup, I'll have to push you out of the car." We both laughed.

"What's the plan for when we get to Fern's?" Fab beat her finger on the steering wheel.

"Since this has to do with her neighbor… this is where I remind you that you're the one with the man skills, no matter their age." I could hear her eyeroll. "Did you tell Gunz about her call?"

She laughed. "Apparently Fern makes his body parts tired and he's happy to have all calls from her go to me so he doesn't have to hear about whatever it is."

She turned off the highway and onto a road that had been paved since we were last here. Single-story homes ran along one side of the road, a forest of trees on the other. She pulled up in front of a lime-green one-story that had undergone a transformation; thanks to Gunz's crew, it was no longer the broken-down wreck it once was. The small front yard had also undergone a makeover, the dead grass and plants replaced by a circular driveway. A beater sedan appeared to be permanently parked off to one side.

Fab and I got out and cut across the driveway to the door. It opened, and Fern gave us a toothy grin, appearing a bit disheveled, as though she'd gotten dressed on the way to the door, her grey hair sticking on end.

"Come in, ladies." She beckoned us inside.

The large living room had undergone an overhaul as well and was no longer a dark tomb that smelled like animal pee. The old furniture and clutter had been hauled away.

"It's nice in here." I smiled at her. "You did a good job."

Fern barked a laugh. "Not me. I'm too damn cheap. Gunz sent some pushy broad, and there was no telling her anything. Have a seat."

I took one of the two chairs next to her recliner, leaving the couch to the mutt dog, who was old but still kicking. Fab walked around, checking out the rest of the house.

"Is she always so nosey?" Fern asked me.

"Yes," I said with a nod. "But she's the best when you need someone to have your back. Or in this case, your neighbor's. Where is he?"

Fab finished her snoop and claimed the chair next to me. "Didn't find any squatters."

"Thank goodness for that." Fern chuckled. "About Bardy… I haven't been able to get ahold of him. Banged on the door a few times and nothing. Thinking something must've happened, as he's lived here as long as I have. Used to see him every day. His car is in the driveway and never moves. Another car comes and goes, but I haven't seen the driver."

"You want us to do a welfare check?" Fab suggested.

I turned to her, telegraphing, *We're not law enforcement*, which she ignored. Guess she forgot we were supposed to be law-abiding these days. If there was no answer, there was no doubt she'd use her lockpick.

"Don't tell anyone, but I did go and peek in the windows. Only one, because it didn't have the drapes drawn like the rest of them. Do you think I could see a damn thing? No." Fern blew out a frustrated breath.

"Why don't the three of us knock on his door like we've got something to sell, and when he throws open the door, you make the intros?" Fab suggested.

"What's his name?" I asked.

"Bardy Dowell. 'Hey you' also works—makes him chuckle. You get to a certain age and remembering names is tiresome."

"On the off chance someone else answers that you don't recognize, we'll tell whoever it is that we're looking for our missing cat."

"Now that's a good one." Fern was clearly impressed.

"Fab thought of it all on her own." I smirked.

"Let's get going," Fern rubbed her hands together, jumped up, and held the front door open. She pointed in the direction of a navy-and-white single-story, the structure appearing identical to hers.

Fab led the way and knocked respectably on the door but got no answer. She tried again, this time with her ear to the door. She shook her head, letting us know she hadn't heard anything. As expected, she whipped out her lockpick and had the door open in a jiffy, pushed it open, and yelled, "Welfare check." Nothing.

Fern swept around Fab and into the house. "Bardy, it's me," she yelled. "Just want to know you're doing okay." Once again, no answer.

Fab headed to the hallway, Fern behind her.

I fisted my hand in the back of her shirt and

held on. "Oh no, you don't. In case we have to make a run for it, we're going to stay here, where we're closer to the door."

"I forgot that you're no fun."

We heard a loud crash, and the distinct sound of a door hitting the wall. "Call 911 for an ambulance," Fab yelled.

I took my phone out of my pocket. Fern took off to what I assumed was a bedroom. I followed her as I made the call, knowing the operator would have questions and I'd need answers.

A white-haired man, who I assumed was Bardy, was on the bed, barely lucid, mumbling incoherently. It didn't take long for the paramedics to arrive, a cop right along with them. I'd already maneuvered Fern outside, where we leaned against the SUV and watched everything unfold.

"FYI, Fab's going to tell the cop that the front door was unlocked," I whispered to Fern.

"Gotcha. What do you think happened to Bardy?"

"Since the bedroom door was locked, it appears that someone didn't want him wandering around, and it's the reason you haven't seen him."

"After finding the front and back door locked, I thought about finding another way in. I'm happy I called you two instead," Fern whispered conspiratorially.

"I'm glad you called us, because if you'd come face-to-face with someone who'd keep a near comatose man, locked in a room, the outcome…" I grimaced. "Also, know that you can call anytime."

The paramedics loaded Bardy into the back of their van and took off.

The cop who'd questioned Fab was now headed in our direction.

"I'm scared," Fern said as she watched his approach.

I put my arm around her and side-hugged her. "Keep your answers short and stick to the truth."

"Ladies," the cop said, "can you tell me what happened here?"

I spoke first and introduced both of us, letting him know that when we first got there, we'd stayed in the living room, and only came running when Fab yelled for 911. I didn't tell him it would've tried Fab's patience to make the call herself because that would start him wondering how many such calls we'd made.

He then questioned Fern about her relationship with the neighbor.

"I was worried, as I hadn't seen him in a while. I had no idea that he…" She winced.

I gave him my contact information and extended an invite to stop by Jake's anytime. "Tell the bartender you're a friend of the owner."

"Heard stories about that place." He scrutinized me with humor in his eyes.

"Florida Keys." I shrugged, as though that said it all, and in a way, it did.

Having retrieved her business card from the

SUV, Fab marched over and handed it to the officer.

Another cop car rolled up, and the first cop went over and talked to the officer who got out; then the two went in the house.

"Are you okay to stay by yourself?" I asked Fern.

"Do I get to go home with you?" she asked, a note of excitement in her tone.

I glanced at Fab: *Come up with something, and fast.*

"As I recall, you like motel life; how about a short stay in one up the road?" Fab asked.

"Thought you sold that one." Fern squinted.

"Not the same one, but just as much fun," Fab assured her.

I couldn't help thinking that Fab had over-hyped No Name, but it would be a short stay.

"I need to get a few things from my house; my dog won't be a problem, will he?"

Fab reassured her it wouldn't be and told her not to worry. She and I waited in the living room while Fern scurried off. Fab got on her phone and called Rollo. "Got another one for you," she said when he answered. "This is a short stay, a week or two." She laughed, and they hung up.

"I'll call Shirl and get her to check on Bardy. When, not if, he recovers, he can't go back home until whoever had him locked in the room is behind bars."

"Even then... Bardy doesn't appear to be in the

best shape. It's going to take some time for him to get back on his feet. Fern knew the man had a problem and wanted our help, and that's what we'll do," Fab said.

Fern came back, dog under one arm, small suitcase in hand. I grabbed the latter and walked her out to the car.

Now that the cops had left, Fab walked back over to Bardy's, which now had yellow police tape across the door, with her phone in her hand. She disappeared around the back and wasn't gone long.

"What's she up to?" Fern squirmed in her seat and looked out the window.

"Fab is a picture-taker. Later, she'll go over all of them to see if she missed anything." I took out my phone and called Rude, and when she answered, I asked, "Can you give your boss the slip?"

"Yeppers. I can put a sign on the gate: 'Come back later.'"

"Meet us at the No Name motel."

"On my way." She laughed and hung up.

I turned in my seat. "You're going to like this place because there's plenty of people to socialize with. It's not your typical motel. It's pay-by-the-week, and you get to stay as long as you behave." *Got it?* in my tone.

"No worries about me. I'm a get-along girl." She tipped her head back on the seat, staring at the ceiling. "Got to find out about Bardy though. I feel bad that I wasn't snoopier."

"Thinking it was better that you weren't, as you might've ended up alongside him. Once Fab and I are able to talk to Bardy, we'll find out what happened and make sure it doesn't happen again," I assured her.

Fab quietly slid behind the wheel, and we took off. It wasn't long before we turned off the highway and around the back of the No Name and parked.

Fern got out and eyed the building. "This might be my kind of place." As we walked through the gate, she set down her dog, who began to sniff around.

"Fernie," Rude squealed from where she stood just outside the office. The two women engaged in a crushing hug.

Seeing the question on Fab's face, I said, "They met when we owned the motel at the other end of town."

"Rude's proven herself to have people skills and is good with other people's problems," Fab said. "Thinking she can handle *Fernie*, and if she's the least bit hesitant, Gunz will make it worth her while."

"If Rude needs any help, I'll have her contact Clive."

"He's going to quit one these days." Fab smirked.

"Doubtful. He enjoys complaining, and his job gives him that outlet. I'm pretty sure it was made clear when he interviewed that he wasn't applying for a cushy office job."

Rollo whistled and beckoned Fab over.

I went over to Rude and Fern. "Okay, you two, you both need to stay out of trouble. If you need anything—" I pointed at Fern. "—Rude can make it happen. If you need brawn, Rollo in the office is your man. Promise you that he can handle anything."

"Don't you worry. I've got this, and if I don't, I'll figure it out," Rude said.

Fab and Rollo joined us, and Fab made the introductions. Rollo nodded at me.

"This way." He handed a key to Fern and led the two women away.

"Aren't we supposed to be at The Cottages for a meet-and-greet?" Fab asked as we headed to the parking lot.

"Got a text—there's been a change of plans. Cruz's kids needed to be picked up, so all of them went along for the ride. My guess is that Cruz wanted to see what his kids were getting into before he let them go. I'd like to have seen his face when the bus pulled up. On the way back, it's lunch on the beach. My guess, a food truck. Try not to turn up your nose, as we have one or two that are favorites." I stared at Fab.

"I'm certain that I've admitted to liking the ones we've frequented here in the Cove," she said once we were in the SUV and headed out to the highway.

"Yeah, sure. Good news: you're off the hook for breakfast at Jake's tomorrow. I've got Cook, Doodad, and Kelpie coming in early, and they're ready to put on a show."

"I still say the parents wouldn't be impressed by your choice of location for your welcome event. You better not need Cruz's lawyerly skills after he hears about the fun *you* have planned, because I have a hunch he won't be stepping up, and I mean ever."

"If you're going to let your kids spend a week with Crum, you can't possibly be surprised by anything that happens. If we're not headed home, you can drop me off in the next block, and I'll walk the rest of the way." I pointed to the side of the road, knowing we weren't far from our turn-off.

"Surprised that you're not trying to figure out a way to get me out of the car and make me do the walking."

"Next time." I laughed and was happy when she took the turn to the compound.

Chapter Sixteen

It didn't surprise me when I got a text from Fab the next morning as I was ready to leave the house: *Hurry up*. I flew out the door and into the car, with her gunning the engine the whole time. We'd both opted for workout pants and tennis shoes. She flew down the Overseas and turned into the parking lot of Jake's, where it surprised me to see the school bus parked in the front.

"How is it that we're apparently the last to show up when I'm the one that extended the invite?" I looked at the clock on the dash as she slid in next to the bus. "Everyone's early."

"Eager to see what you're up to." Fab smirked.

We both got out, and just then, a testosterone truck pulled up and edged its way up to our bumper, missing denting it out of shape by barely an inch.

A muscled jumbo-sized man jumped out, dressed in black jeans and shirt, zeroing in on Fab as he made his way over to her. He glanced my way and dismissed me in a second. I hung back, leaning against the bumper.

"Been awhile." He ogled Fab from head-to-toe.

"What do you want, Booker?" She was already

out of patience, and he hadn't even said what he wanted.

Whatever their relationship had been, it wasn't on the best terms now.

He turned and glared at me. "Get lost."

"Another charmer from your past, I presume," I directed at Fab, not taking my eyes off Booker. "As for you, you can go f— yourself."

He growled.

Fab jumped in front of him as he was about to leap at me.

I had my hand on my Glock—one more step…

"Booker," Fab said with a note of irritation, "she's not going to repeat a single word of what she hears."

That depends. But I knew better than to voice that.

"Just tell me what you're doing here."

Booker got up in Fab's face, his back to me. She backed up. He leaned in and hissed his message at her. If he'd made that move on Fab thinking I wouldn't be able to eavesdrop, he was wrong, as I heard every word: "Raynes wants assurance that there's nothing out there that's going to come back to haunt his daughter, and that includes anyone else attempting to fleece her for cash to keep their mouth shut."

"What I know is that Harris was murdered," Fab told him. "Then his townhouse was burned to a crisp. So whatever evidence he had has gone up in smoke. I'd be surprised if Raynes didn't know all that already. I've got nothing to add. If anything was unclear, he could've picked up the freaking phone and asked me himself."

Booker stared in a way meant to intimidate. It didn't work. "I know the cops questioned you about Harris's death; what did you tell them?"

"If you're asking did I lie about anything, the answer is that there was no reason to do so. When I called Raynes and he didn't answer, I was left with the option of hanging up or leaving a message. As you probably already know, I went with the latter. Raynes knows everything I just told you." Fab turned the tables and got up in his face. "If there's anything else, email me."

"Raynes sent me to deliver a message." Booker's eyes spit fire. "He doesn't want to hear another word about this case from you or anyone else. So stop trying to make contact. If you even think about squeezing money out of him for services rendered or whatever, you're wasting your time. You can't spend it if you're dead. You'd be one of those cases where the body's never found and no one knows what happened." Booker appeared to be enjoying his attempt to scare Fab. He didn't know her very well.

If there were a wager as to who'd end up dead first, my money would be on his early demise. "Okay a-hole, enough of you. Get off this property and don't set foot on it again." I pulled my Glock and pointed it at the center of his chest.

Booker took a step forward. Fab cut him off.

"She's a good shot, so back off while you can still walk away," she cautioned.

"If anything happens to Fab, I can promise that your demise will be slow and painful. Now git." Shooting people dead wasn't my first choice, but with my finger on the trigger, I was ready to do just that if he decided to jump either one of us. "Also know that every second of this chat was recorded…" I nodded toward the security camera on the front of Jake's, not taking my eyes off him. "You so much as lay a finger on either one of us, and all hell will rain down on you."

Booker clenched his jaw, grinding his teeth, then turned back to Fab and glared down at her. "Let's agree that this will be the last time I have to track you down."

"Listen up: I've never screwed a client," Fab told him in a deadly calm voice. "I'm not about to start now. You need to tell Raynes to calm down."

Booker turned to me and continued to glare. "If this building burns down, so much for the security footage." He smirked.

"Like I'm stupid enough to store security footage on-site. Burning Jake's down won't do you any good, and if anything happens to this building or the staff, I don't care if you've relocated to another state, you'll be tracked down and I guarantee you'll be found." I moved my aim from his chest to between his eyes.

"Looks like we both better watch our backs." Booker eyed us both, then turned on his heel and walked away, jumped back in his truck, and roared out of the parking lot.

"I was kind of hoping Booker would push his luck and we'd be dragging him out here." Fab stared after him until he hit the street.

I reholstered my weapon. "The way he looked at you, you should've asked for your clothes back before he got back in the truck. I mean ick!"

"We never… and thankfully we also never had the 'let's try it out' talk." She shook her head. "Surprised that Raynes sent Booker to confront me when all he had to do was pick up the phone."

"I'd like to know how he found you when you don't give out either your home or office address. Plus, this is my business and not connected to you at all. Except that he does know that you live down here, and all it would take is some cash spread around… just happy he didn't show up at the compound."

"If Booker hadn't found me, knowing Raynes, he'd have hired someone else to track me down. Since he went to all this trouble instead of picking up the phone, I guarantee this won't be the last I'll hear of him. The man's paranoid and didn't get what he wanted, and apparently, he's not satisfied with Harris being dead and the townhouse in flames."

"Here's a thought you're not going to like: If you'd recovered the blackmail evidence and handed it over to Raynes, he might've gotten rid of you." I struggled not to cringe. "Since I have no way of knowing, I'm not saying Raynes offed Harris—more like paid for it to be done—but he'd be my number one suspect. And even if he'd gotten the information back, Harris might still have met his demise." A wave of nausea hit me at the thought that we'd be hearing from Raynes again, or someone he hired. Not about to take the wait-and-see approach, I knew who to call so that didn't happen and we weren't stuck looking over our shoulders.

"We should go inside." Fab inched her way to the door. "Someone sees us standing here, staring out to the street, there will be questions we don't want to answer."

"Before we go inside, who's this Booker cretin and where did you meet him?" I asked.

"Booker's been a fixture in Miami for years. He's hired muscle and has worked for Raynes as his private security since I first got down here and started to make connections." Fab grinned at me. "Loved that you pointed your Glock at him and it never wavered."

"I got the feeling if you hadn't warned him that I knew what I was doing, he would've found out for himself."

"When you told him you'd make him disappear—which was gutsy—I'm pretty sure if he hadn't believed you, he would've shot us both." Fab gave me an assessing stare. "I can see that you're planning something. Can't wait to hear what it is."

"Happy it didn't come to a shootout in the parking lot." Very happy. "Here's a promise: that's the last we've seen of Booker, and you won't be hearing from Raynes again either. Sorry, not sorry, if it cuts into your business with your old clients... but you have to admit they're trouble." I held up my hand, cutting her off. "I know you want to know how I'm going to pull it off, but you're going to have to wait. You'll get all the deets when it's a done deal. Also promise it won't take long."

Chapter Seventeen

"Try to behave yourself," I admonished Fab with a grin.

"Me? You're the one who organized a kid party at a bar." Fab pulled open the front door, and we came to an abrupt halt. "I told you you'd regret this one." The smirk in her tone was loud and clear.

Based on the yelling and laughter, the kids and adults were having a good time. One group was sitting on the floor, and all activity stopped as their eyes came up and they stared for a second, checking us out, then went back to gambling. I did a double-take, and yes, they were gambling.

For the second time, I took a head count and came up short—not all the kids were accounted for, the girls nowhere to be seen.

In the middle of the room, Crum was teaching four boys—Logan, 1 & 2, and one I didn't recognize—the fine art of pitching pennies, but using chips instead. A huge pile of chips had been spread out in front of them. The boys alternated between sending their chips flying and hoarding them, laughing the whole time.

"Hey Mom, Dad, I learned to gamble," Fab whispered in my ear.

I attempted to brush her off, but she stepped away with a laugh.

Doodad hung over their shoulders, throwing out tips to improve their chances of sinking a chip in one of the cups. All had beer glasses next to them, and after a triple take, I discerned that they weren't filled with alcohol. At least I hoped not. I'd be double-checking.

"I've got to get pictures of this," Fab said with way too much glee, whipping out her phone. "I'll get them organized into a file and forwarded to their parents, so they can see the level of corruption you're subjecting their children to."

"What's that saying? Oh yes, payback is a bitch." I heard her laughter as she walked away, snapping pictures.

Alex, two boys that looked like Cruz, and a third who was a bit younger alternated between shooting pool and throwing darts, laughing and cheering whenever one took the lead.

I motioned to Alex, who set down his pool cue and approached with a grin. "Three girls are missing — your sister, my niece, and another one — do you happen to know their whereabouts?"

"They wanted to help Cook get breakfast ready, and after we ate, they stayed in there." Alex pointed in the direction of the kitchen, as though I didn't know. "I figured they'd be in the way but knew Cook could speak up about them invading his space, and not a word out of the man. But gotta say, he did look relieved when us guys decided to stay out here and learn new games." He pulled some cash out of his pocket and flashed it at me before it disappeared. "My poker winnings."

"You brought money to gamble?" I asked. Shocked didn't quite cover it.

"Before you got here, Crum gave us each a couple of bucks and a roll of quarters and said we could choose how we wanted to piss it away. His word, not mine." He grinned.

Cootie and Clive entered the main area from the hallway, yelling hellos and waving. The boys called back greetings over one another. I waved to the two men, who nodded back. They stopped at the bar, and it took a second before Kelpie started laughing and dancing. I was relieved to see that she was more covered up than usual.

I turned my attention back to Alex. "Thinking I didn't make myself clear when we talked—"

"This ought to be good," Fab cut me off. Guess she got all the pictures she wanted. She and Alex laughed.

"Who's the oldest here?"

"I am." He returned my stare and straightened a little.

"I need you to keep an eye on things, and if… I'm not sure what, but call me if, at any time, this week stops being fun or you hear more complaining than laughing. I'm not jinxing it, but if things go…" I jerked my thumb downwards.

"I've got it covered," Alex assured me. "Don't think you've got too much to worry about, as Crum has this well-planned-out, and my dad made him go over everything with him… a couple of times." He rubbed his hands together. "For my part, I'm wanting another one of those favor deals."

Not a carbon copy of his father, but close. "With one stipulation—"

"Yeah, yeah, nothing illegal. Pretty sure you'll add more stips if you think of something." Alex smirked.

"What's in the glasses?" Fab asked.

"Please tell me it's not beer." I didn't groan, but close.

"Soda of some sort. Thought it looked like cat pee instead of beer, and when I told Kelpie, I saw her add food coloring. It wasn't horrible."

I chuckled. *That's good.*

"My bros wanted to try one of the bottled beers behind the bar and tried to con Kelpie into believing they were twenty-one. She laughed at them and shook her you-know-whats. I can see what my dad likes about… you know, big ones."

I struggled not to laugh. If Kelpie were to overhear, she'd up her game. "One more thing. If at any time during this week, the cops show up, I want to be the next call after your dad."

Alex laughed. "Oh man, how much fun would that be?"

"Careful there," Fab warned. "Crabby Kevin might be the one to get the call, and he might haul you off to jail."

"My dad would kick his ass."

Fab and I laughed.

"I'm going to go check on the girls," I said, "and make sure they're still having fun and whatever."

"If you're hungry, you may be out of luck, as we ate everything," Alex warned. "There were a few things left, but then we got into a food fight." Guessing he noticed my shock, as he said, "We all pitched in to help clean it up."

"I'm annoyed I was late to my own party and missed out on some of the fun. If you do anything else outrageous—like a food fight, but hopefully not—morph into Fab and take a couple pictures." I grinned at him.

"Crum called Doodad and moved up the time, as we're going on a boat tour later," Alex told us. "Kelpie thought the time change was a good one, as we—how did she put it? — 'could be herded out of here before the regs showed.'"

"She's wearing a big smile, which tells me she doesn't find you guys too nuisancey."

"That chick's fun." Alex cast her an appreciative glance. "Pretty sure my dad would agree."

I refused to think about those two hooking up. "Remember…" I made a phone with my fingers. "I'll wave on the way out."

"We're probably going to sneak out the back," Fab told him. The two laughed.

Fab and I stopped at the bar on the way to the kitchen.

"Love these kids," Kelpie cooed. She'd brought her A-game, dressed in a hot-pink tank top and green net skirt accentuated with flashing lights and bells.

"I can't thank you enough for stepping up at the last minute to help host this gathering. I knew that this location, albeit quirky, was a good choice, as it was guaranteed that you'd all bring the fun. I've heard nothing but laughter since we walked in." I grinned back at her. "We're going to make sure that Cook hasn't been overwhelmed before we sneak out of here."

"Cook upped his game, wanting to impress the kids. Tried to tell him he could put boxed sugary cereal in a bowl and they'd be happy. If looks could kill…" Kelpie chuckled as she checked the watch pinned to her tank top. "I figured traditional breakfast might be dicey and told him so. Took my suggestion… well, not exactly… and whipped up burgers and fries. Not one complaint. Won't be long before they clear out, and I heard the first stop is ice cream."

Fab and I continued down the hall. The door to the poker room was open, and the table was set and looked ready for action. One of Cook's kin was behind the bar, refilling the refrigerator with drinks.

"Is the room booked for a private group?" I asked him.

"They'll be here this afternoon. Late lunch on the deck, and then moving the action in here." He grinned.

I nodded my thanks.

"Leave it to your employees to accommodate any and all requests. Looks to me like breakfast was served in here and they didn't eat on the floor," Fab said, humor in her tone. "Noticed that all the kids had their fortune told by Esmerelda—the cards are sitting next to their fake beers."

"That fortune teller machine has been a hot item since she made her first appearance. Told Clive there's a bonus in it if he can keep it stocked with cards so that I don't have to turn it off, relegating Esmerelda to looking pretty."

"You're really weird."

"Like you didn't know that." I made a shocked face.

Fab and I continued on to the kitchen, where Cook had set up a small table outside his office. He and the girls were having tea, the girls regaling him with stories about school and what their favorite things to do were, all with big smiles on their faces.

I kissed the tops of Mila's and Lily's heads, and they beamed up at me and introduced their new friend, Marlee. I walked around and gave Cook a side-hug, whispering, "You're the best."

"Are you girls having a good time?" Fab asked.

They all cheered.

Doodad came running into the kitchen. "Okay girls, are you ready to show off your talents?"

They yelled yes in unison and jumped up.

"We're having a talent show," Lily announced. "You get to stand in front of the microphone — sing, dance, or just make something up."

"Can we do it as a group?" Mila asked.

"You bet you can," Doodad assured her.

The girls hugged Cook. Then two got on one side, one on the other, wanting him to come with them, and they led the way out.

Now what? I looked at Doodad.

"When I gave my welcome speech, I promised karaoke. Now's a good time, as we have a bit of time to kill." Noting my surprise, he added, "Got the idea when we had a talent night recently and it didn't suck. The drinkers had a fine time."

"The gamblers are going to give up their gig for singing?" Fab asked with a hint of humor.

"The boys think it's a fun idea, as long as they don't have to give up any of their money." Doodad laughed. "I'm also letting them keep the chips, as I'd have a hard time wrestling them away and I'm not interested in any sad faces, since we haven't had a one thus far."

"There's no doubt that the kids are having a great time," I said.

Doodad turned to leave, then spun back around. "Sorry I forgot to call you about the time change, but it was last-minute and an easy fix.

Crum was freaking out about the kids having fun, and it shut up his worrying."

"Please, I appreciate all the hard work." I smiled my thanks at the man.

The three of us walked back out to the bar. The jukebox had been turned on, and Alex was looking for a song. A stage area had been set up in front of the doors out to the deck, and Crum was orchestrating rock, paper, scissors to see who was going first.

What surprised me was that three regulars—or as I referred to them, the beer for breakfast bunch—had somehow figured out we were open early and were sitting at the bar, beers in front of them. If those three had shown up, it wouldn't be long before more filed in.

"Have you sung karaoke before?" Fab asked with a smirk.

"I've never been drunk enough. I'm not even asking you, as I already know the answer."

Kelpie had overheard, having moved up behind us. "The kids are very excited to choose a song, and based on the choices thrown out, I know our machine isn't going to accommodate them, so I'll be finding them on my phone."

"There's an idea I wouldn't have thought of." I shot her a thumbs up, then pulled my ringing phone out of my pocket and glanced at the screen. Fab and Kelpie hung their heads over my shoulder, and the three of us saw Mac's name pop up on the screen. "If it's bad news, can it keep until tomorrow?" I asked when I answered.

Mac laughed. "I had an unexpected drop-off, and I'm not sure what to do. You're my first call. Shirl's here and has an update on someone's neighbor. Pretty sure that makes sense to you."

"About the drop-off—"

"Oh no, I want to see your reaction when you see it."

"Assure me it's not a dead body."

"That would be no fun at all."

"We're on our way." We hung up. "This is a first—Mac didn't hang up on me." I shared the gist of the call with Fab and Kelpie.

"That's all you got?" Kelpie huffed.

"Too many times when something hits the fan, my employees wait until we're face-to-face." I stared her down. It amused me when she blushed.

"Guilty." She reluctantly raised her hand.

"It won't surprise me if you know what it's all about before I get over there."

She grinned.

"Do we yell our good-byes over the talent show?" The boys were grouped around the microphone, singing along to a Jimmy Buffet song; some knew the lyrics, and the rest knew only a few.

"My vote is to sneak out of here and not interrupt a second of the fun." Fab tugged on my sleeve.

We both waved to Kelpie, who'd moved on down the bar and was having a raucous conversation with her regulars, as we went out the front door.

Chapter Eighteen

"I'll drive," I said. "You wouldn't want me to forget how." Fab rolled her eyes at me and jumped into the driver's seat faster than I'd ever seen her do it before. "Hope that I don't make good on my threat to get sick one of these days," I said as she blew down the highway. "You'd have to buy me a new car. The smell doesn't go away, in case you didn't know."

"I'm slowing down." She blew out an aggrieved sigh. "Happy now?"

She slowed somewhat. Then I realized that she was jabbing her finger at a sportscar that had been rolling alongside us and suddenly shot ahead.

"That's the kid." She sped up and managed to get behind the car in question.

"That's too vague for me."

"The car thief," Fab snapped, like I should know.

"Take a breath. Even if you're one hundred percent certain that it's him, you need to call the cops and let them handle it. If you confront a juvenile and try to shake the information out of him, you'll be the one going to jail."

The sportscar made a left into the Publix parking lot and parked. Fab slid into a space one away. A teenage kid and someone who could easily be his mother got out and headed into the grocery store.

Fab waited until they were inside, then whipped out her phone, jumped out, and took a photo of the license plate, then snapped one of the VIN number.

I was right behind her and jerked on her arm before she could run off. "Do not under any circumstances make a scene in the grocery store; it could backfire big time."

"I've calmed down… well, sort of. I'm going to get pictures of mother and son and turn them and the car info over to Xander to track down." When I grabbed a cart, she admonished, "We're not here to shop."

"This is a prop so we look like everyone else," I returned in her snooty tone and followed as she traversed the aisle that ran along the front of the store.

Fab easily found the two, turned down the aisle, and took her pictures, neither mother nor son noticing what she was doing. She pocketed her phone and bumped into the teen, apologizing as she stared him down. There was no recognition on his face.

"Do we have everything?" the mother asked, and without waiting for an answer, she headed down the aisle and the boy followed.

Fab and I hung back, keeping an eagle eye on the pair as they checked out and went back to their car.

"Thought it was a longshot to think the kid might recognize me, since we never met," Fab said as she tapped her finger on the steering wheel while the kid put the groceries in the trunk. "It can't be the first car he stole because he was too good. Did he know who the owner was before he drove off? Probably not."

"Your plan is to follow them to…" I said as she fell in behind their car as it exited the parking lot.

"To wherever they go."

"Let's hope it's not the next state." I pulled out my phone and texted Mac. *Running behind. Fab is in hunt mode.*

Lucky me, we didn't have far to go before the car turned off the highway and onto a residential street. Almost at the end of the street, the sportscar turned into an apartment complex. The driver waited for the security gate to open, went through, and then waited until it closed, which was something we'd do. She passed a long row of cars, rounded the corner, and drove out of sight.

"I wouldn't recommend jumping the fence and giving chase."

"We're leaving. It's just one more piece of information for Xander to follow up on." Fab made a u-turn. "Wonder if the mother knows what sonny boy is up to? I didn't see an adult or anyone else around when my car got stolen."

"Not sure what you plan on doing when Xander hands over whatever he manages to dig up, but my suggestion is that you turn it all over to Cooper."

"When he finds out that I'm pointing the finger at a teenager, unless it's some kind of indisputable proof, I doubt he'll even investigate."

"The Cottages," I reminded her before she got to the corner. "When you get a report back from Xander, talk to Tank. If you get an apartment number, beating down the door isn't an option. It's one thing to think you know and another to prove it."

"Before any of that happens, I'll have shared everything with Didier, and he'll be the voice of reason." She once again flew down the highway. "The Cottages is the next stop. I'm afraid to ask what's going on there."

"As you already know, I got zero info from Mac. Discounted a dead body because I asked outright, and though she didn't deny it, she didn't have the same caginess she'd have if she were staring at one."

Since we hadn't left the Cove, we made it across town in short order. Fab claimed her usual parking spot, backing into Mac's driveway. Mac and Shirl were sitting at the top of the stairs leading to the front door, coffees in hand. Both women were in shorts, with shirts tied around their waists. Mac sported brown leather flats, the toes open-mouthed alligators with fanged teeth ready for a bite. Shirl's...

She caught me looking at her plain blue flip-flops. "I'm not a shoe fashionista like my friend here." She patted Mac's shoulder. "They're comfortable, and I don't give a flip what people think."

"Do yours scare people into thinking they might lose their foot if they come too close?" I asked Mac.

"I got a couple of squeals when I wore them to the bar the other night." Mac chuckled. "They were such a great deal, and you know me—I can't pass up a shoe bargain."

"Tell her why they were so cheap." Shirl nudged her.

"Originally, they had four-inch heels, and one had snapped off. I took them to a shoe repair place and had them made into flats." Mac shook her foot.

"Mac just remodeled her closet and put shelves in so she can scan all her shoes when she can't make up her mind which pair to wear," Shirl told us. "It was a pain taking all those boxes to the dump."

I turned to Fab, who was standing behind my shoulder. *Say something.*

"As always, very cute." She managed to sound sincere.

I thought Mac would faint, but she just unleashed a big sigh and grinned at Fab.

"I've got an update on Mr. Dowell," Shirl told

us. "I got a little bit of the story from one of the nurses."

Bardy, Fern's neighbor.

"He was being held against his will over an issue with his grandson, and it went on long enough that he got malnourished and dangerously dehydrated."

"What did the police say?" Fab demanded.

"Mr. Dowell isn't in any shape to answer questions, besides being afraid of the grandson," Shirl told us. "The cops will have to wait a few days."

"Let's hope that when they're able to get their questions answered, it leads to an arrest," I said and caught Mac and Shirl's nod of agreement. "Now for my surprise, or whatever it is you got me over here for. It's not about the kids, as they're at Jake's — gambling, shooting pool, darts, and who knows what else Crum has come up with by now."

"If any of the kids call their parents and tell them about the welcome breakfast, they'll be gone tomorrow," Fab said as though she expected it to happen.

"We'll still have the local kids, as their parents aren't that prissy." *So there.*

"I don't know the other parents, but if you have a face-off with Cruz, be sure to call him names, letting him know he's *prissy.*" Fab grinned.

"I'm ignoring you." I focused on Mac. "Well?"

"Turn around and check out your property,"

Mac said, and both women smirked.

"Oh cute." Fab had spotted it in a second and pointed it out. "Where did it come from? Does it work?"

"A phone booth?" I checked out the approximately nine-foot red box. "Like the color. Am I the new owner? If so, what are we doing with it? We better be talking legal possession."

"It's for sale, and I'm posting a sign tomorrow. The current owner thought it was a good location for a speedy sale. I'm thinking it has a certain charm and we shouldn't be so fast to write it off and should make a bid ourselves," Mac said.

"Wouldn't shock me if Crum was involved." Both women laughed. "The Cottages acquiring it would depend on getting a good deal. Before making an offer, you need to assure me that it won't be used for criminal activity of any kind, anyone wanting to sleep off a drunk, or anyone wanting to move in and call it home, using the bushes for a bathroom."

"A little small for home sweet home." Fab made a face.

"Very little surprises me," I said with a shake of my head.

"I'm going to enjoy putting the screws to the professor, who's in charge of the sale. It belongs to a friend of some sort." Mac eyed the booth like it was the first time she was seeing it. "I'll make it clear that I get first dibs, and also make it simple for the high IQ he brags about to understand that if he doesn't agree to my terms, payback will be horrendous."

"If it comes to payback, you better get some pictures," Fab told her fiercely.

Mac nodded, and it was clear that she'd enjoy taking plenty of photos.

Fab whipped out her own phone and shared pictures of the kids, and the two women laughed.

"To answer your previous question, there's a phone inside, but it doesn't work—the receiver is missing," Shirl said.

"Do I get it fixed or not?" Mac mused.

"If you could get it working again, and that's a big if, it'll be an invitation to thieves to break into the coin box and steal whatever's inside," Fab warned. "Even if they get nothing because it's credit card only, they may take out their frustration by damaging it. I'd leave it as-is, which gives a clear message: 'Doesn't work.'"

"How has it been with the kids thus far?" I asked.

"So far, they've charmed the guests, and not a single complaint," Mac told us. "Crum's got plenty of activity planned that I'm not a part of, and that suits me just fine."

"How did musical beds turn out?" Fab asked.

"It's only been two nights thus far," Mac reminded her. "But they aren't happy with not having enough bed space and needing to utilize the rest of the furniture. Don't be surprised if they move to Casio's. When he threw out the idea of rustling up air mattresses and sleeping bags, so they could all sleep in the same room, the kids were excited. If you see them running on the beach, you'll know they made the move."

"Very happy that I let you talk me into hiring you." I grinned at Mac. "Don't think anything's ever come up that you couldn't handle. You've managed to hire an eclectic crew to make sure nothing hops off the rails or, if it does, to get it right back on again."

"It's been quiet of late… kind of boring." Mac grinned.

"Don't say that. That's when everything hits the fan." I made a face. "Just know that if you get a whiff of anything going south, the best time to call is when you first find out about it. Don't even think it might be a bother."

Mac nodded.

"Have you dealt with all the drama of the morning?" Fab demanded.

"I'm ready." I stood, waved to Mac and Shirl, and followed Fab back to the car.

Chapter Nineteen

My phone rang before we got to the main highway. It was Cootie, and he never called just to chat, so something must be up. I answered, and he started talking before I could even get out hello.

"If you've got the time, can you buzz by the warehouse? Got a couple of things to show you."

"On our way."

Without another word, he hung up.

"We need to go by the warehouse," I told Fab.

"You really need to start asking questions when you get these 'hustle on over' calls."

"Yeah, okay."

Even when Fab had something pressing, she never opted for the direct route instead of taking every side street she could find. "You've been out cruising the streets again. That was my first time on a couple of the streets you just used."

Fab whizzed into the parking lot of the warehouse, hung a u-turn, and parked. Cootie stood under the roll-up door, eyeing her antics with a smirk.

We both got out and walked over to the man.

"It was probably a good idea." Cootie pointed

to one corner of the building.

"Surprise." Fab jumped up and threw her hands in the air. "It's Didier's and my gift, celebrating your new lame purchase."

Cootie laughed.

I turned to stare at her: *What are you talking about?*

"Seriously!" Fab huffed. "Check out the corners of the building. Now you can spy on the property from the comfort of your kitchen."

"Security cameras!" I grinned at her. "Betting I won't be the only one nosing around."

"Why did you need us to get over here?" Fab barked at Cootie.

"Inside..." He jerked his thumb over his shoulder. "Came upon a cheap-ass coffin that I'm guessing has been stored here for a while. Didn't bother to open the lid, because there's definitely something inside, and I wasn't about to take the chance that it's not someone's idea of a storage container and there's actually a body inside."

I groaned inwardly. "Is there a smell?"

"I sniffed around and didn't catch a whiff." Cootie shrugged.

"Show me." Fab jerked on his sleeve. "Sissy girl can stand here in the doorway."

"If it turns out—"

"You can call the cops," Fab shouted over her shoulder as she and Cootie cut across the warehouse.

Based on our track record, I guessed that dead-body-free was too much to hope for. I listened to a variety of noises and then the two of them laughing. I'd use this as an example the next time Creole brought up hiring someone *normal*. A normal person would have blurted out the news over the phone along with, "I quit."

It didn't take Fab and Cootie long, and they were soon both back standing in front of me.

"The good news," Fab started over Cootie's snort, "is whoever it is in the coffin—more like a wooden box—has been dead a long time, which is obvious, even though they were wrapped in plastic. The bad news is obvious—dead person."

I pulled my phone out of my pocket.

"You need to hold off making that 911 call." Cootie waved for us to follow. "I knew you wanted to get rid of the cars and figured Daddy-O would get you a good price but thought a second opin doesn't hurt squat, so I took a closer look before I made the call to my friend."

I ignored Fab's snicker at the reference to my mother's husband. "Did both men come out?"

"Just my friend, and he thought you'd be lucky to get even a few bucks, and even less for this blue sedan, and then jetted out of here, not wanting anyone to know he was here." Cootie stopped at the bumper of the car in the middle. "On the backseat of this one—" He kicked the flat tire. "—there's a body under a pile of blankets. Considering the other personal items inside, appears someone was living in the car. Knowing what your next question is going to be... it does smell some."

"A twofer, that's great." I turned to Fab, who scooted by me and walked around, peering in the windows of all the cars. "Wonder if the person inside the car owned it?" At their looks, I added, "It might make identification easier."

"So you know, there's nothing to see in the rest of them," Cootie assured me.

"I could shuffle this off on Creole, but he would call the cops, and I can do that." I took my phone out and scrolled across the screen, chuckling devilishly when I hit the number. When Kevin answered, I said, "This call is to test this new relationship of ours."

His groan came across the line loud and clear. "I thought Cooper was your man."

"Got it... sorry to bother you."

"Don't hang up," Kevin barked. "What's going on?"

"Our latest warehouse acquisition—two dead bodies have been found."

After a long silence, he said, "Is this your idea of a joke?"

"Nopers."

"Don't touch anything, which I know you already know. We're on our way." He hung up. I pocketed my phone.

"You probably would've fared better by calling the non-emergency line. That way, they might've sent out someone you don't know. Kevin can be…" Cootie didn't finish, screwing up his nose.

"Attitudinal."

"Pretty much."

"Where did Fab go?" I looked around.

"She's peering over the fence." Cootie pointed. "Since she can't budge those metal steps she found over in the corner — and she tried — she climbed up and, like me, found out there's nothing to see. If she plans to go on a snoop around, she'll need to bring her own ladder."

"Whatever you do, don't suggest that to her, and if she asks, you don't have one to loan her."

"On a fluke, I met one of the guys next door. Not sure how many work over there, as he's the only one I've seen." Cootie continued to keep an eye on Fab.

"How did your meet-and-greet go?" I asked.

"Standing out front, I saw the fence open and hot-footed it over there. My introduction was vague — thinking he didn't need to know any details. Found out it's a body shop, and after a couple more questions, he told me to mind my own business and leave. Friendly guy that he was, he didn't even introduce himself. He hopped in his truck and drove out, stopping with just enough room to get the fence closed and producing a remote-looking gadget. Thinking it locked the place up. Instead of 'Nice to meet you' or some such, even if it was phony, he turned to me before getting back in his truck, a *get lost* look on his face."

It was clear Cootie wasn't impressed with the neighbor. "I'll have to ask *Daddy-O* about him. Since they're competitors, he should know something. What I want to hear is that the guy is low-key and has never been a problem. Cooper told me they hadn't gotten any calls for over there, which made me happy."

"What are you going to do with this place?" Cootie asked.

"I asked her the same question, and she blew me off," said Fab, who'd just walked up and joined us.

I ignored her comment and asked, "You find anything interesting on the other side of the fence?"

"There's a six-car garage at the far end and a warehouse just opposite yours with the same structure as yours. Between the two buildings is a large courtyard—big table, no chairs. No matter where I peek over the fence, I can't see the front entrance to the main building. Directly across, on the opposite side next to the fence, is a small powerboat on a trailer, a flatbed tow truck, and a large enclosed truck."

"Did you get any shoe sizes?"

Cootie laughed, but Fab was disgusted.

"Got to say I peeked over the fence a few times," he admitted. "Nosey as all get out and all. Sounds like nothing has changed."

Fab shot me a smug look. It wouldn't have surprised me if she'd already figured out how to get a look at the inside of their warehouse. I'd remind her to be careful, which she'd blow off.

Two cop cars turned in and pulled behind the fence, and there was no doubt who was behind the wheels. The three of us walked over to where Kevin and Cooper were getting out.

"Dead bodies?" Cooper said, *not surprised* in his tone.

"Hey, Officer Kev." I waved and did a double-take when he laughed. He'd apparently had a hefty shot of caffeine before he got here. Before either could ask any questions, I told them, "It's not my find, so I don't have any answers for you." I pointed to Fab and Cootie.

"I'll tell you what I told these two." Cootie stepped forward and relayed exactly what he'd told us.

"I lifted the lid on the coffin and, just in case, made sure not to leave my fingerprints." Fab demonstrated by pulling her sleeve down over her hand.

"I'll go check the one inside," Cooper said to Kevin and motioned to Fab to follow him.

"I've got the car," Kevin said. Cootie led the way.

I went over and leaned against the side of my SUV. I pulled out my phone and called Creole. "Hey, hon."

"You sound tired."

"It's been a busy day."

"I'm afraid to ask."

"Everything else can wait until later, and so you know, I want dinner tonight to be just the two of us," I said. "As for what's going on right now..." I went on to explain.

"I'll come down and take over."

"No need," I assured him. "As soon as they get the coroner out here, which is probably the next call, Fab and I are leaving and going straight home... that's if I have my way."

"Promise me that you'll only have one drink, so we can enjoy the dinner I'm bringing."

"You're going to have to make it up to me for putting the brakes on my fun." I laughed. "Gotta go. Here comes Kevin and Cooper. If I get arrested, you'll be my first call."

"Not funny," Creole grouched. "Text me when you leave."

We hung up.

Kevin and Cooper met up in the middle of the driveway, talking to Fab and Cootie. I walked over to join them.

"What did you two decide?" I asked, eyeing the officers.

"Coroner is on the way," Cooper told me. The two men walked over to where their cars were parked.

"Once the lid was open, Cooper commented, 'This one has been dead a while,'" Fab told us. "Then went on to say that, after asking around, the consensus was that Logger would store anything. 'No kidding,' he mumbled. The big surprise was no comments about either of us offing the person, which I think might be a first."

"Kevin's only comment was, 'Doesn't appear to be any foul play,'" Cootie passed along.

"Are you quitting on me?" I asked him.

"Oh hell no. I'm not some weak-kneed… you get the gist." Cootie grunted. "Since I've got almost everything boxed up, there won't be any more surprises."

"Let's hope." I shook my head.

"One other thing: I didn't know how you wanted the boxes labeled, so I came up with my own system. Told Rude that when the calls start coming in to Cove Storage about the stuff, they can make an appointment, and I'll be there to make sure nothing flies off the rails. Rude's a tough one and won't like me invading her territory, so I expect that she'll be running me off, wanting to take care of it herself." He grinned. "The woman likes to be up in the middle of everything, and she gets gripey when she thinks she's being edged out."

"Sounds like someone else I know." I glanced at Fab with raised brows.

Kevin and Cooper made their way back over to us, looking less aggrieved than before.

"You going to have the car towed?" I asked. "Think it's one of the ones that is, or was, registered to someone. I've forgotten who."

"We can get our own info," Kevin snarked. "And yes, it'll be towed."

"Well then, consider it a gift."

Cooper unleashed a humorless chuckle. Kevin rolled his eyes.

"Can we go?" Fab asked.

"You sure? Surprised you don't want to be here when they take John Doe out of the car." Cooper eyed Fab.

I covered my eyes with my hands and shook my head, hearing a couple of unidentified chuckles.

"I've got more work to do, so I'll be here and can lock up," Cootie said.

We'd barely gotten out of the parking lot when my phone rang again. "I'm tempted to throw this out the window. But maybe not," I said, after eyeing the screen and seeing that it was Xander. I answered, "Only good news, please."

"I've got a couple of updates for you—"

"Hang a u-turn." I nudged Fab's arm, then told Xander, "We're just down the street, so see you in a few." I hung up.

"Do I need to remind you *again* to ask a few questions when you get these calls?"

"You can call Xander back and ask him yourself." I held out my phone, which she ignored.

Fab got us to the office within minutes. Once out of the car, we headed to the elevator, noting that the first floor was locked up. Getting off on the third floor, we headed straight to the office I shared with Xander and took our usual seats.

"I just flipped a coin to see which update to go with first." He smirked. There wasn't a coin in sight, so he'd picked up my trick—an invisible one worked and got you the desired results. "The sportscar you followed..." He clicked a couple of keys on his laptop. "It was stolen."

"You'd think, if you were going to go to all the trouble of stealing a car, you'd go for something better."

Really! Fab shook her head at me. "It was a Maserati." She used the same tone that Crum did when pointing out low IQ.

"I'd think if you spend that kind of money on a car, you'd want it to be recognizable so people will be suitably impressed." I glanced at Xander, who waved his hands: *Leave me out of this.*

"Stolen!" Fab said in disgust. "So there's no tracking the driver. Wonder if the car is still parked inside the apartment complex."

"Before you race over there and stand by the gate waiting for it to open..." I knew that she was mulling it over as I spoke. "Pass the information along to Cooper, who has the authority to legally get inside the gate, and he'll be able to track the driver. Don't you find it interesting that you thought the teen stole your car, and the next time you see him, he and Mommy are in a stolen vehicle?"

"Maybe mother and son have a lucrative gig going," Fab mused.

"If you're caught behind the wheel of a stolen

vehicle, there isn't an excuse that will get you out of being arrested," I said. "If your kid is in the car, thinking Social Services is going to be the next call. If he's ID'd as a potential thief, then maybe jail for him also."

"More and more kids are committing crimes, and oftentimes, it's linked back to an adult as the one calling the shots," Xander said. "They figure the kid will do minimal time."

"I can't imagine setting your kid up to go to jail," I said in disgust.

"So you know," Xander said to Fab, "I got a match on the picture you sent of the teenager; it's the same kid from the street cameras when your car was stolen. Working on facial recognition for the mother."

"Even if I had the apartment number, I can hardly go and beat on her door without getting into major trouble myself." Fab heaved a sigh, pulled out her phone, and scrolled across the screen. "If I don't make this call, I might do something I'll wish I hadn't." It was immediately clear that she'd called Cooper. She told him about recognizing the kid in the Maserati and following it to what she thought was their home. Surprisingly, he only asked a couple questions before they hung up. "I didn't have the nerve to ask Cooper to let me know what happens when his tone let me know that he wasn't happy with what I'd already done."

"Not sure, if there's an arrest, that it'll make the

internet," Xander said. "You know who could find out? Casio." He grinned.

"Casio would make the call in a heartbeat," I said. "Though you know that once you pique his interest, he always wants all the details about what went down."

"About your client, Bardy Dowell..." Xander looked between Fab and me.

"Yeah, well..." Fab jerked her thumb in my direction. "Fern called *you*."

"Neither of us has actually talked to the man... And since he's artificially related to Gunz, that makes him Fab's client."

"This is what I've got so far," Xander said, interrupting the stare-down between Fab and me. "His house was recently transferred to a Sway Dowell, and after a little digging, I found out it's his grandson."

"Fern told us that he said someone was trying to take his house. And it's a relative?" I felt even worse for the man. "We need some confirmation that the transaction happened against his will and to get a lawyer involved stat."

"It's got to be the same person that locked him up." Fab arched her brow.

"You need to get on it." I returned her stare. "Before you start pointing your manicured nails at me again, Gunz is going to want to hear what's going on from you."

"I've ordered a copy of the document that was filed to transfer the property, and you'll be able to compare signatures," Xander said.

"One family member engaged in ripping another off. This was already ugly, but I'm thinking it'll only get worse," Fab said, exasperated. "I'm ready to go home."

"Keep us updated, and if we learn anything, we'll share too," I told Xander, who nodded.

Chapter Twenty

When Fab and I split up, we agreed that there would be no more drama until tomorrow. I wasn't sure I could hold up my end. I set the table for two out on the deck and maneuvered it so that we would have a view of the water. I knew Creole would have a fit upon hearing about the events of the day, especially the guy that cornered Fab and me outside Jake's. I waited until after we'd finished dinner, which he picked up from Jake's, and he'd downed a couple beers. I restrained myself and drank only two margaritas, sipping the last one, then suggested that we share a chaise.

Right before Creole got home, I'd received an update from Doodad on the kids' party, which I passed along. The kids stayed longer than expected because they were all having such a good time. The older ones were excited to pick up gambling tips from a couple of the regulars. Kelpie kept the younger ones entertained, leaving the jukebox on and getting them singing and dancing, opening it up to anyone else who wanted to join in. It didn't surprise me that she got takers. Especially after it was made clear that knowing the words to a song wasn't required and once the music began, no one was to make a snide comment.

"I still don't know how camping week got to be a thing and the parents actually agreed to it. Wait until they find out that it wasn't all a G-rated beach vacay," Creole grouched. "And *you* helped to make that happen."

"The local parents knew what they were getting into. My bro can try to claim ignorance, but Emerson updates him on everything and keeps him calm. As for the rest, I wouldn't have thought Cruz would let his kids spend time with a man that banged his granny and would assume that he'd have passed that tidbit along to the other parents as a reason not to trust the kids with Crum. But the kids all showed and here we are." I flashed him a phony smile. He wasn't amused.

"When, and not if, the complaint calls come in, be sure you reroute them to Crum so he can mumble some excuse. Tell him to try not to use the same one over and over."

"Stop. What the parents are going to see is happy, laughing kids, and they'll overlook anything they find questionable." I nodded with assurance... I hoped anyway. "If I had to rate the biggest drama of the day, number one would go to... Da-da-da," I yelled.

Creole looked up and shook his head. "Something tells me it was one of those situations where you should've called and didn't."

"What the day was, was one drama after another." I told him about our uninvited guest, Booker. "There won't be any disputing my version, as it can be verified by the security feed at Jake's."

"You don't need to worry about ever seeing that Booker cretin again; I'll take care of it." Creole pounded his fist on the arm of the chaise.

"I've got a better idea."

"You don't know what mine even is."

"It sounds like there's the possibility of it involving jail time if you're found out, so you should hear me out." Creole didn't appear convinced but stayed silent. "It's my opinion that Fab's uber rich client sicced the thug on us, so I'm thinking we call in Fab's papa, who made the last guy disappear and enjoyed every minute of it. He's got the connections to make Booker disappear and ensure that the client never even mentions his daughter's name again, and to do it faster than either of us. The upside is that no one goes to jail."

"I'm assuming that you're going to run this by Fab first and that she'll be making the call."

"That's not what I had in mind when I told her I'd handle it. There was a reason I wasn't specific. Whatever I suggested, I knew she'd turn up her nose at it, as she likes to handle everything herself. Only when everything hits the fan does she call on her resources." I held out my hand and mouthed, *Your phone.* I'd left mine in the house.

He slid it out of his pocket and put it in my palm. "Caspian did whisper the last time I saw him that I could call anytime."

"Let him know that you've compiled all the information he'll need into a file, which you'll forward to him."

"One more thing," I said before I made the call. "When everything is a fait accompli, we'll have a family dinner where Caspian's the surprise guest of honor and let him unveil what a badass he is."

"I've got to admit that Caspian's going to love that he's being called on again, and you know he never turns down an invitation to a family dinner, and for either one, he'd fly in from another country."

"I'll be sure and remind him to schedule time to get into trouble with Mother and Spoon. I know they have a lot of fun together." I scrolled across the screen and found the number. "We need someone that we can brag to that we can get a billionaire on the phone."

Caspian answered and went off in a flood of French. Of our foursome, I was the only one that didn't know more than a few words, most of them not repeatable.

"Bon Cheerios," I said when he paused. I could feel Creole's eyeroll.

Caspian laughed, then sobered. "Fabiana, she's okay?"

"Your daughter is doing just fine and cozying it up with her husband. She doesn't know about this call, and when she finds out, odds are... I'm not betting on this one." That garnered a chuckle. I assured him that Creole knew everything and was in agreement with me calling. Then I told him what had gone down and that he was my first choice to make it all go away.

"You don't need to worry about any of this," Caspian assured me. "You send me that file, and I'll take care of it right away."

Creole flexed his fingers, wanting the phone back.

"My husband is demanding to speak with you." That got another laugh. "You're the best," I said before handing the phone over.

Creole told him there'd be a family dinner in his honor and that he could be the one to make the announcement that Booker was no longer a problem. It was clear from the grin on Creole's face that Caspian liked that idea. They wound up the conversation in French, which had me scrunching up my nose.

"So rude," I said when Creole repocketed his phone. "The last bit, I didn't understand a word."

"I was telling him that I appreciated him handling the situation and keeping me out of jail. He said, 'And doing the same thing for Didier.' He then reminded me that he expected me to call anytime."

"I'm already planning the dinner and thinking that when I put Mother in charge, the location will change to Fab's. And once I tell her it's a surprise, she won't tell Fab anything, no matter how hard she tries to get info out of her." I made a couple of notes, then sent the file I'd promised to Caspian. "There is one more thing." Creole groaned loud enough to bring the house down. I told him about Fab and Didier's gift of cameras on the warehouse.

"Great gift. I'd have had it done somewhere on down the line, but now is better."

"I don't expect any creepers, but if it does happen..."

* * *

I'd been grounded until Raynes and Booker had been dealt with. I knew without a doubt that the news had made it down the beach. I also knew that Creole wouldn't withhold anything from Didier and would keep him updated. Something else that didn't surprise me was that two guards had shown up to monitor the front gate. When asked by my bestie, which I knew would happen, I was going to go with complete ignorance and direct her to Creole.

I took my laptop and a bottle of iced tea out to the deck and made numerous calls, checking up on all of our businesses and making certain that no more bodies had been found.

It was lunchtime when Casio came tromping down the beach, behind him a line of kids with t-shirts over their bathing suits. He laid out a couple of large blankets, and the kids threw themselves down and opened their brown bags, removing a canned drink and dumping what appeared to be burgers and fries in front of themselves.

I was happy to see that Crum had managed to wrangle Lark and Clive into kid-herding. Another young guy that I'd never seen before came trooping down the beach in a red bathing suit and sunglasses, a few items crammed under one arm that were hard to make out. Turned out one was a stool with a back on it that he unfolded and set in front of the kids, sitting down and talking to them while they ate.

Casio turned, spotted me, and waved, then kicked his way through the sand, meeting up with Fab, who was coming up the beach. The two came up the steps.

"If you want anything to drink, grab it yourself." I pointed in the direction of the outside refrigerator. "Has camping week moved to your house?" I asked as the two sat down.

"Yeah, and I'm totally good with it."

"That's because you're the coolest dad."

"I hired a lifeguard, since the plans are to spend the day on the beach. The kids took a vote, and they've decided that, in addition to playing sports, they're looking forward to swimming. That should keep them busy until they drop."

"I've got to say, Crum has brought the fun." I watched as the kids finished wolfing down lunch.

"Came over to find out if we can use the water bikes," Casio said.

"They're chained under the deck at the other end of the beach." I jerked my thumb. "They're not locked, but when you bring them back, make sure they're secure so they don't float off."

"Any complaints from the kids that you're not bringing enough action?" Fab asked.

"The kids have a really good relationship with Crum and are up for whatever he throws out there." Casio grinned. "While they're having fun, Crum is constantly teaching them something and presenting it in such a way that they listen up."

"Like how to gamble?" I flinched at the idea of that making the rounds of the other parents. I'd have my answer as to whether they objected when Crum cooked up another of these ideas and no one showed up.

"Alex has already suggested that, in lieu of movie night at home, once in a while, we change it up to poker night. Got to say I didn't object to the idea… then had to remind myself that I can't clean them out every time."

"Anything we can do—" I flicked my finger between Fab and myself. "—just yell."

Chapter Twenty-One

It didn't take long, just two days, before Mother called and invited Creole and me to a *surprise* dinner at Fab's that night.

When I asked one question after another, she said with a sigh, "Enough with the questions."

"I expected that this get-together would be at my house." Although I'd fully expected the change.

"Fab and Didier have way more room."

"That tells me you invited everyone we know, and probably a few more."

"Don't be late." Mother hung up.

I'd barely put the phone down when I got a notification that someone was at the gate. I looked at the security feed, saw Cooper, and groaned. Just great. My guess was that he wanted to talk to Fab, and when she didn't answer, he called me. I opened the gate without bothering to ask any questions. I had the front door open and was waiting when he climbed out of his car.

"Hello, Officer." I smiled and beckoned him inside, leading the way over to the island. "Would you like something to drink?"

"I'll take a water," he said as he slid onto a stool.

I grabbed a bottle out of the refrigerator and set it in front of him, then sat across from him and waited.

"I was hoping that the reason Fab didn't answer was because she was over here."

"Not here." I smiled simply. "It's a short walk if you want to beat on her door."

"What do you know about the stolen car she turned us onto?"

"I don't know anything more about the Maserati than what she already told you. When she spotted a kid that looked like the one that stole her Porsche, we followed the car."

"If she'd had access to the apartment complex, then what? Would she have snuck around and stolen their car?"

I groaned loudly at the man. "That would never happen," I said emphatically.

Cooper flashed a brief smile. "When we got to the complex, the car was nowhere to be found."

"Did you jump the fence?" I guessed that the eyeroll meant no.

"The office was closed, but we were able to track down the handyman, who hadn't seen the sportscar in the parking lot and didn't know who it belonged to. Where we did get lucky was he was able to identify mother and son from the photos Fab sent over. He showed us to her apartment, but no answer. We went back the next afternoon, and the neighbor told us they moved out in the middle of the night."

"Damn. Someone couldn't wait to tell them the cops had been beating on their door."

Cooper's brow arched at my description. "I'm here because if you or Fab see either of them again, I'd like a call. And as soon as you see them, not when you get around to it."

"So you know, when Fab got the report back that the car had been stolen, you were her first call."

"We did verify that the Maserati was reported stolen, and it still hasn't been recovered. There's been an uptick in high-end car thefts. The reports we've been getting of late have been for cars valued over 100K." Cooper eyed me. "So we're agreed, you see anything, you call? And don't chase a car thief yourself."

"How about if I promise for Fab and me that you'll be our first call?" I'd probably be the one to keep the promise for the both of us.

He stood, and it was clear the jury was out as to whether he believed me. "Mind if I grab another water?"

"Help yourself." I waved my hand. "By the way, thank you for the update. Fab's going to be disappointed she wasn't at home when you came calling." Again, he didn't look convinced as I walked him to the door.

Not long after Cooper left, the door opened, and Creole walked in. "Saw Cooper turning out of the compound; what did he want?"

Not flinching from his glare-down, I slid off my stool and beelined straight for him, grabbed his hand, and pulled him down the hall to the bedroom. On the way, I gave him a brief explanation.

After a long shower and while he sat on the bed, I gave him a longer version of events while I dug through the closet. "I'm assuming that tonight's dinner is about Caspian dealing with Booker. I knew he wouldn't drag his feet, but I'm impressed with his speed, especially if it turns out we have nothing to worry about anymore."

"Be prepared for Fab's annoyance to hit the ceiling when she finds out about everything that went on behind her back and that she didn't get to witness the showdown with Booker." Creole shook his head. "Surprised that Caspian hasn't asked his daughter to let him go along on one of her cases."

"He's hinted that he'd like to come along. And when he finds out that Mother has gunned up and been on more jobs than him, his request will get more insistent."

"Just choose something." Creole stared at me and then at the closet, like a dress would hop into my hand. When I didn't grab a hanger, he came up behind me, chose a short-sleeved black above-the-knee dress, and put it in my hands. "Pretty sure you can easily pick the shoes."

I turned and kissed him, and the two of us

finished getting dressed. The last hurdle was what to do with my hair. I went for easy-peasy and scooped it up into a ponytail.

Creole's phone alerted with a message, and after reading it, he laughed. "Fab's getting two surprises tonight."

"Do I get a preview?" When he didn't answer, I threw my arms around his neck and gave him a big kiss.

"Instead of taking the beach—" He grabbed my hand. "—we'll go in the front door."

"Am I going to need my lockpick?"

"You two have to stop doing that," Creole admonished on our way out the front door.

"You're no fun."

"Pretty sure I can change your mind on that one."

The walk to Fab and Didier's was a short one. You couldn't stand in our driveway and throw stuff into theirs but close enough.

I recognized several of the cars parked on the road in front of their house. I'd been right in my assumption that Mother would invite anyone who had the remotest connection. We turned into the driveway, and I came to a stop. "Wow." Center stage was a black convertible Porsche. "So Fab finally decided on a new ride. Whatever you do, don't touch it; she can spot a fingerprint from a mile away." Creole laughed, but we both knew it was true. "Hope she didn't get it from Brick, as that would mean favors that could go off the rails in all sorts of ways." He was an old client that I didn't miss in the slightest and didn't think she did either. He was also Casio's bro, and they had an awkward relationship.

"Since Fab has been dragging her feet about replacing her car, Caspian did it for her, and it was delivered this morning."

"Looks like her," I said as I walked around. "Want to wager that I have zero chance of getting to drive it?"

"Not taking that bet." He chuckled.

Not bothering to knock—knowing that they wouldn't do it, or Fab wouldn't anyway—I opened the front door and yelled, "We're here."

Spoon was the only one in the kitchen. He turned from filling a bucket with ice, laughed, and pointed toward the patio.

"Heard you and Mother have been busy planning and organizing?" I walked over and hugged the man.

He laughed and whispered in my ear, "Yeah, sure."

"How many people did she invite?" I asked.

"The number isn't important."

"Okay, Mother."

Spoon smirked. "Almost everyone is here. They're outside, soaking up the sun and watching the kids run around. Your mother was smart and organized a separate kids-only party, and they'll be barbecuing and eating down on the dock. It got a thumbs-up reception when she took a vote."

"There's going to come a time when the kids are going to think it's a bore to go home," Creole said, grabbed a beer out of the refrigerator and holding one out to me.

"I'll pass." I made a face. "I'll get a drink from whoever's bartending."

Creole grabbed one of the buckets filled with ice and beer and Spoon the other one, and the three of us walked out to the patio.

"I'll have a margarita." I waved my arms at Casio, who was behind the bar. "I wouldn't be surprised if you won't let anyone park their used car in your driveway, even when your Porsche is in the garage." I winked at Fab, who gave me a squinty stare. I made my way over to Caspian and hugged him hard, whispering in his ear, "Thank you for waving your magic wand."

"Not so fast. You owe me. I was told to hold out for a few favors, and my first one is that I expect, when there's *another* problem, that I'll be your first call."

"You snap your fingers, and whatever you ask—done." I kissed his cheek.

"How is it that I never got that kind of a deal?" the Chief grumbled, coming up behind me. The now-retired Chief of Police from Miami gave me a hug. I wasn't surprised that he'd been invited, as he and Caspian were thick as thieves when the latter was in town. My guess was that the Chief helped Caspian navigate the situation with Booker so it was all legal-like, or mostly anyway.

"Good to see you," I told the Chief, winking at Didier as he handed me my drink.

"Always know you can call me," the Chief grouched.

"I'm going to remind you of your offer when I do call." The two of us laughed.

Of course, Mother had set up a table overlooking the water, as it was a favorite place for us all to sit. Doubly so as we could keep an eagle eye on the kids, who'd been running on the beach since this morning, with Crum, Clive, and Lark keeping an eye on them. I kissed Brad and Emerson before sitting next to my husband.

Caspian, who'd sat at the head of the table, stood and held out his glass in a toast. After welcoming everyone, he said, "To my amazing daughter — you won't be hearing from your client, Austin Raynes, or his gofer, Booker, ever again. I also made it clear that no one else better come around with threats."

I tipped my glass to him, as did the others.

"What's going on now?" Brad asked in exasperation.

Fab stood and gave an abbreviated version of the events that had gone down. "When you had your sit-down with Raynes, did he happen to say if he knew how Harris, the daughter's ex, ended up dead?"

It was clear from Fab's lack of reaction that she'd gotten a heads up about her father's involvement and already knew what would be announced.

"Raynes claimed ignorance about how the man died but made sure that I knew he was out of town when the fire happened," Caspian told us. "He also made it clear that Harris got what he deserved. His only gripe was that the blackmail evidence hadn't been recovered, as he'd have liked to put a match to it himself. I assured him that Fab never had the opportunity to recover anything and didn't want to hear his name mentioned with hers ever again."

"Happy to be rid of Raynes," Fab said.

"What about Booker? Is he dead or still creeping around?" I asked.

"Booker's in jail, where he's going to stay," Caspian told us.

"Turned out he had a couple of outstanding warrants that will keep him there for a while," the Chief informed us.

"One more thing," Caspian said. "If you hear from either man, I want to know immediately."

Fab nodded.

"Do the police have anything on Tech Harris, the man whose house went up in flames?" I asked the Chief.

"Why would you think I'd know?" he asked.

"Because you're thorough and you don't like unanswered questions." I returned his smirk.

"If I hear anything more…"

I nodded.

"Next time you and the sheriff go for a round of golf, ask how the two people whose bodies were found at our new warehouse died," Creole said to his old boss. "Highly doubt anyone will be issuing an arrest warrant for either me or Madison, as I did hear from a good source that both people had been dead longer than either of us have been in town." He told everyone about the bodies discovered.

"Knowing my daughter—"

I interrupted Mother, ignoring her raised brow. "You're right, I've got everything handled. Mostly anyway. Which reminds me..." I banged a spoon on the table. "When you get your invites to the send-off for the ashes, I don't want to hear back that you're busy, and 'I've got a headache' isn't acceptable either." Which garnered a mixture of laughter and eye-rolls.

The kids started yelling, and all eyes turned to them. However, it was easy to see that they'd quickly settled whatever the problem was and gone back to jumping around in the water.

"How are you holding up, now that the kids are staying at your house?" Creole asked Casio.

"I like it better than The Cottages. This way, I know what's happening, sometimes before they have a chance to get into trouble. I also like that the activities were pre-coordinated and none require my input. Here and there, I manage to take credit for the good time they're having." Casio grinned. "Alex knows I'm full of it but doesn't call me out."

By silent agreement, all talk of business was over. We caught up on the latest in everyone's life as we drank, and when dinner arrived, it was spread out from one end of the table to the other.

Chapter Twenty-Two

The next morning over coffee, Creole told me with a grin that he had a message for me from Fab. "'Meeting with Gunz at the office.' Bet you can't wait."

"Any clue what it's about?" I inwardly groaned. "If he actually requested my presence, it's something he thinks isn't up to Fab's standards. Or is it just her, wanting backup?"

"I didn't get the chance to question her smirk when she told me to pass along the info on our way out the door."

"Door? She came over early and left already?"

"Last night, while you were hugging your mother and Spoon, she whispered that she wanted me to surprise you with the news this morning. I quickly negotiated two favors."

"That will come back to haunt her when I do the same damn thing to her. What did Didier say? I expect he was close enough to hear every word exchanged."

"Oh, you know…"

"Shower time." I tugged on his hand.

He scooped me up, threw me over his shoulder, and headed down the hall.

"Letting you know now that you're going to owe me if this is some sucky request," I warned.

After using up all the hot water, I chose a casual green dress and slides. Creole, in jeans and a dress shirt, told me that he didn't have an out-of-the-office meeting scheduled.

"I expect a call if anything goes awry. Better yet, call me anyway."

"Okay, hon."

We grabbed our briefcases and went out to the SUV.

"How long do you think it'll be before Fab takes her car for its inaugural drive?" I asked as he pulled out of the compound.

"I got insider information that it happened last night."

"That doesn't surprise me—Didier and her cruising the streets when the only ones out and about were drunks and criminals."

Thanks to no traffic, we got to the office in record time. Creole pulled through the security gate, parked, and took inventory of the cars.

"Looks like you beat Fab here," I said, looking around. "Works for me, as I've got some emails to send and also need to check in with Cootie."

"Since the warehouse is going to be ready to lease soon, do you have anyone in mind?"

"I'm putting out the word that it's available for a stable business, and not a whiff of shady," I said adamantly.

"On that, we're in total agreement."

We walked into the building together, and after a kiss, I rode up in the elevator to the third floor. Opening the door to the office, I took one step inside and came to an abrupt halt; a cyclone had hit, and based on the mess, I'd bet that the room had been ransacked.

Xander came rushing out of the office that we shared.

"What the..." I waved my hand around.

"If you're meeting anyone, you're going to want to do it downstairs. I called Clive, and he's going to grab a couple boxes from your storage place and help me get this cleaned up," Xander said, sounding frantic.

"Why are you acting like this is your fault? Or did you go off your spool, empty out the cabinets, and throw everything on the floor?"

"Yesterday..." He retrieved a couch cushion and sat down, shaking his head. "This chick showed up looking for a job. I should've had a lot more questions about how she got in the building. But I was finishing up a project and running up against a deadline, so I just wanted her gone."

"Stop. Take a breath before you have health issues." I turned a chair upright and set my briefcase and purse down. "I should give Fab a heads up, but what the heck, let her be surprised."

Xander groaned.

"Don't worry, I won't tell her that cyclone Xander hit." Getting another groan, I walked over to the refrigerator. It was empty, but at least there was no food on the floor. I grabbed a water out of the cupboard and handed it to Xander. "Back to the chick. Then what happened?" I sat down.

"Spacey… hard to believe it was her real name, but I only had one thing on my mind — getting rid of her — and no desire to take the time to ask, 'You couldn't make up a better name?' Got to tell you, she looked like her name."

I chuckled. He stared: *Not helpful*.

"She wanted a job, and I told her that I knew that no one in the building was hiring. She thanked me, and I was about to walk her out when my phone rang. I ran back to my office to grab it, and when I came back out, she was gone."

"You think Spacey had something to do with this mess?" I asked. He nodded. "Wonder what she was looking for?"

"The reason I know it was her is after I walked in this morning and saw this, I opened my laptop and reviewed the security footage. She never left yesterday. What she did was hide in the bathroom. It didn't occur to me to look there."

"Why would you? Don't be so hard on yourself."

"She waited until I left, and then from what I could tell, she rummaged through everything and helped herself to a couple of items off Fab's desk. Wait until she finds out about that." Xander shook his head in disgust. "The footage showed that she camped out on the couch and, early this morning, filled her backpack with food and water and was out the door."

"Did Spacey have a car? Get a plate number?"

"I was last to leave, and a lone unknown vehicle in the parking lot would've stood out to me; I wouldn't have left until I found out who it belonged to. When she left here, she walked out to the road and turned south, toward the Overseas."

"To make sure nothing like this happens in the future, anyone entering the building who we don't have a business relationship with needs to be escorted out when they leave," I suggested.

"I've gone over the footage several times already and can't figure out what she was looking for, if anything. It appeared that she was having a fun time making a huge mess. It did surprise me that she spent the night."

"Compile the footage into a file for Fab, as she's going to want to see it, and make sure that we both get a picture of the woman. I'll show it around Jake's and see if anyone recognizes her, and someone will if she lives in the Cove."

"I'm really sorry—"

"Oh stop. I'm just glad that she didn't catch you by surprise and hurt you."

"I thought about that." Xander winced. "Another thing I noticed from the footage was that she slept sporadically, and when I guess she'd had enough tossing and turning, she snooped around some more before leaving."

"I know you've made a couple of friends on this street—show her picture around and see if anyone can ID her. Also ask if they know if any other places were broken into. How did she get in the gate, do you know?"

"There was a delivery, and she walked in behind the truck. I noticed that she knew how to stay out of sight of the driver."

"Sounds like she knew what the heck she was doing, which would lead me to believe that this isn't the first place she's tossed. Once we get everything put back in the cupboards, we'll have an idea what she took. I don't keep anything here worth taking, and I doubt that Fab does either."

"Me neither. Also thought she wasn't looking for something to pawn, as she barely glanced at the electronics. But then, why waste her time when she was on foot?"

"I'm happy that she didn't take or destroy any of the electronics, and as for the rest of the stuff, it appears she just had fun throwing it around." I shook my head.

The door opened and Fab walked in, like me, coming to an abrupt halt. "What happened in here?"

"Xander and I decided it was time to downsize and get rid of the junk," I said, biting back a grin.

Xander groaned.

"Yeah, sure," Fab said, continuing to assess everything.

"Are you suggesting that there might be more to this?"

"Now I have more empathy for Brad and what

you must've put him through growing up."

"My bro survived all my antics, and so will you." I chuckled.

Fab slammed the door, side-stepped around the disarray, and headed to her desk, which had survived most of the damage. "I don't have all day for an explanation, as my client is going to be arriving any minute."

"While Xander fills you in, I'm going to try to get office space on one of the other floors. The choice of which one is up to you." I took my phone out of my pocket, waiting on her answer.

"First floor, and I want the conference table. Have Lark chase the guys into their office and keep the door closed."

I made the call and repeated Fab's request, which had Lark laughing, especially the second part. I hung up. "Done deal. You can go down anytime. Knowing Lark, if Gunz arrives before you get down there, she'll flag him down. He won't mind, since he thinks she's a hot number."

"I was just about to tell Xander that we're going to have new rules regarding deliveries. This isn't going to happen again." Fab surveyed the room, wrinkling her nose. "A chick on foot — we're going to find her."

"Then what?"

"Lucky her, I just rejected feeding her to wildlife."

Xander's laptop pinged, and he checked the screen. "Gunz is here."

"I'll be here helping Xander clean up this mess. You go solve whatever problem Gunz has now."

"You're coming with me," Fab said emphatically. "And you—" She pointed to Xander. "—sit back and relax. Help will be here soon, and you can tell them what to do." She grabbed her briefcase and had her phone out before she got to the door. She glared, flicking her finger in the direction of my briefcase.

I took the hint, picking it up and meeting her at the door. From the sounds of it, she had Rude on the phone and was organizing a clean-up squad. When she hung up, I reminded her, "She's not your employee."

"Since my bestie is her boss, I knew that it wouldn't be an issue. Why spend all day on the phone trying to enlist help when I can go with a sure bet?" The elevator doors opened, and we rode down to the first floor.

"Can't argue with you on that one, though I'd like to." We walked into the office, and I'd called it—Gunz's big bulk was seated on the corner of Lark's desk as he flirted with her. "I'm going to be reminding Lark that Gunz is a psycho in an expensive suit."

"Be nice."

"Yeah, okay." Noting that the conference table was empty, I passed Fab while she went to snag her client, dropped my briefcase on the table, reserving my seat, and went to look for Creole. Since the guys' office door was open, it wasn't hard to see Brad peering out. "You three don't have anything work-related to do?" I'd interrupted Creole throwing a paper ball at Didier, who tossed it back.

"What are we missing out on?" Didier asked. "We were told to mind our own business, but who listens around here?" His assessing stare dared me to disagree.

"I bet you know exactly what's going on and kept it from your friends here," I said to Didier as I plopped myself in Creole's lap and grabbed a quick kiss.

"I do know, but do you?" Didier smirked.

"You really need an exit besides the windows," I griped. "Because if you had one, I'd be out of here. Not sure whose ride I'd take, as it would be a split-second decision."

"You know what would be fun? Crash the party!" Brad winked at me.

I shot him a thumbs up. "I know nothing." I slid off Creole's lap and headed out the door, which I didn't bother to close, leaving them laughing. I dropped into a chair at the conference table on the opposite end from Fab and Gunz.

"Nice of you to join us." Gunz barely glanced my way.

"You're welcome." I avoided looking at Fab, knowing I'd get the *behave* look.

"Goff is due to appear before a judge in two days, and I need you to make sure he gets there and is appropriately attired." This time, Gunz did make eye contact with me.

"No. In case you didn't understand, N. O. You must've forgotten that Fab is the one who works for you, not me." If Gunz was asking me, then I knew there was going to be a problem.

"It's not that I don't think my girl can handle it, but let's face it, you're able to work with people with… well, issues. I just want this case to be over with; I'm tired of getting frantic family calls. And his mother needs assurance that there won't be any more problems. They're worried Goff's going to end up in jail. It doesn't matter how many times I've told them that he has a good lawyer and if he does as he's told…"

"Doesn't he have a drinking problem?"

"Everything went to hell in his life, all at the same time, and he got on the sauce. I got him a job, which he just started, and his attitude has improved, as in not so down in the dumps." Gunz's look said, *See what a good guy I am.*

"If Goff really wanted to get his life back together, he'd show up in court without having a gun in his back." I tried to dial back the snark and failed.

"You do this, and whatever you want, it's done."

"Done?" I eyed Gunz, and he nodded. He already owed me a couple and better not have forgotten. "Are we agreed that any expenses incurred are on you?"

"You know I'm not a cheap bastard."

Another yes. Of sorts anyway. Rude caught my attention by standing at the elevator waving like a crazy woman. I nodded, and she disappeared inside.

Gunz popped the locks on his briefcase, slid his hand inside, and came out with a sheet of paper, which he handed to me.

I scanned the page, which consisted of the date and location where Goff needed to make an appearance. "Can your guy whip up a suit overnight?" I asked Fab.

"He'll make it happen," she assured me.

"One more thing." I eyed Gunz. "Fairly certain you remember Fern." Just in case… "She's the one that called about that neighbor of hers —"

"She showed up out of nowhere and lied to my face that the man was related, when I have it on good authority that he's not." Gunz appeared to grind his teeth. "I can't fix everyone's problems."

You don't do it now — you have Fab do it… or me. "You need to spell that out to the relatives at the next get-together. I know, have them all take a blood test and get on a special list."

"Are you finished?" Gunz grunted.

"You want us to tell Fern to take a hike —"

"That would be short-sighted," I cut Fab off. "Word gets out that some poor distraught friend of a relative needed help and Mr. King wouldn't lift his pinkie… how's that going to go over? That *is* what they call you, isn't it?"

"*The* King."

First that I'd heard him admit to the title. "I know you know this, but I'll remind you—Fern wants to be the organizer of your family issues. If your response is going to be *no way*, then it's on you to tell her. Neither Fab nor I are going to do it."

Gunz turned his attention to Fab. "I only half-listened when Fern was rattling on about some ideas she had."

Were they exchanging secret code? If so, that was annoying.

"What did you two decide?" I snarked.

"I'll talk to Fern," Fab assured Gunz and me.

"I hope this doesn't mean that Fern's going to be told to take a hike. If you don't think that's imprudent of you, think again." No answer from the man.

"Do you mind if Fab and I have a few minutes?" Gunz had clearly had enough of me.

"You know where to find me." I jumped up and tried not to run into the guys' office. The door was still open, and I beelined straight inside. They'd somehow purloined Xander's flea find, or wherever he found it—a baby monitor—and were fooling around with it to get it to work. Not sure if they'd succeeded, as it was silent for now. I sat on the corner of Creole's desk.

"Does it smell upstairs?" He grinned.

"Didn't take long for word to filter down here. Not even going to ask who delivered the news. Since I don't know how much you already know, you need to listen up. I don't want to hear complaints later about not being in the know." I told them what I knew of Spacey's adventure, all of them snickering at her name. They were certain it was fake, just like Xander and me.

"We're going to do whatever it takes to make sure it doesn't happen again," Creole grouched.

Didier and Brad nodded.

"Just know that Fab's ready to round Spacey's butt up and boot it somewhere, and I don't really care, as long as none of us ever sees her again," I told them.

"We'll spread the word to our neighbors and make sure they keep an eye out, so it doesn't happen to them," Didier said.

"Speaking of being in the know, what did Fat-ass want?" Brad grinned. "This cheap thing was useless." He glared at the box.

"Gunz better not hear you say that and realize you're talking about him, because it'll take him a nanosecond to know you heard it from me," I said with a shake of my head.

"Trust me, I'd make up some believable story that has zero to do with you and me," Brad promised. "Don't worry, it'll make sense, even though it's been a while since I've had to come up with something at a moment's notice."

"Remember the old days, when we pulled a con or two on Mother? There were a couple of times she didn't figure it out." I laughed.

"Speaking of…" Brad pointed out into the main room.

We all craned our heads to see Mother chatting it up with Gunz, the two enjoying each other's company, and Fab sitting back with a huge smirk.

"The thought of those two carrying on like besties makes me nauseous," I said. "I just don't want him to ask Mother to get involved with one of his family members because she'd hop at the chance and sneak around, not telling Fab or me. If that happens, I can promise that one of my bullets will get embedded in one of his cheeks."

The guys all groaned.

"Gunz better remember that he hired Fab as his fixer and leave you and Madeline out of it," Creole grouched. "If you need me to, I'll remind him."

"Blame it on Didier." I flashed the man a sneaky smile. "He's the one who made the rule about Fab and me being a twosome and no sneaking around."

"It's not like I haven't been rolled under the bus before, and so you know, I don't like it."

I winked at Didier as I stood up. "I need to get out there and eavesdrop, make sure Mother isn't signing up to do something that would get her butt kicked." I shot out the door, heading straight for Mother and kissing her cheek. "Behaving yourself?"

"You and I both know that's a big bore." She laughed.

The guys were right behind me. "Pretty much figured your meeting was over," Creole said to Gunz, who acknowledged him with a nod, along with the others.

Brad kissed Mother, and Creole and Didier both winked at her.

"Keep me updated," Gunz said and stood. He grabbed his briefcase, and Fab walked him out.

Chapter Twenty-Three

Whatever Gunz was talking to Fab about must have been intense, as it took her a while to come back inside.

"Madeline's here because she has a job for us," Fab announced as she sat next to Didier.

"Why would Mother come to you when I haven't heard anything about a so-called job?" I eyed the two women, and both were unreadable. The guys sat back and watched avidly. If they were expecting a fight, they weren't getting one.

"Fab and I were talking at the party, and I asked her about doing a favor for my friend, Jean," Mother told me. The two women were known to look for low-level trouble. "Funny thing, I didn't have to undergo any intense questioning from Fab, and I made it clear that I'm more than happy to help out in any way I can."

I shot a glare at Fab, who was enjoying herself way too much.

"Why don't you detail exactly what this favor entails?" Brad came close to a bark. "Or more accurately, what you're involving Madison and Fab in."

"Just Fab," I said.

"Oh stop. Spoon and I were getting ready to leave her house, and Fab was right there," Mother scolded.

"I'm betting that whatever this is about, you wanted to keep it from your loving husband, and hence, he was out of eavesdropping range at the time this little chat of yours took place. You remember your agreement with Spoon? It's pretty much the same one that Fab and I have with our husbands. Also guessing that you never updated Spoon, and he has no clue what you're up to right now." I returned her stare, and having learned from the best, mine matched hers.

"There's no better time than now to find out what Mother is up to." Brad eyed her. "That way, I'll know if I need to secure her to a chair and make a quick call to Spoon."

"If you'd all hold your shorts—" Mother glared. "—you'd find out that it's no different than any of Fab's other jobs." *So there.* "This is where I remind you that it doesn't matter what you think; it's none of your business."

That elicited a couple chuckles.

"You've all met my long-time friend and know what a nice woman Jean is and that she doesn't create drama."

Nice intro, Mother, but what's going on?

"Jean decided to do a little downsizing and called in a woman who orchestrates estate sales and who came highly recommended by another friend of hers," Mother said. "In Jean's case, the woman lived up to her hype, and the sales exceeded expectations. The agreement was that Jean would get an accounting and a check within twenty days. That hasn't happened, and the woman hasn't responded by phone or email. Also, it turns out that the business address was one of those rent-by-the-hour places."

"How much are we talking?" Fab asked.

"Jean estimates the number to be in the thousands, as she sold off antique furniture and collector's items. She's moving out of her large house and into an apartment in a retirement community."

"What about the woman who made the recommendation?" I asked. "Did Jean get back in touch with her?"

"Jean did call her and found out that she was experiencing the exact same scenario and also having no luck contacting the woman. To date, she hasn't collected a cent."

"What is it you want Fab to do? Smoke her out of hiding and kick her butt?" I asked.

"You don't need to be so crude about it," Mother huffed.

"What Mother meant to say was yes, which would've been a lot quicker." Brad looked at me and rolled his eyes.

Mother fished through her purse and handed a business card to Fab. "Thought you could call the estate woman and... well, you know."

"What I'll do is have Xander find a home

address for—" Fab looked at the business card. "—Lynn Wade. In the meantime, you need to get an exact amount that Jean's owed, or close enough so that when I go kick the woman's door in, I'll know how much cash to shake out of her."

I didn't bother to count up the eyerolls at Fab's suggestion. "If Lynn has enough foresight to use an hourly office space, she's probably kept her home address under wraps. When you hit up Xander, have him run a background check, and also ask him to check for a police record."

"Almost forgot…" All eyes turned to Mother. "There was another woman that took Lynn to court and won, but never collected."

"Did you learn all this from Jean?" Brad demanded. "If not, can't wait to hear who did tell you."

"Friend-of-a-friend type of thing. If you don't know how that works, Madison can explain it to you."

"Mother," I said in exasperation, "when you want something from someone, it's not a good idea to roll them under the bus."

"Oh good, you've changed your mind. Best friends and all, I didn't think you'd desert Fab on this case."

I didn't miss that the guys all had smirks on their faces.

"What *we* can do is look into this and get back to you with a preliminary report," Fab told her as she inspected the business card once again. "At that point, we'll know what our options are and how to proceed. If this woman has had success at scamming people, and it sounds like she has, then she's not going to be a sitting duck, waiting for one of her disgruntled clients to find her at her business or residence."

"If this Lynn woman is screwing people—"

"Really, Madison."

"Yeah, I know, language. Maybe next time." *But probably not.* "Now that we know one of her victims sued her and got nothing, I'm not going to say there's no chance of collecting, but it sounds like that's going to be the case."

"Jean knows that," Mother said. "She had planned to confront the woman herself, but when the office address went nowhere, she didn't have another one to check out."

"Knowing you—" Brad gave Mother a penetrating stare. "—you and Jean put on your PI hats and did some investigation of your own. What did you find out?"

"Brad," Mother said in exasperation. If looks could kill, my poor brother. "We didn't do any such thing. We did make a trip back to the office listed on the card and tried to buy information from the receptionist, which was my idea, and Jean thought it was crazy. Turned out to be a waste of money—we got fleeced. She eagerly handed over a bad address. Talking about it after, Jean and I were convinced she knew it wasn't going to pan out."

"If all else fails, a little snooping into the records at the rent-a-desk office might get us the information we want," I suggested.

"There is one more thing."

Fab and I looked at one another. *Of course there is.*

"It's good," Mother assured us. "Jean is expecting a bill for your services, but make it damn little and pass the rest off to me."

"Freebie," I sing-songed.

"How about I offer to pick up the tab, with your promise to stay out of it?" Brad eyed Mother.

"You might not think so, but I can be helpful and manage to stay out of trouble at the same time."

"Uh-huh." It was clear Brad didn't believe Mother's assertion.

"If you think of anything else you might've forgotten to bring up, she's the one to call." I pointed at Fab.

"I say we leave the guys here and go to the Crab Shack for lunch," Mother suggested.

"What we should do is go upstairs and ask Xander to get started on checking this woman out," Fab said.

"I saw Tank's car in the parking lot, and the two of us need to have a chat with the lawyer." I pointed between Fab and myself. "This is one of your cases," I told her, "you should be in on the conversation."

"You handle it, and I may be willing to cough

up a favor," Fab said with a grin.

Mother's expression made it clear she didn't want to hear about a delay in going to lunch.

"Do you think the office has been cleaned up?" I pointed to the ceiling.

"Perfect timing, as Rude just left," Fab assured me.

Mother's phone rang. She pulled it out of her purse and answered, getting up and walking far enough away that we couldn't eavesdrop.

"Anyone want to make a small wager?" I looked around the table.

"It's Spoon," Brad said with certainty.

I turned on my bro. "I don't know how you made that call happen, but if Mother finds out, nice knowing you. I'll come up with something really sweet to say at your send-off."

"I'm requesting a drunken spectacle and that the place be packed. Bus them in; I don't care."

"What you should do is have your final hurrah while you're alive; that way, you can see what your friends have to say about you."

Everyone around the table shook their heads like I'd lost my mind.

Mother came storming back to the table. "I'm going to have to take a rain check on the lunch, and everything else, as Spoon is on his way over to pick me up." She glared around the table as if she wasn't sure who'd outed her… or if any of us had.

"Don't worry about your friend Jean. I'm going

to get right on this, and I'll get back to you in a day or two with an update." Fab stood and hugged Mother, whispering something that had her nodding.

"How about I walk you out?" Brad stood and was at her side before she could answer.

I blew Mother a kiss.

When the two cleared the door, Fab said, "We can put this off for a day or two, since we don't know anything about the woman or where to start looking. It'll take that long for Xander to get us the information."

"My advice…" I grinned at Fab. "Keep Mother updated so she won't beat your door down."

"You two better keep an eagle eye on Madeline," Creole cautioned.

"If she comes up with what she thinks is a great idea, you'll find out when she's more than halfway through the execution," Didier concurred.

"Hate to have to agree, but Mother's a sneaky one." I groaned.

Chapter Twenty-Four

When Fab and I went upstairs, everything that had been scattered all over the floor had been boxed up. We rounded the corner and sat at my shiplap desk, which was long enough to seat a few more people. Fab told Xander about Mother's friend and handed over the business card for Lynn Wade, telling him the information she wanted him to dig up.

"I'll get right on it," he assured her.

"I'll see if Tank has time to talk now." I pulled out my phone.

"He doesn't; he has a client in his office," Xander told me. "If this is about Bardy Dowell, I told him about the man and what little I knew. He told me that before he can get started on anything, he needs to talk to the man and hear from him that he wants representation."

"I'll be checking with Fern to see if Bardy's up for a chat. What we do know is that his property has been transferred out of his name, and before anything further happens, such as a sale, someone needs to put a stop to it," I said.

"Okay…" Fab tapped her watch.

"What are you up to now?"

"I'll fill you in in the car." She jumped up, grabbed her stuff, and was already out of the office before I could object.

Xander laughed.

"I'm hoping this is Fab's way of saying we're stopping for roach coach tacos and heading home."

"Let me know if that's what happens." He laughed again.

I grabbed my briefcase and headed out of the office, where I found Fab holding the door open.

Back in the car, after we passed the turn to the taco wagon and continued going south, I asked, "Knowing I should've insisted on an answer earlier, I'm doing it now — where are we going?"

"Can't believe you forgot." Fab turned off the highway and around the back of the motel.

When I saw Goff leaning against the back gate, I realized I'd pushed him and his problems to the back burner. When Fab came to a stop, he ran over and hopped in the back seat.

"I want to thank you both for not writing me off. After my sit-down with Gunz, I realized I've got to stop blaming life for my problems and get my act together. My first step is to stop complaining and just figure it out as I go."

I didn't know Goff's story or what had gone on and didn't want to know. I turned in my seat as Fab turned back onto the main highway. "Here's the deal. Fab's got a tailor friend..." I nodded toward her in case he didn't remember her name.

"He's going to fix you up with a suit so you present well to the judge. Day after tomorrow, we'll be picking you up and escorting you to the courthouse. Do what your lawyer tells you, and if you start freaking out, know that Gunz only hires the best." And the shiftiest, I left unsaid. "Don't worry about us running off while you're getting measured; we'll wait and give you a ride back to the motel."

"Do you think I'll go to jail?"

"If there was a high likelihood of that happening, your lawyer would've told you already to prepare you. You *have* talked to your lawyer and gone over the details of your case, haven't you?" I asked.

"Rollo let me sit at his desk and use his computer, and I had a Zoom call with the man. He assured me that he was working on a deal with the prosecutor that didn't include jail time. I'm trying not to overthink it but will be relieved when it's behind me. It also helped to talk to a couple of other drunks at the motel who'd sidetracked their lives—made me realize how stupid I was being. They told me if they could get their act together, than so could I."

Fab pulled into a strip mall and parked in front of the tailor's shop, and she and Goff got out.

"I'm going to wait here and make a couple of calls," I told her before she closed the door. She didn't need any input from me to have Goff leaving here looking well put-together. Instead of getting on the phone, I leaned back against the seat and made a list of tasks in my head.

It didn't surprise me that it didn't take long before the two were back in the car, Goff effusive in his thanks.

Fab handed him a business card. "If, for some reason, the suit doesn't get delivered by the time you get back from work tomorrow, give me a call. I think the chances of that happening are slim, but better to be on the safe side."

It was clear from the way Goff looked at Fab that she had another fan.

Once we dropped him back at the motel, I said, "Please tell me we're going home."

"We are, as I'm starving and ready for a drink."

"A drink." I licked my lips and whipped out my phone, placing an order for all our favorites from Jake's and telling them we were on our way to pick it up. "Since I know you were hanging on every word…" I pointed vaguely down the highway.

"You could've asked me what I wanted." Fab sulked unconvincingly.

"On the off-chance I missed something, order it when you get there. Just know that if I have to wait long, I'll ditch you."

"I dare you."

I started laughing, and Fab joined me.

She managed to refrain from driving like a maniac and got us to Jake's in one piece, turning in and cruising around the back to park. We entered through the kitchen, where the line cook waved and held up five fingers.

Cook whistled and motioned for me to come into his office.

"What's up, boss man?" As I sat down, I realized Fab had disappeared to who knew where. My guess, getting the latest street gossip from a couple of regulars that thought she was hot, hot, hot.

"Wanted you to know that the kids are coming for breakfast again. Thinking this time, I'll have them cook their own." Cook grinned.

"You know —"

He waved his hand, cutting me off. "You're thinking it sounds like nothing but trouble, but I'll have it under control. I doubt I'll have a full kitchen, as some will be playing darts and shooting pool."

"I was going to say that it's amazing of you. Also, I'm happy that a couple of those parents don't have my number and thus haven't called to ask 'what the...' But that will probably happen when their kids get home and they find out what their little angels have been up to." I winced inwardly.

"The parents already know. I heard it straight from the kids that they call every night and are anxious to share the details of what they've been doing all day."

"Since all the kids are accounted for, that means none of the parents showed up and dragged their butts home."

Cook laughed as the line cook came into the office. "Your order's ready." At the same time, Cook's phone rang.

"Thanks for keeping me updated." I smiled at Cook.

I signed off on the tab, grabbed the shopping bags and large box, and made my way to my SUV, where I opened the liftgate and put everything inside. Thoughts of getting home and pouring myself a drink to go along with what I knew would be delicious food were swiftly chased away by the sudden appearance of Booker, who seemingly materialized out of thin air. His looming figure cast a shadow over me, anger rolling off him in waves.

"What are you doing here?" I tried not to let my fear take over.

"I'm here to kick your ass. What did you think?"

"I thought you—"

"In jail?" Booker practically spit. "You never hear of bail, you dumb bitch?"

The threat was evident in every word out of his mouth, but I refused to be intimidated. "You're never going to get away with hurting me, so how about a free meal instead?" I suggested as my eyes darted around for an escape route. I needed to keep him talking on the off-chance I could defuse the situation.

"You bitch, you got me fired. Then arrested,"

Booker snarled, thrusting me backward with unexpected force. The bumper of my car ramming the back of my legs, I managed to stay upright and sidestep, maneuvering around to the passenger side.

"I had zero to do with any of that! Raynes wasn't my client, and you know that." I kept backing up, but his advance was relentless. "Why would you come back here again?" I spun away from his grasp, but he managed to snag my sleeve, yanking me forcefully toward him. Reacting on instinct, I drove a swift kick into his shin. Pain contorted his face, and he released his grip.

The quiet parking lot now set the stage for a battle of wills as we faced off. The tension within me ratcheted up as I waited for him to make his next move, knowing he was far from done with me. Like lightening, he suddenly ran at me, growling. I took off running. I didn't get far before he shoved me forward. I hit the ground, and the skin on my hands ripped, pain shooting up my arms.

It had been a while since I'd shot someone, but I knew that getting my butt kicked was imminent, and as he moved forward, growling and spewing spit, I knew it was about to get much worse. Without hesitation, I pulled my Glock and put a bullet closer to his groin than I'm sure he would've liked. He should have been thankful he was alive, as I was an accurate shot and could've made this his last day. I hoped I didn't regret my decision.

Booker's screams could be heard a block away. I backed up and kept my gun aimed at him—if he forced me to take a second shot, it would be the last breath he took.

It didn't take long, after a little gunfire in the parking lot, for Fab to show up, her own gun drawn.

"What took you so damn long?" I grouched.

Fab skidded to a stop and kicked Booker in the hip as he struggled to get to his feet. He groaned loudly. "Why isn't he dead?"

"Less paperwork."

"I'm going to be finding out from my father what the heck went wrong and how he was able to show up here again."

"Pretty sure it was his friend the Chief who stopped him from having Booker killed. A mistake, as Booker snootily reminded me about bail." In most cases, the male ego wouldn't take to being bested and they'd be back to settle the score. "There's not going to be a third time." I only had to make a call, and he'd disappear without a shred of him ever being found, which frankly, I was disappointed hadn't already happened. One might almost feel sorry for him. Except that he'd been warned and showed up anyway.

Both of us heard the sirens approaching, and they were close. Two cop cars rolled into the parking lot and parked in the front. I expected to see them come around the side of the building at any moment, but they must not have realized we were in the back. They'd figure it out soon enough.

I reholstered my Glock, knowing I'd have to hand it over, but I'd wait until asked. "Did you call 911?"

Fab's snort was my answer. "You okay?" She closed the distance between us and gave me a quick once-over.

"A little banged up is all." I held out my hands, and Fab winced. I told her what Booker had accused me of. "I thought, between your father and your client—"

"I thought the same thing. My father isn't going to be a happy camper, and if it was the Chief that advised restraint, it won't do him any good to make that suggestion a second time."

"How about you don't make that call, and I'll call Toady? Then you can share the story after…" We both knew that once Toady got his hands on the man, no one would ever hear from him again.

"Let me call my father and run the options by him. Let it be his decision." Fab opened the back of the SUV and gestured for me to sit. "At the sound of a gunshot, the phones came out, and you know what that means—business is going to go through the roof. Was anyone racing for the exit? Nope."

Kevin and Cooper came out the kitchen door, and their eyes landed on Booker, who'd stopped moaning and hadn't moved for several minutes.

"Booker's his name," I told the two. "I put a bullet in his groin, or close enough anyway."

With a shake of his head, Kevin walked over to Booker, and bent down to check him out.

Cooper approached Fab and me. "So you were the shooter?" I nodded. "How are you doing?"

"This is the worst of it." I held out my scraped palms. Before he could ask, I told him what had happened, leaving out Booker's first visit.

Fab told Cooper about Raynes, the client who hired her, and that Booker had worked for the man for years. She didn't come right out and say "Thug for Hire," but he got the gist.

The paramedics arrived, loaded up Booker, and off they went.

Kevin made his way over to us. "Booker came to as the paramedics were checking him out. He's worried you shot his dick off."

"Maybe if my aim had been a little more to the right." I restrained myself from making a finger-gun.

"Don't leave town. In case we have more questions."

"I can't be responsible for the demise of every a-hole in this town," I snapped, but calmed down a tad when Fab put her hand on my back.

"If any part of Madison's version of events needs clarification, there's security footage," Fab told the two men.

"Figured as much," Cooper said. "I plan on

going back inside and getting a copy of it."

"Can I go home now? I've got food in the back, and it's getting cold." I knew I sounded excessively whiney, but my excuse: my palms were on fire.

"At least we'll know where to find you." Kevin smirked.

"I've got a question, off topic. Did the kids ditch The Cottages because you scared the devil out of them?" I asked him.

Cooper laughed.

"See what I have to listen to when I go the extra mile to be a nice guy?" Kevin snorted. "For your info, Cooper and I had a sit-down at the pool with the kids and answered all their questions about being a cop." *So there* in his tone.

"That was very swell of both of you." I smiled at both men. "If you're hungry... free food." I pointed to the building. "If you want to be a favorite, while you're waiting for your order, sit at the bar and regale Kelpie with a rundown of events."

Cooper shook his head. "Cook's putting together a to-go surprise."

"Cook is really good at remembering what everyone likes, so you're going to enjoy," I assured them.

With a nod, they went back inside via the kitchen, and we got in the car.

I pulled out my phone as Fab turned onto the highway. "Got to give the husband a jingle with an update... unless you did it."

"They're in a meeting, and a good thing, as I only had about two seconds."

"Just so we don't have to listen to any crabbing later on..." I called, and it went to voicemail. "Shot a guy in his man goods, and he died. Fab and I are on the way home with food." I hung up.

"You forgot to mention Booker's name." Fab retrieved her phone and made a call. "What Madison said... sort of."

We both laughed.

Chapter Twenty-Five

"You're not one bit funny," Creole bellowed as he followed Didier into the house. Fab had sent another message that the two of us were at her house. She'd gotten me there by bribing me with a margarita and promising that I could stretch out on the couch.

"Please use your quiet voice," I said in a feeble tone. I caught Fab's smirk, from which there was no telling if I'd done a good job whining or not.

Creole threw a manila envelope on the coffee table, leaned down and kissed me, then scooted me over and sat next to me.

Before he could ask, I held out my scraped palms. "Fab cleaned them for me and put some kind of sauce on them. You tell him," I told Fab, who at my suggestion, hadn't wasted any time getting the two men each a beer. My rationalization: it would soften them up.

Fab pieced together what she knew and what she'd heard me say and gave a good recitation of events.

"Booker blamed me for losing a lucrative account and getting arrested, even though we all know that Caspian, or more likely the Chief, made that happen," I said. "We should check to see if he died on the way to the hospital; if not, he'll be back. Especially if his you-know-what doesn't work anymore."

"I'm surprised that Booker got out of jail *and* that when it happened, Caspian didn't send one of his guys to escort him out of the state," Creole said. "He must not know that the man was released."

"You know those wagers you like to make?" Didier asked me with a raised eyebrow. "Here's one for you. The bet is that once Caspian gets the call, it's the last we'll be talking about Booker."

"I still haven't gotten used to the fact that my father can be such a badass," Fab said with a shake of her head. "When Madison nodded off, I called Raynes at his office, and even though I lied and said I was Caspian's assistant, he wouldn't take the call. Pretty sure he was there, because otherwise, why put me on hold and then come back online and say, 'He's not in at the moment.'?"

"Bet you've got Raynes wondering what's up," Creole said with a knowing nod. "You need to give your father a heads up before Raynes calls him back... if he does."

"I did put a call in to my father, and when he calls back, I'm going to let him know what happened. Then volunteer to be backup." Fab grinned.

"I'm on board with that," Didier told her.

"Because I know it'll be an emphatic, 'In no way are you getting involved.'"

"You're no fun." Fab pouted.

"There's food," I announced. "It just needs to be reheated. In the meantime, I'll have another margarita." I reached for my empty glass, which Creole intercepted.

"How many of these have you had?" He stopped short of growling but just barely.

I held up one finger. "Meanie over there cut me off."

"One more, and that's it." Creole took my glass and stood. "I'll be back with food and drink."

"That would make you my favorite husband."

The guys went out to the kitchen, and from the banging around, it was clear that they weren't wasting time getting dinner ready.

With a glance over her shoulder, Fab came over and sat on the coffee table, picking up the envelope. "What's this?" She fingered the flap.

"Since Creole was the one to throw it down, you should ask him." I tried to slap her hand away. "If it doesn't have your name on it, it's none of your business."

She held it up, and there was nothing written on the front. "No name and in my house, I'm thinking that gives me the okay to open it."

Before I could warn Creole, Didier appeared and grabbed the envelope out of Fab's hand. He made a tsking noise, and they engaged in some kind of silent communication.

"It could be for me," Fab said in a sneaky tone.

"You know full well—"

She stood and cut him off with a kiss, attempting to grab the envelope.

"Stop, you two." I was tempted to cover my hot cheeks. "Hon," I yelled, "Fab wants to open your envelope."

"Not until after dinner," he yelled back. You'd have to have been deaf not to hear the smirk in his tone.

"I'll keep this with me." Didier walked away with the envelope in his hand.

"Something tells me that Didier didn't trust you not to take a peek when his back was turned." I grinned at Fab as she scowled at her husband's back.

"One of these days…" She let the threat hang in the air.

My guess was that she couldn't think of anything… nothing impressive anyway. "Where are we sitting for dinner? In or out? The table needs set, and I can direct you on how to get it done." I loved setting the table; she didn't care for it at all.

"Let's eat on the patio, since it's a warm night, with the perfect amount of breeze so we don't sweat to death. I'll throw the silverware in the center of the table, help-yourself style. And stack the plates up." *So there*, on Fab's face.

"I so dare you. I'd relish telling everyone that you really don't know how to set a table."

In the end, it was Didier that set the table. He and Creole carried out plates and served Fab and me. Eating on the patio turned out to be a good choice, the water that trickled up on the shore making the night perfect. Instead of any serious conversation, the guys joked around and made us laugh.

Once we were finished, we took our drinks and sat at the far end of the patio overlooking the water—the perfect spot for enjoying the view of the lights that flickered across the blue-green water.

"So what's in the envelope?"

Didier shook his head at his wife.

"We got an offer for the new warehouse acquisition," Creole told us. "A Jackie Troy walked into the office today—guess she didn't think she needed an appointment—and after a brief conversation with Lark, she pitched her offer to Didier, Brad, and me, as we were at the conference table."

"Did she have any idea who she was supposed to be dealing with?" I asked.

"At first I didn't think so, but then she singled me out."

"Did she happen to mention what her plans for the property were?" I asked.

"Jackie was upfront almost immediately, saying that the plans were to expand the family business. Turns out that she and the husband own the body shop next door."

"It would've made more sense to buy from Logger's daughter," Fab mused.

"Apparently, she wasn't able to make contact with Troll. It surprised her that the sale happened so fast."

"Can't wait to hear how you left it with her," I said.

"That it was a gift and the decision wasn't mine to make, but I'd get back to her." Creole winked.

"It was clear to all of us that Jackie didn't like that answer," Didier told us. "Guessing she thought she'd get an immediate acceptance, and the frustration rolled off of her."

"Don't be mad…"

All eyes turned to Fab.

"Honestly, I wasn't holding back… but after all that's happened today, I thought I'd save it for tomorrow, which would give me some time to do a little more investigation."

I knew I had *speed it up* on my face, as did Creole and Didier.

"As you both already know, Didier's and my gift was adding security cameras to the property. Made sense, since I'm Head of Security and I've had them installed on all your other properties."

"As I recall, my thanks were effusive." I grinned at her.

"Not quite the way I'd describe it." Fab restrained a snort. "Late last night, not able to sleep, I did a little security snooping, and after checking out every property the two of us own, ended up at the new acquisition. You know how the property next door is dead during the day…? The times I've peered over the fence, anyway, there's not been a soul creeping around. Well, not last night—it was a busy place."

"Afraid to ask. What happened?" Creole stiffened.

I reached over and rubbed the middle of his back.

"Around three in the morning, the gates opened, a white Porsche rolled inside, and a guy standing at the gate locked it up. Another dude appeared out of nowhere and talked to the driver, and then he got behind the wheel and drove it into the warehouse. About the same time, a Mercedes coup was driven out of the same warehouse and into the back of an enclosed trailer. Though I couldn't get a clear view, I'm positive that it wasn't the only car in the trailer. The driver of the Porsche reappeared, jumped up in the cab of the truck, the gate keeper swung them open, and he was gone."

"No auto body place that I know of does business in the middle of the night. Not legitimate ones anyway," Creole said.

"Thought the same thing when Fab showed me the footage." Didier side-hugged her. "After thinking about it, it's possible that it had something to do with a good client."

"Cooper told me that car theft wasn't a common occurrence here in the Cove, but he did say that of late, they'd had several reports of high-end autos going missing," I threw out. "When I asked Kevin or Cooper — can't remember which one — about the properties on either side of ours, they said that they hadn't been called out to either property. I was told that the guy on the south side inherited the property and lives there because he's dirt poor and has no other options."

"Surprised you haven't been over there making a deal with the man." Creole gave me a questioning look.

"Once all the dead people have a final resting place, I'll have my friend here jump the fence, check the place out, and give me a thumbs up or down." I winked at Fab.

"I'm not dragging a ladder around," she huffed. "What we do is go to the gate first, maybe get lucky with a bell, and if not, then the lockpick." She made a key-turning motion. "All else fails, there's pole vaulting."

"The pole business sounds dangerous," I teased. "I'll help with the ladder."

"Ssh." Fab crossed her lips with her finger. "You can't be outing us before we've had our fun."

"I'm available in the morning to go and remove all ladders from your property," Didier told Creole. The two laughed, but it was easy to see that it was under consideration.

"Before we do anything, I'm going to suggest–" Fab waved her hand. " — that I continue to monitor the footage and report back."

"If it looks illegal—"

"And it doesn't matter what Fab sees on the footage," Didier cut her off. "You will not be investigating on your own. Right?" He glared at her.

"Yeah, okay."

Didier continued to glare.

"That was a yes."

"Back to the offer we got…" Creole nudged me. "Think on it and let me know."

"My answer is no. If that's too abrupt, how about, 'Thanks for thinking of us…' blah, blah, blah."

"I knew chances were zero but had to bring it up." Creole grinned.

"If whatever her name is—"

"Jackie," Fab cut me off.

"Now you remember a name."

"It's happened before… once or twice." Fab smirked.

"If *Jackie* doesn't want to take no for an answer, we'll have Fab take care of it, and you can bet that's the last we'll hear from her." I air-boxed.

Fab and I laughed.

"Since we're all together, let's take care of our morning get-together now, since I'm thinking it's about time for another one," Fab said.

"Let me guess…" I rubbed my temples. "Mother."

"Madeline wants an update that I don't have.

Told her that Xander hadn't had the time to get back to me, and she wanted to know what the holdup was. I reminded her pulling these reports together takes time and said as soon as I got it back, she'd be my first call. But knowing Madeline, it won't take her long to get one step ahead of me. I immediately called Xander to warn him that she'd be calling, and she already had. He got her off the phone by telling her a client had just shown up and he'd get right on her file."

I laughed and got a glare from Fab. "I know what she was up to." I was about to heighten Fab's frustration. "Mother wants to morph into you and needs info to get started. Then you, babes, will be told to get in the back seat."

"And get blamed for everything that goes wrong?" Fab huffed. "Not going to happen. My secret weapon is Spoon. She's going to have to do some heavy duty sneaking around to get by her husband."

"Don't underestimate Mother when it comes to doing what she wants, though I do give Spoon credit for slowing her down on occasion. When she was relaying Jean's situation, she had that glint in her eye, wanting to be ringleader. Brad noticed the same thing, and though I didn't see him do it, I'm certain he's the one that managed to contact Spoon, which brought him to the office, looking for his errant wife."

"Creole and I thought the same thing and questioned Brad after everyone left," Didier said.

"He didn't hesitate to tell us that he pulled his phone out unnoticed and sent a text."

"He better hope that Mother never finds out. She'll lay on the guilt."

"Let's say we get an address for the shyster woman, then what? We track her down and shake what she owes Jean out of her? What if she doesn't have it?" Fab waved off Didier and Creole, who were trying to speak at once. "You two are going to say, 'Call the cops.' My guess is that she already knows that they'll tell us that it's a civil matter."

"What good is another judgment if you can't collect?" I threw out.

"Or when the cops get there, she reports the two of you for harassment." Didier glared.

"What would our excuse be for showing up and wanting money—that we're collectors?" I asked.

"Hello, jail," Creole said, not amused. "The only way you get money out of the woman, if that's the goal… you'll have to threaten her."

"Once again, you risk getting arrested." Didier said with a shake of his head, showing that he didn't like the idea any more than Creole.

"Or spread the word in a highly visible way, letting people know not to use the woman. The neighborhood apps are a good way to get information out there," Didier suggested.

"I got a little info out of Xander, and the reason he's still checking into the woman is because she's got quite the track record for swindling people using the estate sale con. Judgments haven't stopped her—she's gotten them under a couple different names and just starts another business and changes her name."

"Compile all the information, turn it over to Kevin or Cooper, and they'll arrest her," Creole said. "If her track record is as clear as you say, then a judge might make it damn expensive to get out of jail on bond. If he held her pending trial and her victims testified, she might be behind bars for a while."

"You should get with Mother, or better yet Jean, and find out what she wants," I said. "As for Jackie, turn the story over to a local reporter, who maybe can get it on TV and warn people that way. I can see where someone who's winding up an estate wouldn't think to check out a company before doing business with them. If they're running off referrals and the non-paying part hasn't caught up to them, then they're going to continue using her until it does."

"If she's smart, she'll be running several businesses at the same time. When she gets wind someone's planning to sue, she'll move on and hope they don't look for her," Fab said.

"Free advice," I directed to Fab, "don't give Mother any clue how to contact this Jackie woman."

"Better yet, don't give Madeline any information at all," Creole said. "Dance her around like you do Didier and me."

Didier grinned. "Or your backup plan—make stuff up."

"Listen up, everyone. Mother's good at ferreting out BS, so you have to keep any kind of con job subtle."

"How about I trade a favor or two and you—"

"No," I cut Fab off. "If just no wasn't clear, no way!"

"What happened to that infamous clause of yours—no dancing someone around when said person wants to cash in a favor?" *So there* on Fab's face.

"That's not the exact wording, and you're out of luck on this one."

"You're mean."

"I know."

The guys laughed.

Chapter Twenty-Six

Thanks to Creole, Fab and I got a couple days' reprieve, as he'd told Mother that I was resting and he was making sure that I did. He also informed her that he'd confiscated my phone; she didn't need to know that I handed it over with a grin, happy for him to be the bad guy in all this drama. Mother wasn't happy that Jean's case hadn't been wrapped up and didn't want to accept that more investigation needed to be done. Before she could create more havoc, Fab called Spoon and ordered him to keep his wife busy for at least two days, and not one word that he'd gotten a call. Or else. She wisely didn't elaborate. He laughed.

Three days later, I got a heads up from Fab that she was out of excuses and Mother and Jean were showing up in the morning, and if we weren't ready to hit the road, then we better have a damn good excuse. Or just hide. I told Fab that she was going to have to give bad-ass a rest and trot out nice-girl. She groaned and hung up. The next morning, I put on my workout pants and slipped into tennis shoes. I'd bet that Fab was similarly attired.

I looked out the kitchen garden window, finished my coffee, and picked up my phone, and just then, Mother roared into the driveway, Jean in the car. Fab walked into the driveway and, seconds later, got into a face-off with Mother. I grabbed my purse and ran out. Mother had the back door of her Mercedes open and was motioning for Fab to get in. Fab's militant stance clearly said, *No way in wherever.*

"Okay, ladies," I said as I walked up, just a smidge short of running. "What's going on?"

"I'm driving, and you two need to get in the back." Mother flicked her finger for me to hustle it up.

I leaned in and kissed her cheek in case a full-blown fight broke out. Then I waved to Jean through the open door, and she rolled her eyes in return. Guess she didn't know about Mother's belief that doing that would cause your eyeballs to stick, never to be seen again.

"Mother dear, we're going in my car." I waved off her sputter. "There's way more room, but the primary reason is if anything goes awry on the road, you want Fab behind the wheel. Trust me, I know. Now ladies, let's get going." I got a dirty look from Mother, but Jean was getting out of the car. *Get behind the wheel,* I telegraphed to Fab. She didn't hesitate and stomped over and climbed inside. "Be nice," I said to Mother. "You need Fab, and she's easier to deal with when she's not irked off. Riding in the back of your car would do that... unless you somehow morphed into Didier."

Mother and Jean, both in their sixties, had kept themselves in shape and were dressed in workout pants, long-sleeved tops, and tennis shoes. They huddled by the car in an intense conversation. Finally, both nodded and grabbed their purses out of Mother's car.

I opened the back door for Jean and went around to open the door for Mother. I got a squinty stare as she climbed in. I really wanted to run back into the house but managed to get into the passenger seat without any further drama.

Fab backed out of the driveway and, to her credit, didn't squeal all the way to the gate.

I turned in my seat. "Would you ladies like anything to drink before we hit the road?" I glanced over my shoulder at the GPS and squelched a groan at seeing our destination was Miami. I hadn't had time to read the latest in the file that Xander had sent over.

"I wouldn't mind a coffee," Jean said.

"We'll take you to our favorite place." I smiled and sat back in my seat.

Fab pulled into the drive-through, and everyone got what they wanted.

I figured a few sips of caffeine, and everyone's mood would lighten up.

Once we were on Highway One headed north, Mother hung her head between the seats and asked Fab, "What's the plan?"

I'd heard that Jean wanted an accounting of all items sold and to recover monies owed. As for anything else, she didn't want to end up in the middle of drama that she couldn't handle.

"You're going to wait in the car while I go to the door and demand payment," Fab told her.

Mother's snort clearly told her, *Not happening*.

"We don't have any legal standing here," Fab said with an edge to her voice. "The last thing I want is for one of us to go to jail."

"You're going to knock, ask for money, and you think this Lynn Wade woman is going to just hand it over?" Mother's tone conveyed, *Fat chance*.

"What would you suggest?" Fab asked, barely managing to control her snark.

"Be aggressive. Let her know that not paying up would be bad for her health."

Instead of snapping *Have you lost your mind?* at Mother, I said, "The reason you called on Fab was for her experience, so you need to let her take the lead." I knew Mother wanted to be the lead, but that wasn't going to happen.

"I don't want any trouble," Jean said in a soft tone. "The last thing I want is for any of us to go to jail."

I shot her a reassuring smile.

"You think going in all nice-girl is going to get Jean what she wants?" Mother demanded.

"There are no guarantees on any job. But here's one for you: I barge into the woman's house, and you can bet the police will be called. Have you come up with an idea that guarantees that that won't happen?" Fab challenged.

"I'll try to calm down," Mother said. "I don't want Jean to be screwed over and the Lynn woman to walk."

Jean tugged on the back of Mother's top, and she sat back.

"Even if we had a court order…" Fab went on to caution the women not to get their hopes up.

I side-nudged her. *What are you going to do?*

Fab shrugged. *No clue.*

The drive north was a quiet one. Mother and Jean were in constant conversation. Fab and I didn't say a word.

Finally, Fab pulled into what appeared to be a quiet neighborhood and parked in front of a beige duplex with a brick roof. "Try to behave," she lightly admonished, which was mostly meant for Mother. She scooped up an envelope, shoved it under her arm, and got out of the car.

Just as Fab hit the walkway, Mother jumped out of the car and was hot on her heels. Fab stopped and turned toward her, and whatever she said, Mother stayed put.

Before I could caution Jean to stay in the car, she was out and standing on the sidewalk; at least she hung back. Was this what those two had been cooking up on the drive up here?

The last to get out, I released a breath and said to anyone listening, "I'll be hanging out here by the car, in case you need bail money." I knew, though, that if the worst were to happen, I'd be arrested along with the rest of them for being at the property.

The scenario at the door went exactly how I expected. As planned, Fab went with the nice-girl routine and handed the envelope to the woman, who laughed in her face and, after a glance, threw it on the ground. If Fab had a Plan B, other than to go all thug, she didn't get a chance to trot it out, as Mother bolted forward.

"You damn well aren't going to cheat another person out of the money you owe. You pay up or else," Mother snarled.

So much for staying out of the fray. I started up the walkway.

The woman laughed in Mother's face, went inside, and slammed the door.

At Mother's side, I tugged on her arm. "Hate to be a party-killer…" Though not really. "We need to leave." I turned and made sure Jean had heard. She nodded, but before she could start back to the car, I asked, "Was that Lynn Wade?"

Jean nodded reluctantly.

I looked at Fab, who'd backed off the doorstep. *Well, say something.* She wore the same militant expression as Mother. "Okay ladies, listen up. Figured this was a wasted trip but also knew you needed to see it for yourself. What you need to do is talk to a lawyer. Though even doing that, you still might not get what you want."

"I thought getting a recommendation was all

I'd need for there not to be any problems with the sale of my household items." Jean sighed.

"If there's a next time and you need someone checked out, or a recommendation, call Fab or me," I told her. "How about we go and have lunch? A drink would be just the thing about now." I turned to see that Mother and Fab had just ended another intense discussion. I'd ask later… maybe. Before I could tell them to get their butts in the car, Mother sidestepped Fab and started towards the front door.

Fab fisted the back of her shirt, bringing her to a halt. This time, after an exchange of words, Mother nodded. Fab went back to the door and was about to knock when it flew open, Lynn in Fab's face, forcing her to back up to the start of the walkway. Lynn leaned in and appeared to have a few choice words for Fab, who so far, hadn't said anything or lost her patience.

None of us noticed the approaching sedan until the passenger window went down and someone leaned out, gun in hand, and let loose with a hail of gunfire, all aimed at Lynn and her house. Fab jumped at Mother, pushing her to the ground and holding her down with one arm around her.

As I hit the ground, I yelled to Jean, who'd already dropped, "Keep your head down."

Tires squealed as the car sped down the block.

Lynn, who'd dived onto the grass, got up, cast a glance around, and stumbled inside her house, holding her arm. The door slammed, rocking on the hinges.

Fab helped Mother to her feet and motioned for her to follow as the two made their way over to me. Jean and I were already back on our feet. Jean didn't wait to be told what to do and dived into the back seat of the car. Mother followed suit.

"It appeared that Lynn took a bullet, but since she got to her feet so quickly, I'm thinking it's not life-threatening," Fab said as the two of us took cover behind the SUV.

Chapter Twenty-Seven

Fab and I scoped out the street in both directions, and there was no sign of the car. In fact, all was eerily quiet. Only Fab would be able to provide a complete description of the vehicle.

"Surprised they didn't make a u-turn and come back for round two," I said. "We ready to get out of here?"

Before Fab could answer, Mother yelled from inside the car, "Let's go."

"Thinking that's a bad idea," Fab said with a disgusted sigh. "When the cops show, and they will, we don't want Lynn pointing the finger at us."

Before we could flip to see who'd call 911, two cop cars flew around the corner and parked in front of the house.

"We should've gotten out of here when we could," Mother grumbled.

Really? I shook my head at her.

Fab leaned her head inside the car. "When questioned by law enforcement, keep your answers short and to the point. And be truthful."

Two officers got out of their cars, and Fab and I met them halfway. "A call came in about a shooting," one said. Fab gave them a quick recap. He ran to Lynn's door and gave it his best cop knock.

It surprised me when Fab moved closer, hanging back on a strip of grass. I turned to the other cop. "Officer Tarlow, nice to see you again," I said and reintroduced myself.

He eyed me intently. "Thought I recognized you." He made it sound like it wasn't a good thing.

"I'm friends with your previous chief," I reminded him so he wouldn't think that I was someone he'd arrested. "Fab was chaperoning sorority girls…" I jerked my head in her direction. "You responded to a call and scared the devil out of them so we could get them back to their billionaire daddy without further incident."

Tarlow nodded with a smirk, and it was clear he remembered and was back to business. "Did you recognize the car? The shooter?"

I filled in a few details about why we were there that Fab had glossed over. I pointed to the open car door and the back seat, which he'd already eyed several times. "The blonde is my mother, Madeline Spoon, and the other is her friend, Jean Winters, the one defrauded by Lynn Wade." I nodded to where the women were huddled together, looking pale. Then I cast a glance at the house and told him about the estate sale scam the woman had going. "From what we've heard, Jean wasn't her first victim. Fab has a list of people that filed police reports, and some have gone on to get judgements. There's a complete report on Lynn Wade in the envelope lying on the ground over there."

"What's your part in all this?" Tarlow asked.

"I'm here to post bail, if necessary." I got a chuckle off that one. "Fab's Plan A was the nice-girl approach, and that was a flop, though we both pretty much gave it a zero before it got out of the gate. My mother was insistent that we try— anything to get her friend's money back. Ever say no to your mother?"

"I try not to," he said. "You got a gun on you?"

I lifted my shirt and turned my leg so he could see it outlined on my thigh. "We both do, and we both have permits to carry. Also, Fab has a PI license. If the con artist's story is that we pulled a weapon and the bullets were from our guns, I'm pretty sure my friend's got a camera on the front of her shirt." When his brows went up, I added, "She's been doing that of late so there's no question as to who's telling the truth."

"I play golf with the Chief on occasion, and he told me that he sprung you from jail once after you landed there because another cop's kid made claims against you."

"Yes, Alex. He was quite the handful for being seven years old, or close enough." I'd blocked all memories of the trip to that backwater jail. "The best thing to come out of that situation was that it was the start of the Chief's and my frigid relationship beginning to thaw. Now he comes to family get-togethers."

"Uh-huh." He didn't believe that for a second.

"Just ask Mother…" I cast a glance inside the car. "She's the only chick in a dude group that consists of her husband, the Chief, and Fab's father. They all go fishing together on occasion."

"You're good with the stories." Tarlow chuckled.

"It's doubtful that Mother is actually holding her own pole or casting a line… but she does make sure that all aboard have plenty of food and drink."

"I'll believe it when you get me an invite." He took a couple of steps away and turned back. "Try not to run off."

I laughed.

Tarlow stuck his head inside the car and asked Mother and Jean a couple of questions. He then met up with the other officer, who'd just come out of the house.

An ambulance came around the corner, parked, and two paramedics got out, grabbed their bags, and headed up the walkway. They exchanged a few words with both officers, and the one led them to the door. He tried the knob, and it was locked. He knocked and knocked again, then yelled, "Miami police," and Lynn finally opened the door. They disappeared inside.

Tarlow bent down, picked up the envelope, and pulled out the report.

Fab came over and stood next to me.

"Will we be able to leave soon?" Mother called out.

"Once they're done with their questioning," I said, thinking it wasn't an answer but better than, *Hell if I know.*

"I saw you getting all friendly with the other officer —"

"Seriously?" I cut Fab off. "You've apparently forgotten Officer Tarlow." I nodded in his direction. "He came to our rescue on the sorority girl job, and lucky us, he remembered. Turns out he's friends with the Chief."

"Here's one for you," Fab said. "Prior to the shooting, Lynn called 911, then hung up. I'm guessing that was right before she came back outside. A second call came in about the shooting from one of the neighbors. Told the officer I haven't had time to check out the block but that I hadn't seen anyone lurking about since we got here."

"Thinking if you're sitting in your house, game show on, and hear rapid-fire gunshots, you wouldn't hesitate to call the police." Over Fab's shoulder, I noticed Tarlow flicking through the information Xander had compiled on Lynn. I nudged Fab as he shoved the papers back in the envelope and walked over. "Is Lynn okay?" I asked Tarlow.

"She's lucky it was only a grazed biceps."
Ouch.

"If one of these victims had pursued criminal charges, we'd have arrested her. Unfortunately, based on this report, the cases were all dealt with in civil court. I asked Ms. Winters, and she's not interested in pressing charges."

The other cop was back and shaking his head as he motioned Tarlow over. After a short discussion, Tarlow turned back to us. "Ms. Wade told my partner that she called 911 because she was afraid you were trying to break into her house. While she was on the line, she decided she'd overreacted and hung up." He eyed the pin on the front of Fab's blouse. "If you'd forward me a copy of the footage you got, then I won't have to be questioning you should the accusation arise again."

Fab whipped out her phone, called Xander, and made the request. "Your email?" Tarlow told her and she repeated it. "It won't take long before it'll be in your box." She hung up.

"If Ms. Winters changes her mind about pursuing a case, have her contact me, and I'll investigate. Fraud is a crime." He handed me a business card.

I went to the car and came back with cards for both officers.

Tarlow took them and eyed one. "If I have any further questions, I know how to contact you. You're all free to go."

He got back to the front door as it opened. The two paramedics exited. The four had a short conversation, and the paramedics got back in their ambulance.

"Wonder if it was Lynn's plan to have us arrested, and then she got cold feet?" Fab whispered as we walked back to the car.

"Even though Lynn's wound didn't sound serious, I figured they'd be taking her to the hospital."

"Neither of us would go."

Agreed.

"Let's get the heck out of here." Fab tugged on my arm.

My hand on the car door, I looked around and noted that both officers were now inside Lynn's house.

"I'm sure that it doesn't come as a surprise that Lynn never had any intention of paying you or anyone else she ripped off," Fab told Jean as she headed down the street. "Based on her previous moving around, and after what went down today, it wouldn't surprise me if she packs up and is out of here tonight. And for two reasons: you found her and so did whoever it was that wanted to kill her, and if she's smart, the latter has her shaking in her shoes."

Jean scooted up and stuck her head between the seats at what appeared to be Mother's prodding. "I'm going to chalk this up as a loss and move on. I don't like being cheated, but thankfully, I wasn't depending on the money for anything. I've never been this close to a shooting and don't want it to happen again." A shudder shook her body.

"From the little I saw peering over her shoulder, Lynn's not living the high life, so I doubt that she's got any money we could shake out of her," Fab told her.

Jean patted her shoulder. "I wouldn't want to risk anyone getting hurt."

"Adding to what Fab said, once the shooter finds out that they missed, if it was their intent to kill her, chances are high they'll be back," I said.

"Listen up, you two," Fab said in a stern tone, eyeing Mother and Jean in her rearview mirror. "*Do not* come back here for any reason. The last thing you want is to get into the middle of something you can't handle. If Lynn should see you again… there's no telling what she would do. It was clear that the woman has self-entitlement issues. When we were face-to-face, she threw a couple of threats my way."

Jean was only too happy to agree. After some hesitation, Mother nodded reluctantly.

Back at the compound, I turned to the two women and grinned. "How about lunch?"

Both groaned.

Guess all the action killed their appetites.

I was relieved that Mother and Jean had decided they'd had enough and were ready to call it a day. I knew Fab felt the same way. After hugs and kisses, Mother and Jean got in the car and roared off.

"Before you go…" I told Fab about Booker getting released from the hospital.

"I'll call my father when I get home."

"Surprised…" I arched my brows, figuring she'd initiate a hunt for the man.

"I had to swear more than once that if I got an update, he'd be my first call."

"Be sure to remind him you're available for backup." I almost laughed when she shook her head, *fat chance of him accepting the offer* on her face. "One more thing before you skate off—I need a day off."

"You're doing a lot of that lately," she grumbled with a smile, then grabbed her stuff and headed home.

Although Jean had been resigned, Mother clearly wasn't going to be happy letting Lynn skate. Once inside my house, I dumped my purse on the bench in the entry, got out my phone, plopped down on the couch, and called Spoon.

"This call is to be kept secret," I said when he answered.

"Now what?" he groaned.

"You didn't hear this from me…" I updated him on the morning's activities. He was so silent, I checked the screen to make sure we hadn't been disconnected. "You need to keep a vigilant eye on your wife, and at the same time make sure she doesn't figure out what you're doing."

"Don't be worried when you don't hear from her for a couple of days," Spoon chuckled humorlessly. "I know just how to keep my wife busy."

Since I wasn't about to ask, we hung up. I threw the phone to the other end of the couch and stretched out.

Chapter Twenty-Eight

Looking forward to a drama-free day… I laughed and hoped that I hadn't cursed it by even thinking such a thing. I'd gotten up before Creole, made us coffee, and brought it back to bed.

Creole eyed his mug suspiciously. "Thinking all hell broke loose somewhere, and you just now remembered."

"I can be a good wifey on occasion without an ulterior motive." I made a face at him. "I can assure you there were no more shootings after yesterday's."

"I'm going to tell Spoon, before your mother gets a wild hair—"

"No, you're not." A finger-shake in my tone. "He's got it handled. Bet you that he's taking her for a weekend away, they've already left town, and any schemes she's concocted are forgotten."

My phone rang, interrupting our kiss. I rolled over and grabbed it off the nightstand, seeing Cootie's name flash on the screen. I flipped it around so Creole could see. It was rare that something came up Cootie couldn't handle himself. "Should I be afraid to ask what's up?" I asked Creole. Not waiting for his response, I answered the call and put it on speaker. "Heads up: Hubby is listening in."

"Greetings." He unleashed a growly laugh. "I need to be assured by both of you that this call never happened."

Now what? "Pinkie swear."

"What she said," Creole told him.

"Your friend—you know, the Frenchie one—well, she brought that security weirdo friend of hers back..."

Creole nudged me with a grin.

"Dude's adding cameras to the front of the warehouse and got all gripey when I asked what the hell he was up to. The whole time, Fab's been crawling all over the fence, and at least once, she ended up going over."

"To do what? Did she get back over in one piece?" I asked.

"Dude tossed her a rope, anchored it to the back of his truck, and here she comes like some monkey."

Creole turned away and laughed.

"What was she looking for? And no, I didn't ask. She wouldn't tell me anyway. I did see that she came back over empty-handed. It went off so smoothly, one might think they had it planned." Cootie snorted.

"How am I supposed to find out what she's up to without outing you?" If something on the neighbor's property had caught Fab's attention, she wouldn't give up until she got an answer. She might need a reminder that trespassing was a good way to get her butt kicked or worse.

"If I had to put money on you coming up with a cockamamie story, I'd ante up a few bucks."

Creole covered his face, laughing again.

"What you could do is hustle your pokey over here and *Surprise*," he yelled.

I shook my head in an attempt to stop the ringing in my ears.

"Then you feign shock when you catch her snooping around where she shouldn't be."

"I need a shower and more coffee, and I'll practice my facial reactions on the way over. You better be working on your surprised face when you see me park and get out."

He grunted, and the line went dead.

Creole turned the screen toward him. "What happened to good-bye or something?"

"That's so overrated. And it cuts down on awkward moments when you just hang up."

"I've got some time before I've got to be at the office."

"You're off the hook. I've got this handled. Both of us show up, and she's going to know we were tipped off."

He jumped out of bed and lifted me up, carrying me into the bathroom.

Once out, knowing there was no need for dress-up, I put on a comfortable black t-shirt dress and paired it with slides, while Creole donned jeans and a dress shirt. I grabbed my purse and briefcase, he hooked his arm around me, and we went out to my SUV. He kissed me and got in his truck.

A strong shot of caffeine was needed before going to see what Fab was up to, and I cruised through the drive-through before heading to the warehouse. My guess was that she'd found out something about the neighbor and hadn't bothered to share. After some investigation, I planned to stop by the office and grab another kiss from Creole.

When I reached the warehouse, I came to a stop and waited for Fab's security guy to turn onto the road so I could turn in. I rolled down my window and waved. He waved back. I parked next to Fab's new Porsche, leaving plenty of room. A dent would mean certain death. Except for the day it arrived, it was the first time I'd seen it out of the garage since she'd gotten it.

Fab walked up as I got out. "Why more cameras?" I didn't waste time asking.

"Surprised you noticed." She stood back and took stock of the building.

"Your friend was leaving as I got here, and after a quick scan of the building, I saw the new additions."

"Just me being thorough," she said as she eyed every corner of the property.

"No one knows you better than I do, and right now, I know you're full of baloney." I knew she'd turn up her nose at the pedestrian lunch meat reference, and she didn't disappoint. "Since you've been here working and snooping and... did you go inside and check out the progress that Cootie's made?"

"Let's do it now." Fab linked her arm in mine with plans to tug me all the way.

I disengaged my arm. "Be secretive. Fine with me. But I'm telling you now that I'll find out what you're up to."

"Do you have to be so annoying?"

"Yes." I gave her an assessing stare before heading inside. "Wow..." I came to a stop just past the threshold and checked out the stacks of boxes lined up against one wall from one end to the other. I didn't miss that they all had identifying markings on them. "You got a lot done." I smiled at Cootie, who'd walked up to join us.

"Got behind, as I ended up doing it all myself and repair calls cut into my time."

"You've done a great job," I assured the man. "When all of this is ready to be moved to storage, I'll get some muscle and a truck big enough that it'll only take one trip. Which reminds me, I need to get with Rude and see where it's going to be stored."

"Rude's got that all figured out. She came down here to check everything out. The two of us made a master list based on how I marked each box, and each one will be individually numbered so it's easy to find. That way, if someone *does* show up to make a claim, we won't have to search for days."

"Doodad put out the word—*Come pick up your stuff*—and so far, no takers," I told him. "Tank's advice was to keep the items for at least six months before we dump anything. I'll check back with him when time runs out. Then, instead of dumping, we'll donate."

Fab was done with her inspection of the warehouse, including making a check of all the boxes, and was back.

"Do you know why more cameras were needed on the property?" I asked Cootie, ignoring Fab poking me in the side.

"If I had to guess, I'd say your friend here found out something about the auto body place and plans to get the goods on them."

"Are you done?" Fab snapped at Cootie, which didn't slow him in the slightest.

"No, he's not. What else?" I prodded.

"What stands out to me is that I've yet to see or hear one person over there working and not a single sign of anyone coming or going. Kind of odd, don't you think?"

I nodded. "I did ask Spoon what he knew, and he told me that he'd heard it was a one-man operation and, other than that, he didn't know anything. He also hadn't met the owner in all the years he's had his business, which he found odd, as he's met everyone else on the block at least once. No gossip either, as that would've made the rounds."

"I can't prove anything... yet." Fab's tone told us that she was determined to figure out exactly what was going on. "What auto repair business has the majority of their comings and goings at night? None that I've ever heard of. From the footage I've scanned, it's busy over there at night. Last night, I got a glimpse of a kid who reminded me of the one that jacked my car. It frustrated me not to get a close-up."

"A bit of advice, girlie..." Cootie raised his brows at her. "If you do lay hands on the kid, try not to kick his butt or wring his neck before you call the cops." He eyed her: *Are you listening?* "I'd be interested to know what the kid planned to do with the car — just a joyride and then dump it? Or perhaps he had a buyer waiting in the wings? Can't believe anyone who buys stolen cars would deal with a kid. If that's the way it played out, they'd get the car without paying a dime, and the kid would end up face-down in a ditch."

"In addition to adding cameras, did you jump the fence?" I eyed Fab. "Share what you learned and don't bother to deny it, as I saw a ladder propped up against the fence that doesn't belong to us."

"After a quick look at the property, you'd never know it was an auto body shop. There's not a single car anywhere in sight, which is unusual. Or maybe that's just because they keep everything locked up. A quick peek inside the warehouse and garage would answer that question. But if they're smart, any attempted break-in would trigger an alarm. I'm not going to try my luck so I can find out if they're dumb-asses or not."

"You could stake the place out, and when the gate opens, rush inside and introduce yourself as the new owner of this property. Just don't use my name," I admonished lightly. "You know what you should do? Mind your own business." Fab glared. Cootie laughed.

"One thing I know about this street—people do mind their own business, and expect others to do the same," he said in a crabby tone. "Good way to get shot… just because."

"Continue your snooping, since we know that's what you're going to do and you loathe an unanswered question," I said to Fab. "But instead of creeping around the property, increasing your chances of getting hurt, comb through the footage you're collecting with the same intensity that you do all the other properties. If you find something that smacks of illegal, give Cooper a call. You might just earn yourself a brownie point."

"He's easier to deal with than Kevin, but I think he wouldn't mind it at all if someone else was assigned to take our calls."

"To speed you along in your snooping endeavor, I can ask around to a few of the locals I know—only those that I know can keep their mouths shut—and see what they know." Cootie arched his brow. "I'll be very casual, as I don't want my ass handed to me."

My phone rang, and I pulled it out of my pocket and looked at the screen. "Your lovely wife." I held it up so Cootie could see.

"She's up to something." He cackled.

I answered and barely got out, "Hello," before I was interrupted.

"Bardy's out of the hospital and staying with Fern," Rude said breathlessly. "Besides being scared, he's got problems, and my guess is he's going to need a lawyer. He's open to a chat, and you know where to find him."

"Appreciate you letting me know. Once Fab and I are done arguing over whose client he is, we'll head on over." We hung up.

Chapter Twenty-Nine

Since we both had our cars, we headed back to the compound. Fab flew ahead of me and was waiting impatiently when I pulled in. By the time we got to the motel, which was a short drive, nothing had been decided as to how to deal with Bardy's situation. Fab pulled around the back and parked in the space clearly marked "No Parking."

"The ticket and tow job are coming out of your pocket," I said as I got out and pointed to the sign. Unable to identify the noise Fab made, I ignored her. "You might want to tell Gunz that this place really does need a name. The Motel is just damn weird."

"He's well aware, and I'm not sure why he hasn't done something about it already," Fab said as she headed through the gate.

"I'm assuming you've got a plan for how to proceed?"

"We're here to find out the latest, which know is that Bardy's out of the hospital. After we introduce ourselves, we say... well, something nice, and then find out what the grandson's role was in what went down or if it was someone else that locked the man in his room." *So there* in her tone.

While Fab went into the office, I scanned the pool area, checking out the upgrades to the exterior. Whoever was hired did a good job. It surprised me that, even though the pool water was now blue and inviting, there was only one person stretched out on a chaise, who had a newspaper over their face. I assumed they were asleep since I hadn't seen any movement.

Glancing back to see what Fab was up to, I saw Rollo pop up from behind the counter and join her in the small lobby area, where the two talked. A shrill whistle from the corner of the building had me turning. I was impressed to see that it was Fern who'd unleashed the obnoxious noise. She waved me over.

"You need bail money?"

Fern cackled, then made a face. "Last year I think it was, the seniors went on a jail tour. I was glad when it was over and most shared my sentiment."

"Agree with you." No need to tell her I'd been behind bars — innocent, of course — and it sucked.

"I'm really hoping that you two can help Bardy and make sure that he doesn't lose his house."

"As you know, Gunz's girl can be relentless." Fab would kill me if she heard me refer to her that way. "We're here to find out exactly what happened and the players involved, and then we'll know where to go from there."

Fab showed up at my side. "What did I miss?"

"Me heaping accolades on you for being a superstar."

Yeah, sure—she rolled her eyes. "Do you know if Bardy's awake and ready for guests?"

"He's over there." Fern pointed to the man I'd spotted earlier. "He's a bit twitchy about being cooped up inside. I would be too, if I were…" She shook her head. "There's a few perks here, and besides the free coffee, there's a stack of newspapers in the office. They're old, but still good for shade and the crossword."

Fern and I fell in line behind Fab as she made her way over to Bardy. I slowed to dip my foot in the pool—not as warm as I'd like but not frigid either.

Fab tapped Bardy's shoulder. It took a minute before he lifted the corner of the newspaper, peeked out, and gave her an assessing once-over. Then he sat up and threw the paper on the ground. Fab introduced the two of us and pulled up a chair. I dragged chairs over for Fern and myself.

"We're here to find out what you need us to do so you can go back home," Fab said.

It would have been hard to miss the shudder that shook the man's body or the fear etched in his face.

"My grandson, Sway, showed up at the door, claiming that after an argument with his parents, he needed a place to cool off and he'd only be staying a day or two. It took about a week before I was tired of him underfoot and asked when he was going to fix things with his parents; I still hadn't gotten the whole story. When I brought up his sneaking around in the middle of the night, that's when I found out the little shit had a temper. He went off and scared me so bad, I backed off without another word. Called my son and asked him to come get his kid, and he asked for a little more time, saying that Sway was just frustrated at not carving his own path as fast as he'd like. Whatever the hell that means." Bardy went into a coughing fit, his cheeks flaming red.

"I'll get you some water." Fern jumped up and ran for the office, yelling on the way, "Don't choke to death before I get back."

She returned just as Bardy's coughing fit subsided, twisted the cap off a water bottle, and handed it to him. While he drank, she rubbed his back. "Don't go gulping it," she lightly admonished, taking the bottle back and sitting on the end of his chaise.

"I'd heard, though no one wanted to talk about it, that Sway had gotten into drugs but had since sworn off them. Since he was acting so cagey, I convinced myself he was doing them again, so I decided to do a little snooping. I had pangs of guilt, pretty sure my son wouldn't agree with what I was doing, but if I hadn't done it..." He grabbed the water bottle back from Fern and lay back, unleashing a big sigh.

"Just take your time," Fern advised the man. *Right?* She eyed the two of us.

"I stumbled across some legal documents that he'd stuffed in a drawer, and what caught my attention was that they had my name on them." Bardy finished off the water.

"Another one?" Fern asked. He nodded. She grabbed the empty one and sprinted off.

"Grabbed up the paperwork, ran to my neighbor's, and paid her to make a copy for me. Then I went home, put the originals back, settled back in my recliner, and read every word."

Fern was back and, this time, scooted her chair closer. He reached over and patted her hand.

"Take your time; there's no hurry," Fab assured him.

"The gist was that Sway planned to sell my house out from under me," Bardy continued. "Funny thing, but not really—he had a checklist of everything he needed to do to make the transfer happen."

"How far has Sway gotten?" Fern asked.

"After some investigation, we found out that your property is now in Sway's name," Fab told them. "What we didn't know was if it was done with your approval."

"He forged my signature. I guess no one noticed that it didn't match?" Bardy shook his head as though he still couldn't believe it.

"No one's comparing signatures on things like this. It either means that Sway has a fake ID saying he's you or a partner in crime willing to notarize anything," Fab told him. "This whole situation was brought to a head because Sway —" She arched her brow. " — caught you snooping?"

"Before I confronted Sway, I talked to Fern." He smiled at the woman. "I hedged around, not able to admit how stupid I'd been."

"That's nonsense," Fern sputtered. "The last thing you were expecting was that snot-nose stealing from you."

"When I did confront Sway..." Bardy blew out a labored breath. "Never thought he'd attack me, kick my butt to the floor, and drag me to my bedroom. You don't know how many times I asked myself if I'd ever walk away."

"You're lucky you have a snoopy neighbor." Fern winked at the man, getting the first smile we'd seen. "I got worried, and not one to sit around, I called..." She pointed to the two of us.

"From what we've been able to find out, a sale hasn't happened yet," Fab told him. "What we need to do is find out if the realtor representing the house has a pending contract, and if so, we need to put a stop to it."

"If the deal is cash, you're going to need to hustle." I left unsaid that anyone involved, whether they knew the truth or not, was unlikely to cooperate. "We have a number of connections in the real estate field that will make it easier for us to find out where everything stands," I assured him.

"The other problem that needs to be dealt with immediately is your grandson. Have you filed a police report?" Fab asked. "Any chance you told your son what his offspring did?"

"My son, Jasper, came to the hospital every day, and I told him what Sway had done to me. I don't think he believed me at first. Then, when I mentioned the police, he begged me not to make the call, saying that he'd deal with everything. After that, he apologized numerous times, to the point I didn't want to hear it anymore. I bought myself some time to think by telling the cops, when they showed up, that my memory was fuzzy. I knew that to do anything else would tear my family apart."

I was surprised that his family's first concern wasn't protecting him but the kid who put him in the hospital. He could've died. Then what? Would they have stepped forward then?

"When the cops asked a question, I hedged so much they probably thought I was senile. Didn't help that I wouldn't make eye contact—that's a trick of liars. They were patient, more than I deserved, and they didn't call me out, just said that they'd speak to me again." Bardy squeezed his eyes closed, then looked at the ground. "I have two granddaughters, Sway's sisters, and part of me wonders if I'd ever see them again if I pressed charges."

"Your son isn't doing his kid any favors, letting Sway get away with committing multiple crimes.

If you'd died—"

"Right before you showed up, I thought it was the end and wondered how long it would take," Bardy said, cutting Fab off. "I closed my eyes for what I thought would be the last time, and when I opened them, I was in the back of an ambulance. I was flooded with relief."

"Out of curiosity, how did your son find out you were in the hospital?" I asked. "Did Sway visit?"

"Jasper was at my bedside when I opened my eyes. I didn't ask how he found out." Bardy appeared to be frightened by the memory. "Don't know how long he stayed, as I closed my eyes and went back to sleep. The next day, Sway came with his father and didn't say a damn word or make eye contact. Tired of waiting for someone to say something, I asked him if he'd sold my house yet, and he walked out. Jasper appeared not to know what was going on, and that's when I enlightened him. On the verge of storming out, he said he'd get to the bottom of everything. I remember mumbling, 'Hope I have a home to go home to.' Whatever he was about to say, he thought better of it and walked out."

"Does Jasper know that you've been released and where you're at now?" Fab asked.

"I'm struggling not to be angry, but it's hard. I assumed that Jasper would figure it out when he showed back up at the hospital and found out I'd been released. I know it was cowardly, but I didn't want my son pressuring me into recuperating at his house." Bardy shuddered. "So happy when Fern showed up and told me she had folks lined up. Hard to believe, but I've seen the woman in action and know she can make things happen. Then she went on to sing you two's praises and relayed the squatter story. Most would think she's crazy, but I know her." The two smiled at one another.

"Here's the deal…" Fab leveled a squinty stare at Bardy and Fern. "You're both going to promise not to go looking for trouble. You're going to stay here with your feet up, and no wandering off. That would include not going anywhere near your house until we've made certain that Sway is no longer a problem, and the property is back in your name."

"Do you feel safe here?" I asked.

Bardy nodded as he looked around. "How much is this going to cost me?"

"You get the family discount—Gunz picks up the tab," Fab assured him.

Bardy leaned toward her. "I'm not related," he whispered hoarsely, loud enough for anyone in the pool area to hear. Good thing it was empty other than us.

"Yeah, well, that's not what Fern told him." I eyed the woman, who didn't look the least bit embarrassed.

"If asked, all you need to say is 'cousin,'" Fern rasped. "That's vague enough, and who's going to do any checking? No one. The man's got dough coming out of those big butt cheeks of his and won't miss a penny of it."

"Make sure that Gunz doesn't hear butt cheeks and his name in the same sentence." I struggled not to laugh and noticed Fab doing the same. I made a mental note of that descriptive tidbit and would make sure it got announced at a family dinner. But only after everyone had eaten. "As far as payment goes, you can rest assured that you don't have anything to worry about, as Gunz never complains, even about the ones who're only vaguely related."

"It's taken care of," Fab brushed it off.

"Thinking that if you're going to go by the house, you'll need a key, and I don't have one," Bardy told Fab. "You also need to watch your back if Sway answers the door."

"No need to worry." She smiled sneakily. "I'll check it out, and if Sway is there, the last thing I want is a confrontation with the man."

Why tell him who needs a key when you have a lockpick? Or, if there were a confrontation, Sway wouldn't come out on the winning side?

"I'll need a couple of days to do some more investigation, and when we meet again, hopefully I'll be able to answer all your questions. You can be assured I'll keep you updated on everything," Fab said. "If you need to talk to me about anything, Rollo in the office can get ahold of me. He knows that I'm working on your behalf, and it won't be a problem."

"Same goes for you." Bardy patted Fab's hand. "If I can be helpful in any way, let me know."

I leaned over and whispered in Fern's ear, "You hear all the *behave* talk? It also applies to you. If anything hits the fan, you better damn well call."

"I'm no stupe. You don't need to be worrying about anything," Fern whispered back. "My eyes will be wide open, and if anyone shows up that shouldn't be here, I've got Rollo's number, and he's told me, 'Don't hesitate.'"

"One more thing," Fab told Bardy, "your lawyer is Patrick Cannon, and he'll be giving you a call to get the paperwork started to get your property back in your name." She stood and assured Bardy again that she'd be in touch.

I nodded to the man and followed her out.

Once outside the gate, Fab slid behind the wheel. "I've got Xander doing some more digging to make sure any potential sale gets stopped. Got to call Tank and tell him to hustle on his end of the paperwork. As for Sway, I'll drop-kick his butt to the street if he's still in residence."

"You need to be careful, since the property is in Sway's name. Save the butt-kicking until after the transfer back to Bardy." I eyed Fab, who easily ignored me as she turned onto the Overseas. "The kid's father isn't doing him any favors, trying to cover up multiple felonies. If he'd rip off his grandfather… he just might try it again and with a non-family member, thinking he'll have better luck."

"I told Rollo to keep an eye on the man and, if anyone shows up, to scare the hell out of them. His grin told me he'd enjoy every minute of chasing someone off the property."

"Knowing you as well as I do, we're on the way to Bardy's house. Good thing you have your backup with you." I pointed to myself. "While there, we need to check out Fern's place and make sure no one's taken over her house."

"Just a drive-by, not going to the door. I want the first time I introduce myself to be when I have legal papers to serve."

"Enroute, why don't you tell me how the conversation with Caspian went when he got the news about Booker?"

"He had a major fit in multiple languages. Though I'm not fluent in all of them, I was able to piece together enough to know what he was fuming about. If he knew..." She chuckled. "It was the Chief that convinced him that, based on a couple of outstanding charges, Booker'd be in jail for a while."

"So the Chief basically saved Booker from being erased from this earth?"

"Papa assured me that that was the last I'd ever hear the man's name."

It was a short drive before Fab turned off the highway and cruised Bardy's block twice. The second time, she slowed to take a picture of the license plate of the car in his driveway. All looked quiet at Fern's.

"We know several a-kickers who would enjoy heaving Sway to the street by the back of his neck." I smiled, liking my idea.

"Agree with you but wouldn't want it to come back on Bardy. I didn't want to tell the man, but I'm pretty sure he figured out for himself that the kid is a big problem. A stern 'behave yourself' isn't going to stop him from doing squat."

"If anyone deserves an oversized boot up their ass…"

Fab laughed. "I'm over this day; let's go home."

"I second that."

Traffic cooperated, and we were back home in a flash. Fab pulled into my driveway and jumped out, but before she disappeared, she told me, "I'm the one who needs a day off this time. If something comes up, put it off."

"Got it." I mentally saluted.

Chapter Thirty

Needing some sunshine, I packed up my office and carried it out to the deck, where I spread my paperwork out on a chaise. Several cranes landed on the sand, catching my attention, and I watched as they walked along the shore, looking for food, I presumed.

Just as I flipped up the lid on my laptop, Fab came romping up the stairs, her laptop shoved under her arm. She set it down and went to retrieve a water.

"Did you miss the part where you mandated a day off for yourself?"

"Sometimes..." Fab maneuvered a chair around so she could look out over the water and still make eye contact. "As you know, things don't always go as planned. Knowing how you loathe recycled information—just as much as I do, in fact—" She toasted me with her water. "—I thought why not make my calls here, where you can eavesdrop?"

"You're not the only one hard at work. I'm about to find out if Bardy's house has a contract on it." I opened my laptop and typed in the address. "Found the listing." I picked up my phone off the side table, called the realtor listed, and put the call on speaker. I knew speaking to the realtor directly would be a longshot but figured I could still get a couple questions answered.

A woman answered the phone, and I gave her the address, asking, "Is it still available?"

After muttering a couple of indecipherable things, she said, "I'll need to put you on hold."

"You'd think if she didn't have the information at her fingertips, she'd have a vague idea," I said to Fab.

It took the woman so long to get back on the line that Fab and I traded raised eyebrows more than once. I also checked the screen a couple times to make sure we were still connected. Finally!

"If you give me your name and number, I'll have the agent call you."

After giving her the info she requested, I asked, "Could you tell me one way or the other if the property has a contract on it?"

"I'm sure you'll be getting a call shortly." She hung up.

"Why not answer the question?" Fab grumbled. "She had to know if it's still available. Wonder why she wouldn't answer. You'd think Sway would want it sold as quickly as possible before everything blows up in his face, which is about to happen."

"It wouldn't be the first shady real estate agent we've dealt with," I reminded her.

"With all the work you have to put in to get your real estate license, why jeopardize it on a shady deal? Claiming ignorance doesn't keep you out of big trouble, as in jail."

"We need to know if there's an offer, and ASAP, before everything gets more complicated." I picked my phone back up and called Xander. When he answered, I said, "I've got an illegal favor to ask, and I'm more than happy to take it up with one of your shadier friends. I just need the number."

"What is it you need so I know where to route it?"

"This call is on speaker —"

"When isn't it?" Xander cut in.

"Fab just rolled her eyes, so she's thinking you're going to do it yourself. I'd rather someone who knows the risk and does it anyway." I filled him in on the new information from Bardy Dowell and told him about the call I'd just made.

"I know just the guy to call," Xander assured me. "I'll call back with the info."

After we hung up, Fab said, "You do know that Xander can dig up just about any information you need, as he's proven in the past?"

"I don't want to be the one responsible for getting him sent to jail."

"That's not going to happen; he's smarter than that," Fab assured me. "Once Xander gets us the info we need, we'll take over and give the information to Tank, so he can kill whatever

Sway's next move is. Based on what's happened thus far, he'll want to hurry the process along."

"Damn! This would be so much easier if Bardy'd reported Sway to the cops. If he was too afraid to, then Sway's father ought to have. Letting the kid skate on a major felony only teaches him he can do it again."

"Sounded to me like Bardy thought he wouldn't have a family if he pressed charges."

"What if Bardy had died? Would they have helped bury the body? Stand around, sniveling what a great guy he was?"

"Yes and yes," Fab said in disgust. "I get that Bardy doesn't want to lose his family, but I think that ship sailed when his son sided with the grandson, despite the fact he almost killed him in an attempted swindle. If that was my kid, I'd be worried. What if he turned on me?"

"I'd think it would be normal to ask that question… unless you had your head shoved up your… backside." Phone back in hand, I scrolled across the screen, showing her that I was calling Tank. "Speaking of lawyers…"

"No, we weren't," Fab snarked.

"Tank's name did come up." I matched her tone.

I was mildly surprised when he answered. "Let me guess, another dead people problem?"

"Sorry to disappoint. This one's a little more pedestrian—fraud—but there's the possibility that other charges could be heaped on." I reminded him about Bardy's case and told him about the calls I'd made and the favor I'd just asked for.

"I've been waiting to hear on Bardy's condition, then planned to stop by and introduce myself. I want to be sure that he wants my services and I'm not pushing myself on some old man."

"You don't have the reputation of a slime."

"Good to know." Tank laughed. "Once I get Bardy's okay, I'll get the documents drawn up and filed with the court to bring this deal to a halt. It's bad enough that the title has been fraudulently changed; the last thing we want is for a sale to happen, which would really complicate the issue. Then I'll get Clive to run the paperwork over to the courthouse."

"I appreciate your speediness in this matter."

"Word of warning: If the kid is willing to commit felonies to get his hands on the property for a quick profit, Grandpa needs to be careful. And so do the two of you when he finds out you're helping the man."

Fab and I exchanged raised eyebrows, knowing he was right.

"I'm going to run upstairs and find out what Xander's dug up." Tank hung up.

Shouts from the sand drew Fab's and my attention. The kids came trooping down the beach, all with what appeared to be ice cream in cups, spoons sticking out of the tops, and sat down. Crum was dragging a canvas bag, which he upended in front of them, an assortment of balls tumbling out.

"Isn't it a bit early for all that sugar?" Fab asked with a raised eyebrow.

"Crum probably figures the kids are going to need the energy to run up and down the sand for however much time he needs to fill. You know he's got something planned — you can bet he's not going to stay out on the beach all day."

"Any calls from an irate parent, or all of them perhaps?" Fab asked with a chuckle.

I looked down to the sand and took a head count. "I'm safe with this bunch. Appears the northern bunch has hit the road. I had heard that Crum might have a day or two of killing time with the local kids after the others went home."

"Who lets their kids go off for a week with someone they don't know?" Fab asked incredulously.

"I know they wouldn't have sent the kiddos around the block with me... Well, maybe if I'd gotten Cruz's stamp of approval. I can just see asking and him laughing. But they all had a relationship with Crum. He must've refrained from looking down his nose and mumbling about IQ."

"I'm amazed that there wasn't some surprise drama that necessitated them all going home early."

"Let me guess, all of you bet on just such a drama behind my back."

Fab made a zip-lip motion.

So the answer was yes.

"In the spirit of updating and not the best news—"

"I wondered what got you over here, interrupting your day off." I swallowed a groan.

"Booker walked out of the hospital and disappeared."

"How is that even possible? Wouldn't the cops have taken him into custody? Or did he sneak off?" Not giving her a chance to answer, I added, "Hoping this means Caspian took care of the problem and in the future, it'll be *Booker who?*"

"Really, Madison."

"Your huffiness is a put-on. We both know Caspian is a badass, especially about anyone who would think about laying a finger on his daughter. I realize it was me he attacked, but still… I don't like Booker's chances of walking around sucking air if your papa thinks he'd even look in your direction. He's as tough as his daughter."

"I've got a call into my father and am waiting to hear back."

"I'll call Xander and have him do some digging. I don't know how long it would take for the cops to find out if Booker did walk, but hopefully he's in custody."

"If he's found to be lurking around the area, give the information to Toady. Think of it as doing something nice for the wildlife." Fab grinned, liking her idea.

"I'd like to know if the rumors of Toady feeding people to alligators has any validity." I looked at her, figuring she'd know for certain.

"Overheard him boasting of his accomplishments a couple of times, a big grin on his face. I've never known the man to be full of himself. If he tells you he's going to get a job done, it's done."

"You can count on Toady always coming through on whatever he promises." Fab nodded.

The kids had finished their ice cream. Crum whipped out a large bag and stood about a foot back from the older ones as they pitched their cups into it, then moved closer for the younger ones. All of them hit the mark.

My phone rang, and I answered, putting it on speaker. "I was about to call you," I said to Xander.

"Booker's out of the hospital," he told us.

"Does that mean he's back in jail? Not out on bail, I hope."

"So you know, all this went down just after midnight and I forwarded both of you a copy of the security footage. You'll see that Booker was wheeled out, slumped over in a wheelchair, by a hulk of a man who made sure his face was never seen on a single camera. Then thrown, and I mean literally, into the back of an SUV with tinted windows. The man drove off. And guess what? No license plate."

"Sounds like good news." I eyed Fab.

"Let's hope."

"Just now got an alert and can answer one of your questions—there's a warrant out for Booker's arrest."

"I appreciate you being on top of everything," I said. "And so does Fab."

"Don't make it sound like I don't know he does a damn good job," Fab crabbed.

"No fighting." Xander chuckled. "Something tells me you'll hear what happened to the man before I do. But if his body turns up somewhere, I'll let you know. Until then, keep an eye out wherever you go." We hung up.

"Let's hope that's the last time we ever hear about or see Booker," Fab said.

She and I watched as the kids bagged up the kickballs and jumped with excitement over wherever they were headed next.

Not sure how much time went by, but it wasn't long before both our laptops pinged with an incoming message.

"From Xander," Fab told me. "Bardy's property has a contract on it—cash deal. Buyer is a corporation, and they want a two-week closing."

"That gives us time to make sure the deal is killed."

"Just forwarded the file to Tank. Speaking of… just got an email from him." She scanned her screen. "He's on his way to a meeting with Bardy, and if all goes well, he'll have the paperwork filed and ready to serve on all parties by tomorrow."

"You'd have thought, when I called the real estate office, that whoever answered would've said, 'There's an offer.' Makes one wonder about the agent's involvement and whether they know the deal's not on the up-and-up."

"You know what this means for tomorrow?" Fab eyed me.

"I'll have my a-kicking clothes on and be ready to go when you blast the horn."

Chapter Thirty-One

We'd managed to get a fair amount of work done when Fab got an alert that someone was at the gate and, after a quick glance, said, "Husbands are home early." She jumped up and gathered her stuff together. "I'll text a time for tomorrow." She ditched me and hustled back down the beach.

I hurriedly cleaned my paperwork off the chaise and moved over, making room for Creole, knowing he'd find me. Sure enough — he changed, grabbed a cold drink, came out on the deck, and sank down next to me.

"Your update on the day…" I turned my laptop screen so he could see the emails in my inbox.

He scanned the screen and opened the one about Booker. "There's a story here, as no one gets released from the hospital in the middle of the night." Then he scanned the emails relating to Bardy. "You're forbidden to get hurt," he admonished.

"No need to worry, as I'll stand back while Fab kicks the door in." Noting that Creole didn't think I was one bit amusing, I toned it down. "A legal document is being drawn up, and we'll be serving it on Sway to let him know his criminal gig is up."

"Aren't you over the limit on how many papers you can serve without a license?"

"That's why I'll be doing my best to look fierce while Fab sticks them... you get the idea. Even though we haven't talked specifically about who's doing what, pretty sure she's ready to butt-kick if the opportunity arises."

"Why am I just learning about this?" Creole asked, not quite grouchy but close.

"It's not that I've been dragging my feet, it's that the info dump just went down this morning." I eyed him. "Back to Booker—who do you suppose is behind his ride to wherever?"

"It wasn't law enforcement, and I'd discount a friend springing him, because why would they send him airborne into the car? My guess is that his chances of sucking air for much longer are slim."

"Hope we're done having to worry about him... and Fab's client can be included on that list. Change of subject... did you tell the woman who made the offer on the warehouse to take a hike?"

"I did, and to say Jackie was none too happy is putting it mildly."

I arched my brow. "Did you run a background check on her?"

"Why, when we're not doing business with the woman? After I rejected her offer, I watched her struggle not to go off and wondered if she was going to hold it together. She finally managed a fake smile and told me not to be hasty and think it over, as it was a good offer."

"You need to forward me the woman's pic, which I'll send to Fab; she'll get gripey if I leave her out."

"Sending it now." He took out his phone, and after a few swipes, said, "Done. So you know, I told Jackie that we didn't want any trouble and there better not be any. She got the unspoken message that if there was, she'd be at the top of my suspect list." Creole stopped short of growling. "Thought I'd let you know that, since I haven't stopped by the warehouse in a while, I'll do it tomorrow and see for myself how it's going."

"You might want to wait a few days."

"Afraid to ask."

"The good news is that there's been no more dead bodies—"

"Oh yeah, got an update of my own." Creole wiggled his brows. "Heard from a connection in the coroner's office regarding the body found— the one in the wooden box. There's a ten-year-old death certificate on file. Turns out the woman died of natural causes, and her husband died shortly after."

"Do you know where his remains were tossed?"

"When I call back, I can ask, but don't be surprised if I don't get an answer to your question."

"When you get your friend on the phone, if he

does know the location, maybe the lovebirds can be reunited." I leaned over and kissed his cheek. "Promised Kevin and Cooper that we'd make sure the ashes didn't end up at the dump. Pretty certain they weren't including the actual bodies in their admonition... but covering my bases so I don't get any gripey calls."

"Those two bodies aren't our responsibility." Creole's tone said I should know that. "As for the other body—the one in the back of the car—he OD'd."

"Yikes. I'm relieved that neither person was murdered."

"You didn't say why I shouldn't be paying a surprise visit to the warehouse," Creole said, staring me down.

"You don't want to be in the way when my favorite cleanup crew gets started with the power washing, smell removal, and whatever."

"Weirdo has a crew?"

"That's not nice." I made a tsking noise. "If that were to get back to him and you were in need of his services to remove smells from something, you'd be out of luck."

"Yeah, okay. Wouldn't want to lose that contact."

"Sarcasm isn't necessary." I wagged my finger, which he nipped at.

"Have you spread the word about when the warehouse is going to be available to lease?"

"I've been dragging my sandals, as I'm a bit

fearful about who might come calling. One business taking over the entire building would be ideal. We're not interested in dividing up the space to house several different businesses, are we?"

"Recently had a meeting with a man that heard about the space, and the location is ideal for him."

"Hmm… and I wasn't invited to said meeting."

"Very last-minute. He'd heard the warehouse was available from… he wouldn't say, which I didn't like. It felt like I was the one being interviewed, and I had no clue if I met his standards or not. I sat through his pitch, and he's interested in turning the building into a pawn shop."

I laughed. Then realized Creole was serious. "What did you tell Mr…?"

"Smith." He grinned.

"You would be so flipping out if it were me feeding you this… oh yeah, pitch. What did you tell him?"

"That I'd check with my partner and get back to him."

"Your partner's answer is no. In fact, *hell no.*"

"I figured as much and already told him just that, although I was a lot nicer."

"Aren't you hilarious."

Creole grinned. "I do know of someone else looking for a large space, though they haven't approached me. Thinking if we're interested, we could get in contact."

"Maybe if I knew what you were talking about...?"

"What do you think of a wrestling gym?"

"That's an interesting option."

"Give it some thought, and if you're interested in pursuing it, I'll set up a meeting."

"Sounds like a really fun idea. Set it up; I'd like to hear the pitch." Before I could forget, I opened my email to send the neighbor's picture to Fab. "This is the woman who wanted to buy the warehouse?" I looked at it sideways.

Creole peered over my shoulder. "That's Jackie. You know her?"

"This is the woman Fab followed back to her apartment building in the stolen Maserati." I looked at the image more intently. "Then she managed to vacate the premises one step ahead of the cops."

"The same person whose kid Fab suspected of stealing her Porsche?"

"That would be the one."

"You can forward this only after extracting a promise that Fab won't go off half-cocked," Creole cautioned.

"I'll wait until we're face-to-face so maybe she'll listen." I shut the lid on my laptop. "Did I remember to tell you that she installed more spy cameras on the warehouse, all directed at the neighboring property?"

"Good thing that friend of hers knows what he's doing, so hopefully the cameras aren't easily detectable." Creole unleashed a grumbly sigh. "If they're running an illegal operation, they're going to protect what they've got going and not just roll over. They won't be able to pack up and leave that warehouse like the woman did her apartment."

"I know you're about to suggest 'call the cops,' but what do we have other than accusations?"

"Just because I'm a retired detective doesn't mean I don't have the chops to do some investigation."

"Please don't. If I can't put myself out there and risk getting hurt, then neither can you." I stared back unflinchingly.

"Neither of us has a clue what we're dealing with, but I've got an uneasy feeling. If they discover that we're investigating them, even in the slightest, all hell will break loose."

"I'm hungry."

"You're trying to distract me, and it's not working. We'll table this discussion for now, but not for long, as we need to come to an agreement on how to proceed." He leaned in and kissed me.

Chapter Thirty-Two

The next morning, Creole had no sooner walked out the door for an early meeting—and only after an admonition to not look for trouble—than my phone rang. Twice.

"Got the docs ready for you," Tank informed me when I answered. "I'd bring them by, but I've got to be in court. Left the papers that need to be served in an envelope on my desk."

"I don't have a problem picking them up," I assured him.

"One more thing, a copy of the file was also sent to your email, and when I get the proofs done, I'll be sending those over for signature."

"Kick ass in court."

Tank laughed, and we hung up.

The second call was from Cootie. "Got a call that there's water everywhere at one of the Boardwalk businesses. Would you meet the cleaning crew at the warehouse? They said they'd be done today." He sounded harried.

"I'm on it," I said. We hung up.

I raced to the bedroom, donned workout pants, a t-shirt, tennis shoes, and tucked my gun into the side pocket, though I didn't anticipate having to use it. I grabbed up my briefcase and keys and flew out the door. As I roared across the highway, I realized my phone hadn't rung again. That meant that Fab hadn't seen my getaway on the security feed.

I made a parking space for myself inches from the driveway of the warehouse going in the wrong direction. Two trucks were waiting to get inside. I hopped out, unlocked the fence, pushed it back, and waited while they drove inside. They waved as they passed me and parked. I'd met these two on a couple of occasions, so I walked over and re-introduced myself. "If you need anything and you can't reach Cootie…" I handed them each a business card.

From there, I headed to the office. There were two cars in the parking lot, which I recognized as belonging to Toady's men. The building was quiet as I got off on the second floor and waved to the guys, who were having a meeting with someone on their laptop at the conference table. I ducked into Tank's office and grabbed the envelope sitting on the corner of his desk.

On the way back to the compound, I cruised through the drive-through and ordered Fab's and my favorite coffees and muffins. No matter how much coffee she'd already drunk, she wouldn't turn her nose up at a triple espresso. Before getting back on the road, I flipped the lid off my latte, licked the whipped cream off the lid, and took a long drink. I sped back to the compound, turned into Fab's driveway, and laid on the horn. I jumped out and took my assigned seat, then reached over and hit the horn again, and this time didn't let up until Fab slammed out the door.

She threw the car door opened and roared, "Where the hell have you been?"

As I handed her the coffee, I noticed that we were similarly dressed. "I wasn't gone long."

Fab flipped the lid off her coffee, took a sniff, then a sip, before she downed a good portion.

I gave her a quick recap of my morning, then grabbed the manila envelope sitting on the dash. I opened it and pulled out the paperwork, scanning the instructions. "First stop, Bardy's house, where we serve Sway—or rather, you serve him. If he doesn't answer the door, you've got time to come up with something… other than kicking it in, which I'd be tempted to do," I said as Fab flew out of the compound.

"If Sway's home and not answering… it can't be about the court summons, as there's not been enough time for him to find out."

"Then knock until he can't stand it anymore or the cops show up."

"No more coffee for you." Fab owned the road today as she headed south.

"Just know that if Sway takes a step in your direction, I'll shoot him."

"If the opportunity should arise, I want to be the one to do it. You can't suck all the fun out of the day."

"Oh, I can and I will." I flashed her a demented smile. "I'm thinking that whether Sway's home or not, we go ahead and serve the realtor, then head over to the prospective buyer's office and do the same."

"After serving the papers at the corporate office, I'd like to ask what they had planned for the property, but I doubt I'd get the question out before they told me to leave."

"Any friendliness the real estate office exudes will be gone in a flash when they get a glance at the paperwork and realize their sale is about to blow up," I said. "If I were the one being served, I'd have a few questions of my own. My guess is that once their lawyer finds out there's fraud involved, they'll want to distance themselves from the property as quickly as they can."

"Just great—we'll be dealing with a bunch of unhappy people today." Fab grinned.

"You're one of the few who that wouldn't faze." I laughed. "The only one I can work up any empathy for is Bardy; who knows what the rest of them knew and when they knew it. If they do come at you with questions, refer them to the attorney on the docs."

It wasn't long before Fab turned onto Bardy's street and slowly cruised the block before making a u-turn and parking across the street, barely avoiding the weedy overgrowth.

"You suppose there's any dead bodies in there?"

"Would you stop?" Fab said with a shake of her head.

"The pickup in the driveway suggests that you might get lucky."

I looked over at Fern's house, and all appeared quiet. I'd already separated the documents and handed Sway's copy to her.

Once out of the car, Fab hot-footed it up the driveway, the papers behind her back. I stood at the driver's side of the truck. It surprised me when she knocked on the door like she wasn't out of patience. It took a minute or two before Sway answered in pajama bottoms and no shirt. He checked Fab out and clearly liked what he saw.

Fab verified his identity, then shoved the papers at him. After a quick glance, he threw them back at her and was about to shut the door. Faster than him, Fab's foot stopped him from shutting it in her face. She kicked it open, and he stumbled back. She scooped up the papers and pitched them at him, and they landed on the floor inside the house. She turned and headed back down the driveway.

"Fab," I yelled and pointed.

She glanced over her shoulder as Sway ran after her, waving the papers and unleashing the same four-letter word over and over. Fab turned and stared him down. He threw the papers at her and took a swing. She grabbed his fist and sent him flying backward to land on his butt. She drew her weapon and yelled, "Dare you," pointing it at him.

Sway inched his way backwards, scrabbled to his feet, and yelled several unintelligible things before running into the house.

I jumped back in the car, and Fab was right behind me. She squealed down the street.

"You okay?"

"That was fun."

"Of course it was." I tried not to laugh. "You better stick to the speed limit in case he called the cops. You don't need a speeding ticket in addition to attempted murder."

"You're hilarious today."

She's grinning, so score one for me.

"When you're doing something illegal, the last thing you're going to do is involve the cops," Fab said with a knowing nod. "Got a quick peek inside the house, and the place appeared to be cleaned out."

"What I don't understand is why Sway would still be at the house after all he's done. Especially when he knows that he's been found out, by his family anyway."

"There was never a police report, so he probably thinks he can do what he wants. Since Sway is in residence, odds are good that his father hasn't stepped up and kicked his butt. Wouldn't surprise me if he doesn't suffer any consequences, and if not, then he'll almost certainly do it again."

Fab gave a knowing nod.

"Even if Bardy doesn't press charges, it wouldn't surprise me if the corporation files an action."

"Maybe," she mused. "The real estate company isn't going to want any press, and as for the corporation, they're not out anything."

Fab cruised to the real estate office, turned into a strip mall, parked in front of the door, and was in and out quickly—document free. "The receptionist sneered at me and turned up her nose like I was smelling up the office," she said as she got back behind the wheel.

The next stop was Homestead and turned out to be a high-rise. Since the only parking spot was in the last row, I got behind the wheel while she ran into the building. I coasted up and idled in the loading zone in front of the entrance. If a cop turned into the parking lot, I'd claim that space in the last row.

Fab was back in short order, and I traded places with her. "That went smoothly; got the impression it wasn't the first time they'd been served. The receptionist took it and, with barely a glance, tossed it into a basket."

"Be interesting to know if there was a takeover of the whole block in the works." I stared out the window, happy that getting rid of the papers had turned out to be a one-day job.

"Ask Fern to see if she was contacted."

"Speaking of… She wants to be Gunz's fixer,

behind you, of course. She's been wanting this for a while now and keeps bringing it up, so I doubt she's going to give it up until Gunz tells her 'Hell no,' and I hope he'd let her down gently. You should put in a good word for her." I ignored her snort. "You can assign her all those menial tasks you're not interested in doing."

"Fern's also been bugging Gunz non-stop, and he's over it. However, he's come around... sort of — how and why, I wasn't about to ask. He did throw out the idea of having her field the family calls and then pass them my way." Fab made a face.

"What did you do, threaten to quit so he'd back off?"

"Told him that he needed to be specific about what he'd want from her, and he laughed. Then hung up. Once I started thinking about all the messages I get, most of them about nothing, I came around to thinking it wasn't the worst idea. Fern's first task could be to return all the calls and only forward me the five-star alarms." Fab nodded, liking her idea.

"What you should do is take her on a test run and see how that goes. She's going to be excited to work for you, and my best advice is to try not to scare her when she gets on your last nerve."

"That's why—"

"You've come up with an alternate plan already? Taking my job from me?"

"Can I finish?" Fab said, trotting out a superior tone.

"Sure, why not?"

"Since we're partners, back-up, and of course, friends..."

My laughter only slowed her a bit.

"You have the talk with Fern, and I'll handle Bardy."

"I was about to suggest an early lunch, my treat. But I'm changing it to dinner, with alcohol, at my house, and bring Didier. By then, I'll have an answer for you."

Chapter Thirty-Three

"What are you up to?" Creole asked, having made his way out to the patio as I was putting the finishing touches on setting the table.

I blew him a kiss and eyed him up and down.

He smirked. *Like what you see?*

"Our guests will be here soon."

"Let me guess…" He pointed in the direction of Fab and Didier's house.

I knew everyone's favorites, so I had the drinks ready and the food ordered, which had been delivered by one of Cook's nephews.

Once we were done eating and the table cleared, I made sure the guys had beers. Fab and I hadn't finished our half-pitchers.

I tapped the tabletop with my spoon. "Had this great idea to change up the breakfast meeting to a dinner one."

"Isn't that something that should be subject to a vote?" Fab snarked.

"Too late now," I sing-songed and was even more pleased when she flinched. Didier grinned. "Now where was I? Oh yes… busy day and so many updates, one of them really big."

"Can you dial down the dramatics and get to it?"

"What fun would that be?" I shot back at Fab. "Anyway…" I leaned over and brushed a kiss on Creole's cheek. "You're up, babes."

"What?"

I made a camera with my fingers and made clicking motions.

Another laugh from Didier.

"Why didn't you just forward the files?" Creole asked me.

"What the hell are you two talking about?" Fab demanded.

"Tsk, tsk. You're falling behind in policing the naughty language," I said to Didier, who shook his head.

Creole pulled out his phone and scrolled across the screen. Not long after, an alert sounded on Fab's phone. "I'm not going to update anything until Fab tells us what she thinks."

"Whatever this is about, something tells me it's something you could've already updated me on." Fab eyed me as she pulled out her phone.

"And miss the opportunity to have the two of you for dinner?"

"This invite was last-second, and we both know it," she said as she scrolled across her screen and scooted closer to Didier. "This is the pic I sent of the driver of the Maserati."

"Open the next file."

"Where did you get this one?" Fab asked.

I nudged Creole.

Didier spoke up. "That's the woman who wants to buy the warehouse."

"He stole the retell from you." I shot Creole a surprised look, and he laughed.

"Jackie Troy is her name, if you're interested–"

Fab cut Creole off. "She owns the shady business next to your property?"

"From what Madison filled me in on, that would be her. Have your cameras picked up exactly what they're doing over there?" Creole asked.

"I don't want my wife involved in whatever it is," Didier snapped.

"Feel the same about Madison." Creole nodded. "That said, if they're operating a car theft ring over there, they need to be stopped. Not by our wives but by law enforcement."

"Your hot idea is to call in a friend or two, and they do what exactly?" Fab demanded. "Just because we think they're engaging in illegal activities, that's not evidence. You and I both know that if law enforcement shows up over there, they'll be gone and move somewhere else."

"I'd heard it mentioned a couple of times that there was never a hint of illegal activity over there," Didier reminded us.

"Before you make any calls…" Fab eyed Creole. "We need to be certain what we're accusing them of, and that's why I'll continue to monitor the security footage and find out exactly what's going on."

"Unfounded accusations could explode in our faces." I made a shocked face, thinking about it. "There goes neighborly relations, and that would include everyone on the block, as word would spread like wildfire."

"Good point," Didier said. "What do you have? A picture of the woman who claims to own the property next to yours, but have you verified that?" he asked Creole, who shook his head. "It appears that the woman driving the stolen car that Fab followed and your neighbor are one and the same. But since there's no proof, the cops may or may not question her." He raised his brows and looked around the table. No one said anything.

"What I do know is that the kid in the car stole my Porsche—I've got pictures of him running from the scene and no one else anywhere around. It's interesting that the next time I saw him, he was in another stolen car."

"When Jackie came over to pitch buying our warehouse, did she leave a number, anything in writing?" I asked.

"She went the friendly route and pitched her offer by writing the amount on a piece of note paper and said that if I was interested, she'd have a contract drawn up," Creole told us.

"The question of how she tracked you down was brought up a few times, but we didn't come to a definitive answer," Didier said. "Your properties are held in a corporate name."

"When you've had a business on the block as long as they have, you know where a newbie came from," I said. "Even though the people on that street aren't a friendly bunch, they still manage to know everything that happens."

My phone rang, bringing all eyes to me as I pulled it out of my pocket and looked at the screen—Xander. Creole leaned in for a look.

"You better put that on speaker."

"Probably not, since you didn't ask nicely." I ignored whatever noise Fab was making. "This must be good," I said when I answered.

"Remember Spacey?" Xander asked in an excited tone.

I groaned. "It's just the foursome tonight; should I put it on speaker?"

"Saves time."

"Be nice, everyone." As I hit the speaker button, I heard Xander chuckle. "You've got the floor, so to speak."

"Spotted Spacey—"

Fab cut in. "The chick that trashed the office?"

"No, the other Spacey." Everyone but Fab laughed at my snark.

"She was standing out in front of a gas station, thumb out, and I waited to see who'd pick her up, since it wasn't going to be me. Didn't have to wait long. Do you want to guess where I followed the car to?"

"Our warehouse? And she jumped the fence?"

I rolled my eyes. "If any of that happened, we're renting a dog, maybe two, and mean ones."

"Calm down." Creole chuckled.

"Close. The repair shop next door," Xander told us.

No quick comebacks. We all just stared at each other.

"Spacey whipped out her phone, and minutes later, the gate opened and she slipped inside. I got the heck out of there before someone saw me idling down the street."

"If you see her again—"

"Already know what you're going to say," Xander cut in. "No worries about me following her anywhere again. Not into crazy."

"Good to hear."

"Appreciate the update," Creole told him.

I pocketed my phone.

"We've got Jackie, the kid, and now Spacey linked to the property next door," Didier said, mostly to himself.

"What makes no sense is that when I watched the footage of the woman tearing up the office, it looked like she was having fun making a mess, as opposed to looking for anything of value. She even passed over a couple of small electronics she could've put in the tote bag she helped herself to," Fab told us. "What she did steal was food, a couple of pens—nothing of consequence. So what was she there for? Information? If so, what in particular and did she find it? Surely she didn't break in just to trash the place."

"I don't like the bits of information we're collecting, none of it good," Creole said with exasperation.

"And so? You're stepping in and pushing me aside?" Fab challenged.

"I'd never hear the end of it, so don't think so." Creole stopped short of a growl. "You think this is funny?" he said to Didier's big grin.

"Just waiting to see where you go next." He didn't bother to tone down his grin.

"One suggestion: team up with Casio. You and he join forces, make a case, and call in law enforcement." Creole nodded at Fab. "I can guarantee that they're not going to like not having been called in at the beginning so they could do their job."

"Hey." I waved my hand. "Don't leave me out. Since it sounds like you won't need backup, I'd be satisfied being kept up on the latest as it happens."

"You know what I want?" Didier asked Fab.

"For me not to get hurt." She gave him a quick kiss.

Chapter Thirty-Four

The next morning, I was surprised to open the door to incessant knocking. "Neither of you put your pick in your pocket before leaving home?"

"That wouldn't be mannerly." Fab skated by me and into the kitchen. She immediately went to the cupboard and pulled out the coffee pot designated for sludge.

"Careful," I cautioned Casio. "One cup of that, and you'll get hair on your head."

"Nothing's ruining my bald coif." He ran his hand over his head.

"Since I didn't know the two of you were meeting…" I raised my eyebrow at Fab. "Before you pull up a stool, help yourself to something to drink," I told Casio.

"I'm going for a cup of whatever that is. Heard stories and thought I'd check it out for myself." He slid onto a stool at the island.

"Where are the kids?" I asked.

"Back in school—fun time is over. But next time there's a break, I know who I'll be calling."

"How did you two end up here?" I asked.

"I called and, before he could say anything, asked, 'Do you have food? Because I don't.' Was about to suggest I order something when I remembered you had leftovers, and here we are." Fab grinned.

"Have you two had time to come to an agreement on anything?" I asked.

"We're going to build a case and turn it over to the locals. And *everything* on our part will be legal." Casio eyed Fab.

"That will appease my husband," she said with a snort as she set two coffee mugs down.

"Don't say you weren't warned." I eyed the concoction in front of Casio.

Fab slid onto a stool across from me. "Okay Mr. Legal Eagle, how are we going to get a look inside the two buildings and the truck?"

"We'll come up with something."

"I'll remind you that the word *legally* was thrown out, and you two traipsing around the neighboring property is anything but."

"First, we'll see what kind of evidence we can compile from the security footage," Casio said.

"Kind of surprised that you teamed up with Fab."

"Already warned your girl here that I'm not putting my butt on the line… gotta think of my kids and all. From what I've heard, it does reek of criminal activity, and it's got me jacked up and ready to build a case… for once, not from the front line." Casio grinned.

"Just be careful, you two." I looked at them.

My phone rang, and I flipped it over—Fern. I

put my finger across my lips, answered, and put it on speaker.

As soon as the call connected, Fern rasped, "Heard shots."

Before the line went dead, I heard sirens in the background.

Fab whipped out her phone, oozing frustration when her call wasn't answered. "Rollo, what the hell is going on? Call me back."

I hurriedly gave Casio the slim version of Bardy's problems.

"The old man should've made a police report, and one of you needs to encourage him to do so now. Let the kid deal with the felonies he committed. If not, the man will always be looking over his shoulder," Casio warned.

"Sorry you didn't get your food, but we need to go check this out." Fab downed the rest of her coffee.

"I'll take a raincheck." Casio stood. "While you're doing that, I'm going to go snoop around Madison's warehouse and get the feel of things."

"Cootie's supervising the crime scene cleaners, so there won't be any problem getting access," I assured him.

"Cootie, huh? He'd be a good one to talk to... see what he knows." Casio nodded at Fab and me.

Fab went out the deck doors, Casio out the front. I ran down the hall, slipped into some tennis shoes, grabbed my bag, and was back outside in minutes. It was one of the few times I beat Fab to the car, but I didn't have long to wait.

Fab jumped behind the wheel and squealed out of the driveway, talking to someone on her earpiece. I deduced from her clipped responses that it was Gunz. "Call you back." She didn't waste time getting out to the Overseas and heading south. "What irks Gunz off the most is that the motel will become the talk of the town and end his 'under the radar' ride."

"Tell him criminal activity is good for business and it doesn't require a dead body to get a line of people wanting to check in. Except... he doesn't want walk-in business and whatever it is he does want, he hasn't spelled out."

"You need to be nicer." Fab smirked.

"That nice stuff is a two-way street."

Fab came close to shrieking as she caught sight of a police car blocking the turn-off. She slowed and inched past. "Now what?"

"You go back, turn on your charm, and tell the officer that you're the property manager and here to help."

Fab hung a u-turn and pulled over as an ambulance approached, lights flashing. It turned off the highway, and the cop flagged them around the back. She rolled down her window and gave him the manager spiel; he directed her to park in the front, something that I'd never seen anyone do.

"You wait here while I turn on the charm and maybe trade a little information." Fab jumped out and headed over to the cop.

I got out, phone in hand, and leaned against the side of the car, taking a couple of pictures. Then I called Creole, and it went to voicemail. I left a message: "Shooting. We're not hurt. Tell Fab's husband." He wouldn't appreciate the lack of detail, but I'd remind him, "I did call." I called Fern, and it went to voicemail, and the same with Rollo.

Fab was back and not happy. "He didn't throw me off the property but did tell me to stay out of the way. Then went on to say that an older man had been shot, but it wasn't life-threatening. I asked if it was Bardy Dowell, and he didn't know but said the man would soon be on his way to the hospital. I filled him in on everything I knew."

"Hate to point the finger without knowing for sure, but where's Sway? If it was Bardy that got shot, who else would shoot at him? And if I'm right in my assumptions, how did Sway find out that Bardy was staying here?"

"Brendon didn't know."

"The cop? First-name basis, huh? That was fast. You need to turn that charm on Kevin." I didn't see her eyeroll but heard it.

"Morphed into you, got all friendly, and gave him my business card. Also told him about free food and drinks at Jake's."

"Did you flash your ring so he didn't think you were coming on to him?" I turned so she couldn't see my grin.

"You're disgusting."

"Thank you. I'll forego the curtsy… this time."

Fab whipped out her phone and made a couple of calls. "About time you answered," she snapped and shot several questions at the person, ending with, "Sorry, have Rollo call me."

"Assuming that was the kid that mans the front desk?" I asked. Fab nodded. "If he quits, I'm going to suggest you fill in until a replacement is found."

"When Rollo's done laughing, he'll unequivocally say, "No chance in…'"

"Did you get anything out of the dude? Probably not, since it didn't sound like you gave him a lot of time to answer the questions you fired at him."

"Impressed his answers were short and clipped. Remind me to gift him a free meal at your joint."

"Once Kelpie and Doodad find out he works here, they'll exhaust him with questions."

Fab's phone rang, and she glanced at the screen before answering. "About time." After a minute of intent listening, she said, "I'm on my way." She pocketed her phone. "Let's go." She backed out onto the highway and went a couple of blocks before making a u-turn.

"It's mean of you to make me ask where we're going."

"There's another entrance to the motel. Can you believe I missed it? I can't." She turned again, this time on what appeared to be a dirt path to nowhere.

"You're the only one I know who'd turn in without hesitation. Warning: You blow a tire and you're picking up the tab."

The dirt stretch took her past the back parking lot, where she made a sharp turn, and then another, then pulled in and parked as the ambulance pulled out. We both got out. Rollo had appeared out of nowhere and was waiting on us.

"Was it Bardy that got shot?" Fab asked.

"The guy sitting next to him." Rollo shook his head. "Luckily, he was only grazed. A man crept onto the property decked out in black, wearing a ski mask. I didn't know anything about it until I heard the shots and screams. I came out of the office to find out what the hell... and the guy pointed a gun at me. Had a weapon on me but didn't want to start a gunfight with half a dozen people running around in circles. I stepped back. When I did, he ran out to the parking lot and jumped in a grey Nissan—got a partial plate and will text it to you. Bastard didn't bother to brake when he turned onto the Overseas and almost broadsided another car, which barely managed to get out of the way."

"There are security cameras on all corners of the building," Fab reminded us. "I'll go over everything and see if I can turn up anything useful. Gunz will be on both of us until the shooter is found and in jail."

"One of the cops that showed up is a friend of Gunz's, and I promised to send a copy of the footage and anything else I found out," Rollo said. "Told the man that this was a quiet place and had been for years, which he already knew. Also shared info on Bardy, who also answered questions. I kept an eye on the man, worried about his health, as he'd gone pale and was shaking. The consensus was that Bardy was the target and the shooter missed."

"That means we've got to ID the shooter before he comes back," Fab said.

"In the meantime, I suggest a beefy bodyguard or two and can arrange to have them here in short order," I said.

"How many do you think you need?" Fab asked Rollo.

"One will work."

I pulled out my phone and stepped back, calling Toady.

"Hey girlie," he answered.

I told him what happened and what I needed. "My first choice would be Birch. No offense to any of your other guys; it's just that I know him."

"No offense taken," Toady assured me. "I'll make a call, and if he's not on another job I don't know about, I'll send him over. If not him, I've got a couple of men that are equally badass. I'll keep you updated."

I pocketed my phone and walked back to Fab and Rollo. "On the way."

"We've got to find the shooter, as this can't happen again," Fab said and turned to Rollo. "Be prepared for Gunz to burn up your phone until he's caught."

I followed the two, who continued to talk as they walked into the now-vacant pool area. I ventured over to Fern's room and looked in the window, seeing it was empty, then made my way over to Bardy's room. He and Fern were asleep on the bed. I caught sight of a couple of people with their noses between the drapes. When they saw me looking, they jerked their heads back.

I made my way back over to Fab and Rollo and interrupted the intense discussion on how to ID the shooter. "How about I call Shirl and have her check everyone here out and refer any that need additional medical services? You can shut down any talk of them not being able to afford it and assure them it will all be taken care of." I shot Fab a *you tell Gunz* look.

"Thanks for that, as there's a couple of them that I planned to keep my eye on." Rollo nodded.

"I'll make sure you get Shirl's number. Know that you can call her anytime." I stepped away and made the call.

"You're good for business," she said when I answered.

"This could be a 'Hi, how are you?' call. But it's not. Next time."

Shirl laughed.

I told her about the shooting. "Would you

come to the motel and give everyone a once-over? Fat-ass, as I like to call him, would flip if someone died in their bed."

"Can't have that."

"Bring a business card and make sure that Rollo gets it. Told him not to be shy about calling. You can send your bill to me or Fab, and it will get forwarded to Gunz. Rumor has it that he's a speedy payer. If not, you let me know."

"I'm on my way."

We hung up, and I grabbed a chaise and watched Fab prowl around. Rollo had disappeared.

Done scanning every corner of the property, Fab dropped down across from me. "Gunz is livid."

"Not surprised."

"I forwarded the partial plate number to Xander to see what he can come up with."

"Since the same info was handed over to the cops, aren't you treading on their territory and hence looking at trouble?" I asked with raised brows.

"My excuse will be that I don't know who knew what."

I shook my head. "You should introduce Shirl and Gunz through business cards, or whatever, and let him know that she's someone to have on speed dial."

"Good idea. Is she on the way?"

"When she gets here, we'll leave, as I know the

last thing she wants is to have someone following her around."

It wasn't long before Shirl showed up with her sidekick, Mac, who hated to be left out of anything. We left as Rollo and the two women hit the first door.

Chapter Thirty-Five

The next morning while Creole was making coffee, I finished dressing, choosing a short-sleeved black dress with a full skirt and low heels. Out of patience, I scooped my hair up in a ponytail, all the while practicing my smile. I grabbed my purse and walked out to the kitchen, where Creole eyed me from head to toe.

"Where are you going?"

"Can you keep a secret?"

"That depends…" He eyed me again.

I held out my little finger. "You either pinkie swear or wait until later for the replay."

"We're here," Fab called out as she and Didier walked through the deck doors.

"See what happens when you leave the sliders open?" I nudged Creole.

"You want a cup of coffee? Or did you bring your own?" Creole called out as they claimed stools at the island.

Fab set her laptop down in front of her. She eyed me pretty much the same way Creole had—trying to figure out where I was going—then waved at Creole. "I'll take coffee."

"You're not going to demand your favorite brew?" Didier eyed his wife.

"If whatever he's brewing is terrible, I'll spit it back in the cup."

The guys laughed. I shook my head.

"Did we have a meeting?" Creole asked, making another pot of coffee.

"That's what I heard." Didier quirked his head at Fab.

"I called the meeting—short notice. If the rest of you didn't get the invite, it's because I didn't send it." Fab flashed a smile.

Wonder what she's up to now?

Creole and Didier talked about a work issue until the coffee was ready and everyone had a cup sitting in front of them.

"What are you up to?" Creole directed at Fab. "A straight answer would be appreciated."

"Thinking the same thing could be asked of you." Fab singled me out.

"You're the one that orchestrated this meeting." I waved my hand: *You're up.*

"Since when do meetings take place that I'm not invited to?" Fab flipped open her laptop and hit a button. The screen showed me sitting in her chair at the office, laughing it up with Mac, Shirl, Xander, and Clive.

"What, no sound?" I asked.

"Asked myself the same question several times and thought you'd have an answer as to how that happened."

Creole and Didier grinned and watched, eagle-eyed.

I shrugged, shaking my head: *No clue.* "And what?" I asked.

"What the hell are up to?" Fab snapped.

Hell, I mouthed to Didier and pointed at Fab.

"Well?"

I couldn't see Fab's foot, but it was probably jumping up and down. "Here's the deal. In the spirit of partial honesty, I've been working on a project that I have no intention of sharing. The reason for the secrecy is that I know not a one of you would support the idea and don't want to hear about it. But to assuage any bad feelings, I'll get a couple of pictures." I'd try for a video replay that I'd spring at a later date.

"Do I have to worry about your safety?" Creole asked.

"I can assure you that there's no need to worry." I smiled at him. A change of subject was needed. "How's everything going at the motel?"

"Bardy's shaking in his tennis shoes and was ready to go on the run when the bodyguard showed up. He calmed down then, as did the others," Fab told us. "Turns out that Rollo knew the bodyguard, and they laughed it up. Haven't heard back from Xander on the partial plate number but expect I will soon."

"How's it going with Casio on the warehouse surveillance?" Creole asked.

"Not sure why Fab needs to be involved,"

Didier grumped.

"The level of her involvement is up to her," Creole said.

"Since it's my security cameras that have the property covered from one end to the other, Casio's going to need me." Fab smirked said, *Not going anywhere.* "We exchanged a few emails and decided on a course of action. We're going to start gathering the information we're going to need to get law enforcement interested."

"When did all this happen?" Didier demanded.

"You know I do my best work in the middle of the night."

"Did you get your questions answered?" I asked Fab.

She gave me a major eyeroll, and Didier laughed.

I slid off the stool and put my mug in the dishwasher, then turned and kissed Creole, who'd come up behind me. "Don't let her follow me," I whispered.

He laughed in my ear. "I'll be shocked if she doesn't track you down," he whispered back.

"It's been fun; let's do it again." I beelined for the entry, grabbing my purse and briefcase. Creole had the door open and escorted me out to the car.

"Are you going to give me a heads up?" he asked.

"I'm going to a funeral."

He laughed, clearly not believing me.

Chapter Thirty-Six

There weren't a lot of cars in Tropical Slumber's parking lot, and the school bus parked at the far end stood out. When I'd approached Mac about planning a funeral send-off, she was all in, and when Shirl heard, she wasn't about to be left out. I'd loaned them Clive, telling them if they needed anything, he was the man to call.

Raul was beyond excited to plan a service for the boxes of ashes but had lamented that no one would come. He'd contacted the families of the deceased and extended an invite, but got a frosty reception, even after assuring them there would be no charge. As for the two bodies, his coroner friend had assured him that he'd be their first call if their relations didn't step up and expressed that he doubted they would.

When I called Mac, Shirl, and Clive to the office, none of them had asked why, and I hadn't seen a reason to be forthcoming with information. When they filed in, Mac and Shirl were excited, as they knew it was about the group funeral – what else? They hadn't contacted Clive yet, and when he heard funeral, 'Here we go' was written on his face. He'd worked in the building long enough that nothing should surprise him.

"Okay..." *I went over the details and who would do*

what. "You two — " *I pointed at Mac and Shirl, who were grinning.* " — are in charge of the guest list. Be sure you mention free food and drink."

"We're not going to have a hard time filling the seats," Shirl assured me.

"I'll be giving Raul a jingle to find out the maximum head count and run everything by him," Mac said. "Not sure if he'll want entertainment, but on the off chance..."

I didn't want to laugh, but it escaped me. "Don't do too good a job, or he'll be wanting to steal you away."

Mac digested the thought and shook her head.

"What about me?" Clive grouched.

"You're the go-to guy for whatever needs to get done and to make sure it all goes smoothly. Dickie and Raul are long-time friends and have always been accommodating to us, and I want this to go off without a hitch." They all nodded. "When I talked to Raul, he told me a reporter friend was coming to do a story. Apparently, she's done a couple in the past. I suggested that he have her call you — " I looked at Mac. " — and you can make sure she gets whatever..."

I parked and walked across the parking lot as Mac came around the side of the building and met me halfway.

"Today is going to be a little different than the service we originally talked about." She gyrated her hands in circles.

I glanced over my shoulder. *Was it too late to go home? My feet up on the deck railing, a cold drink in my hand...*

"Caught your cut-and-run look, and no need to

worry." Mac unleashed more hand gyrations. "The three of us agreed that what we originally talked about was rather vague, and soooo... We invited Dickie and Raul to dinner at The Cottages and served it out by the pool. Raul was fun and charming, and even Dickie... I'm not going to say he was outgoing, but he didn't creep anyone out. And yes, before you ask, I put the invite out to the rest of the guests to join us."

"You're lucky there wasn't a first-time guest that flipped their stick."

Mac snorted. "You know it's not like first-timers aren't welcome..." she blurted. "But we stay pretty full with returns, so if there's someone new to the circus, and they're all invited, what the heck. I've yet to have someone ask for their money back."

"When I dumped everything in your lap, there were no restrictions. I probably should've mentioned no fist or food fights. Or shootings." My brows went up.

"Now wouldn't that be something?" Mac's hands shot up the air. "You know... Raul should list a no-holds-barred option. Bet it would be popular." She nodded, liking her idea. "Back to the dinner—at my urging, Raul told some funny stories... and maybe a few that weren't, but I noted that the folks with the horrified expressions, of which there were only a couple, didn't cut and run."

"If they were Cruz's relatives, they wouldn't

dare, or they'd bear the brunt of family humor for eons." The two of us laughed.

"Where's your sidekick?" Mac scanned the parking lot.

"Watch your back if she hears you called her *sidekick*." I sliced my finger across my neck. "Ditched her and drove myself."

Mac got all wide-eyed. "Nice knowing you when she finds out. In case you forgot, she has to know *everything*."

The two of us walked over to the outdoor patio and bar, where the tables were more than half-filled and a quick headcount told me twenty-five were in attendance, which was more than I expected, all with drinks in hand. I recognized some as cottage guests, some locals, and others that lived down the street, who smiled and waved back.

"How did you transport so many people here?" I asked.

"Took two trips." She sighed. "My first idea was to cram them all in—standing room only. The only thing that stopped me was that if we got pulled over, losing the license might be on the line, and you've got to admit the bus has come in damn handy."

"If I agree, are you going to suggest that we get a full-size one?"

"Oh hell no." Mac shook her head furiously. "Once word got out, you can bet it would be filled to the gills."

Raul and Dickie came rushing out the side door from the main viewing room, and Raul thanked me profusely for involving Mac, as she'd upped the fun. Mac wore a big grin. He stopped himself from hugging me in time, as he knew I didn't do touchy-feely, and held out his knuckles for a bump, which I reciprocated. I smiled and waved at Dickie, who smiled back.

"We finally got the names of every single deceased, and I'm in the process of having a plaque made. I decided to go with opening the bottom row from end to end, so they'll all be stored together." Raul smiled: *Great idea, don't you think?*

"I can't thank you enough for taking over after the discovery, because if left on my own, I'm not sure what I would've come up with."

"Pfft. What better way to introduce our newest addition? As for the reporter I told you about, she's going to get us coverage in a couple of senior magazines." Raul broke out into a big grin and started waving.

I turned, and here came Fab.

Raul hugged and heaped thanks on her, assuming she was part of making everything happen, which she graciously accepted. I shot her a slight head-shake and caught her smirk.

"Knowing your preferences, I saved you seats in the back row on the lawn. They're the only ones with reserved signs on them." Raul smiled at the two of us. "I'll see you after the service."

"What are you doing?" Fab took a step closer and snarked in my ear. She reached out and grabbed Mac's arm before she could take off. Shirl showed up at that moment, made a quick assessment, and stepped closer to her friend.

"Fight time," Mac whispered hoarsely, jerking her head at Fab and me.

I squinted at Mac. *No fighting today.* "I'm not even going to ask how you managed to show up here and just at the right time. I'll go first. Remember the ashes? This is their send-off."

Fab covered her mouth and laughed. "Of course it is." She shook her head. "No invite for me?"

"Since I didn't want to listen to endless complaining, no. But don't feel bad, I didn't ask any family or friends, saving myself from listening to a list of pitiful excuses, only to be told, 'Thanks for thinking of me, but hell no.'"

"What's your part in all this?" Fab eyed Mac and Shirl.

"We were the planners." Shirl swept her hand around. "Clive's motioning to one of us; I'll go." She shot off across the lawn.

"The original plan was short service, food, and git. But now you'll have to wait and see." Mac grinned at Fab's glare. "We'll talk later." She took off after Shirl.

I turned to Fab. "Whatever happens, it was the *best* funeral ever. Got it?"

Fab unleashed an eyeroll. "Like I'd say

anything else."

From behind the microphone, Raul asked everyone to take a seat. Fab and I walked across the lawn to where there were several rows of chairs in front of the mausoleum, the urns displayed on a table. We easily found our reserved seats. Mac and Shirl entered the row from the other end and sat next to us.

Fab leaned over and asked Mac, "Is the service going to be over in five, and then we're on our way?"

"We're going to sit here and be respectful for as long as it takes."

I grinned at Mac's admonishing tone.

"There will be no gunshots or antics of any kind, due to boredom and your desire to skate out of here." *Got it?* Mac eyed Fab.

Trying not to laugh, I moved up, blocking the glare-down between the two.

"I want to thank you for coming," Raul welcomed us, then introduced the preacher, who walked over in an oversized suit and took the microphone.

"Aren't you curious—"

I put a finger across my lips and tried not to show my amusement at the knowledge that Fab wanted me to ask how she knew where to show up, and it wasn't happening.

After scanning the faces in the crowd, the minister gave a short service.

I was happy, as a couple of guests had nodded

off already. At least no one was talking.

Next, Mac went up to the podium, sheet of paper in hand, and adjusted the microphone. "Never met Mr. Reely, but I'm thinking he'd be pleased at the turnout. I mean, wouldn't you?" She grinned.

Almost everyone nodded and mumbled something in response.

Mac left the podium, and Shirl took her place, a big grin on her face. "Happy it's not me in one of those boxes." She wrinkled her nose. "Who am I here for?" She looked at the list. "Oh yes, Mr. Kirk. One thing I noticed—the men on this list outnumber the women. Wishing them all the best in heaven."

"What about hell?" someone yelled.

"Not a one in this group went there," Shirl said with assurance, giving them a stern stare, then left the podium, someone else replacing her.

I leaned over to Mac, who'd just sat down, and was about to whisper when she furiously shook her head. Minutes later, she pushed back her chair, got up, and went to the podium, standing off to the side until Clive finished.

Mac walked back to the podium. "For our last..." She waved to the urns. "Fab Merceau would like to say a few words." She made eye contact: *Well?*

Everyone turned to see who Mac was singling out.

Fab stood and turned, hissing in my face. I

grinned. At the podium, she scanned the list. "I want to thank you, on behalf of all that knew Mr. Jacob, for coming to his funeral. I'm certain he wouldn't have expected such a big crowd, but you know he's waving." She waved to the crowd like a princess riding a float.

Raul cut off Fab's exit from the podium, hooking his arm around her shoulders and waving along with her. He thanked everyone for coming, and the guests stood.

"If Fab asks, I just disappeared," I said to Mac, who growled. Overhearing, Shirl laughed.

"I'm so rolling you under the bus," Mac promised.

Chapter Thirty-Seven

Fab ignored me for a day. I'd heard that she'd been the hot topic of gossip amongst the funeral goers. They were all anxious to meet her and exchange a few words, some having heard stories and wanting to know if they were true. She charmed every one of them with a non-answer. Mac had gushed with appreciation when she called to report in.

Fab had plenty of time to be dressed and ready for the day when I texted her: *Coffee on me. Your choice.*

Her response was almost immediate. *Pick you up in ten.*

I knew without a doubt that she was up to something. I hoped she'd choose our favorite place before the by-the-way news. I grabbed my purse and was waiting in the car when she got behind the wheel.

When she didn't say anything as she flew out of the compound, I broke the silence. "You ever going to speak to me again?"

"I was planning your death, and by the way, no funeral for you. Then, when Raul went on and on about me making his day by stepping up to the podium, I decided to take all the damn credit and told him I volunteered."

"You were already his favorite, and I'm betting you just moved higher on the list, if that's possible."

Fab cruised through the drive-through and ordered our favorite coffees in extra-large. Another red flag. Back on the Overseas, she headed south, which was a relief. So we weren't head out of state, but intuition told me we weren't going home.

"When are you going to tell me where we're going?" I asked.

"Xander came through—"

I cut her off, just managing to control my snark. "When doesn't he?"

"The information guys we used in the past boasted about being the very best. They weren't, and that's the reason I never fail to show my appreciation to Xander."

"I'm ecstatic that we found someone we can trust and never have to worry about him screwing us," I said. "What did he find out and about who?"

"He pulled all the security footage from the cameras on the front of the motel, easily found the car we're looking for, and grabbed the whole plate number. He laughed that it was one of the easiest retrievals he's done."

"That means we're headed to… where exactly? And who's the registered owner?" I hoped it had nothing to do with Bardy's grandson but found it hard to believe he wasn't somehow involved. I mean, who else?

"Registered to an Arch Bowan, and we're about to confront the man."

"Betting that Didier has no clue what his wifey is up to. If he did know, he'd have made you call the cops, and there'd be no handling it yourself." Fab's silence told me I was right. "If they don't already have this information, the cops aren't going to be far behind. My suggestion is that you be prepared in case Arch has his gun on him."

"Dude's in his twenties, with no criminal record. I asked Fern to find out if there's a relationship between this Arch fellow and Bardy. She got back to me, saying, 'Bardy never heard of the guy.'"

"I was going to call Fern for an update on Bardy and forgot to follow through. During your conversation, did she say how he was doing?"

"Hiding out in his room. I told her to keep an eye on the man, and she promised she would."

"Gunz must be burning up your phone." It wasn't the first time I was happy he wasn't my client, and despite that, I still had plenty of interaction with the man.

"Here's a first. Gunz wants any information we uncover about the shooter to be turned over to him, and he'll deal with it."

"When he asks why you totally blew him off, you're going to say…?"

"You'll figure something out."

Fab turned into a quiet neighborhood and cruised the street, checking out the houses on both sides, a mix of one- and two-story homes. She slowed, passing the driveway that held the car she was looking for... or one damn close.

"Now what? Since you haven't asked, I assume you must have a plan."

"You can sit in the car." Fab smirked.

"That's not happening. When Didier or anyone else asks why you're in jail, I want to be able to belabor the details."

Fab u-turned and parked one house back, then got out, cutting across the street. I was right behind her and, like her, checking out every inch of the property. On the way up the driveway, she stopped at the car, whipping out her phone and taking pictures, which she compared with the information Xander had sent over.

Instead of hiking up the stairs to the front door, Fab opted to check out the garage area, which had been turned into a seating area with a bar.

"I don't know why you don't just go to the door. Creeping around the property might get a gun in our faces," I hissed at Fab as she headed out to the backyard.

In the back, a man lay sleeping on a chaise in shorts and a t-shirt, a towel over his face. He was faintly snoring, oblivious to the approaching footsteps.

Drawing her Walther, Fab approached with her

gun at her side and stood over the sleeping man. She lifted the corner of the towel, turned and nodded that it was Arch Bowman, and let it drop.

So we'd found who we were looking for... now to find out what he knew about the shooting at the motel.

Fab kicked the chaise, sending it rocking.

Arch finally stirred. He lowered the towel and blinked blearily at her. He spotted the gun, jerked upright, and put both hands in the air. "Who... who are you? I don't know what you want, but there's not much here to steal," he sputtered.

"Listen up. I'll be the one asking the questions, and if you want to walk away in one piece, you'll answer truthfully," Fab said in a steely tone.

Arch's eyes widened in fear. He tried to stand up, but Fab shoved him back down, her hand on his shoulder, and kept him in place.

"You shot up the motel, and I want to know why." Her voice was hard.

Arch's expression flickered with fear and guilt, which he quickly covered with a mask of defiance. "I don't know what you're talking about," he spat. "I was just... I was just in the wrong place at the wrong time."

Fab leaned in, glaring. "Did you already forget that I specified the truth?"

He leaned over and emptied the contents of his stomach on the concrete.

Fab stepped back with a glare. Even though I wasn't in the line of fire, I also stepped back.

Neither of us said a word while he struggled to get himself together. Finally, he sat back up, his face white as a sheet. He caught sight of me, and that sent fear skidding across his face as he stared, wide-eyed.

"If you're going to be sick again, make sure it's in the same direction." Fab tossed her head. "You listening?"

He nodded timidly.

"I've got evidence linking you to the scene," she continued. "Witness statements, security footage—you name it. You're going to jail for a damn long time."

"If you're smart, you'll tell the truth," I told him. "If not, all it takes is a phone call, and you disappear."

For a moment, silence hung heavy between us, broken only by the distant sound of a couple of barking dogs. Slowly, the man's resolve crumbled, and he slumped flat on his back, his arm draped over his face.

"Okay, okay," he muttered, his voice barely audible. He lowered his arm. "I was there. But I didn't pull the trigger. I swear."

"So what were you doing there?" Fab demanded.

"A friend asked for a ride—"

She cut him off. "Tell me everything," she demanded, her tone leaving no room for argument. "Start from the beginning." She lowered her gun to her side and sat on the opposite chaise. "Does this friend have a name?"

Looking at Fab, I could see her mind already racing with speculation about what the man could reveal, now that she knew someone else was involved.

"He swore he had nothing to do with the shooting," Arch muttered.

Fab leaned in and got in his face, while he tried to inch away with nowhere to go. "He who?"

"Sway Dowell. Told me he needed a ride to check on his grandfather, who'd just gotten out of the hospital."

"How long did you hang around after you heard the shots?" I asked.

"At first, I was in total denial. Didn't believe what I'd heard were gunshots. Rather than find out I was wrong, I hung a u-turn, and as I did, that's when Sway came running out of the building. Not proud to say it, but if he hadn't shown up when he did, I'd have left him. But fear was talking, and I was about to jam on the gas when Sway jumped in the car. When he realized I was about to leave him, he went off and didn't stop until I told him to shut it or get out."

"What was Sway's version of events?" Fab demanded.

"All he said was that some guy showed up out of nowhere and started shooting. He hadn't gotten to check on his grandfather but knew the man would want him to run rather than risk getting shot at."

"Why didn't Sway drive his own car?" Fab asked.

"I assumed car problems but didn't ask, as it wasn't that big a deal."

"What was Sway wearing?" I asked.

"Black jeans and a jacket. I had on blue jeans and a shirt." *Why?* was written on his face, which I ignored.

"You want some free advice?" Fab asked.

Arch mumbled something unintelligible.

"Stay away from your friend Sway until an arrest is made. I'm not pointing fingers, but you just never know."

"Don't be surprised if the cops come knocking," I told him. The way the man went ghost-white, I expected him to be sick again. But thankfully, it didn't happen. "Be straightforward and truthful in your answers, and they won't be thinking they need to take a closer look at you."

"As a thank you for your cooperation..." Fab handed him a business card. "Any problems at all, give me a call."

Arch eyed her business card and then her. "Nice."

I headed back to the car, knowing Fab would catch up, and she didn't disappoint. Once inside, I said, "You threaten to shoot his ass, and you're a delectable morsel?"

Fab laughed. I joined her.

Chapter Thirty-Eight

While I was replaying the events of the day before for Creole, the gate buzzer sounded and a breakfast that neither of us ordered was delivered. I licked my lips at the sight of the logo on the familiar pink box and had no intention of refusing it, since I knew the food was excellent.

"This tells me that someone is on the way over and wants to make sure there's something to eat," Creole snarked as he set the large box on the counter. "The question is who?"

"I've got my top two picks."

"Greetings," Casio yelled as he strolled through the sliders like he'd knocked and been invited in. "Coffee. That's what I need." He headed straight for the pot.

"Do we barge into your house?" Creole demanded.

"You could. But if you're the slightest bit picky about your brew, like you-know-who, I suggest you bring your own." Casio filled a mug and took a long drink, then headed to the bakery box and flipped the lid.

Creole closed the lid on Casio's hand, which he snaked out. "Were you invited? If so, by who?"

Casio claimed a seat at the island. "Dude, what crawled up your..." He took another swig of his coffee. "I was invited to a meeting... coffee, food..." He pointed at both. "Betting I'm at the right place."

Creole and I looked at one another and said at the same time, "Fab."

Right on cue, Fab and Didier entered through the sliders. "We're here," Fab yelled, setting down her briefcase.

"Keep it down," I admonished. "If you'd like a drink of whatever, get it before you sit down."

"Not friendly," she tsked.

"Anyone else showing up for this *meeting*?" Creole asked.

Fab looked around and made a show of counting heads. "As it stands, we're two over, but neither of you will be booted." She eyed Creole and Didier.

Creole checked his watch. "We've got some time before we've got to be at the office, so make it quick." He exchanged glares with Fab, then turned it on Casio, who'd filled a plate from the bakery box when no one was looking.

"As you know, Casio and I are working on devising a plan to find what the neighboring business is doing."

I waved my hand. "What's my part in all this? Figuring it must be something or you'd have had this get-together in your kitchen."

"It's your business," Fab reminded me in a

snooty tone. "Someone needs to represent whatever you're going to call it."

I saluted. "Any questions from the two of you, to give you peace of mind, before you head off to the office?" I eyed Creole and Didier.

Didier snorted. "I'm holding you responsible if my wife gets hurt." He eyed Casio. "Even though she'll be the one to drag you into the fray."

Casio licked his lips, finishing up his breakfast, and with a bored look, said, "Yeah, sure." He got up and refilled his coffee mug.

Fab pulled her ringing phone out of her pocket. A quick glance at the screen, and she answered. "Didn't expect to hear from you so soon."

To me it sounded like she'd never expected to hear from whoever it was.

"When do you plan on confronting Sway?" Fab asked and, after a pause, said, "You need backup. I'll be at your house in an hour to fix you up with a camera so you get the proof you need. Don't do anything until we get there." She pocketed her phone and said to Didier, "That was the driver I told you about."

"The same one I told you to tell to call the police, and you ignored me?" Didier stared her down.

"I'd just finished telling Creole, who didn't have time to unload what he thought, so how about a quick recap for our guest?" I asked Fab.

When Fab finished with her slick version of events, Casio said, "If you could get the Sway kid on video admitting to the shooting, closed case for the cops."

"What about your client, the grandfather — does he want the kid arrested?" Didier asked.

Creole shook his head in annoyance. "Thus far, I haven't heard that the man has filed a police report from when he was held hostage. Now, though, he won't have a say in whether his grandson gets arrested. He's fired a gun in a public place and shot a bystander — it's no longer up to his grandfather."

"If Arch thinks that his friend was the shooter, why would he risk setting up said friend and getting his butt handed to him?" I asked. "Is he afraid to go to the police, thinking they won't believe him?"

"Not sure why you're not calling Cooper and letting him deal with it," Creole said to Fab. "As for Gunz, the last thing you want to do is hand over information and have this guy end up dead. Unless he's a family member? If so, not sure why Gunz didn't take care of it before it got this far."

"How about you introduce me to... Arch, is it?" Casio asked. Fab nodded. "I'll hang out in another room, the other kid confesses, and I'll call the cops. If things go south, I'll kick some butt and then call the cops."

"If you've got a mic and camera on Arch, then it's not like you're going to miss a word," I pointed out.

"I'll owe you one," Fab said to Casio. He

grinned. "I want this case over with, and if Sway is the shooter, the thought of him skating after all he's done is sickening. Not sure what Gunz is thinking, but I'll talk to him after there's some kind of resolution."

"We'll take separate cars." Casio stood. "Text me when you're ready to go." He put his dishes in the sink, winked at me, and headed out the sliders.

"Well cool, I'll have the afternoon off." I'd go out on the deck as soon as the house cleared out.

"You're coming with me and making sure I don't go off course," Fab said.

"I'd at least like a promise that you'll listen should I have some good advice."

"You've got her promise," Didier answered for her.

* * *

Fab flew down the Overseas. "Where did Casio go?" She glared into the rearview mirror.

I flipped the visor down, and when I saw who was behind us, I laughed.

It didn't take long before we were back at Arch's house. Fab parked one house down, and Creole and Didier pulled in behind us.

"Try to be nice. Our hubs are taking time out of their day to make sure we… well, you don't get your ass handed to you. Once you find out what's up, send my husband back to me, and we can fool around in the car while we wait for you and Didier." I laughed as she mimicked getting sick. "Since you're miked up, if someone shows up, I'll let you know."

"You'd think that Didier could trust the promise I made not to get hurt," Fab sulked. She got out and met up with the two men. "What are you two doing here?"

Didier ignored the attitude oozing off her and pulled her into a hug. The three had a short conversation. Then Fab and Didier crossed the street and went up the stairs.

Creole knocked on the car window. I waved, and we stared one another down for a minute before I hit the unlock button.

"Beginning to think you were going to let me stand out there all day." Creole slid behind the wheel.

I jerked on his shirt, pulling him over to me and laying a kiss on him. "I don't care why you're here, just happy to see you." I handed him an earpiece and twisted around my iPad so we could watch the action.

"Didier called Casio and told him, 'Change of plans.' Casio just laughed and said, 'Better get my favor.' Didier told him he was getting two."

"So you know, the little woman wasn't happy with the change of plans."

"The *little woman* can hear you," Fab growled. "Didier and I are both miked up. Try to behave yourselves until we're out of here."

"Yeah, okay... for both of us," I told her.

Fab knocked on Arch's door and made the introductions. The man didn't cover his disappointment that Didier had been added to the equation but invited both of them inside.

"Since we're going to need proof..." Fab quickly outfitted Arch with a mic and camera.

"If you think Sway's going to get violent, just know we've got your back," Didier assured him.

"Not sure how Sway would react if he knew I was trying to prove he was the shooter." Arch shuddered.

"My partner and I are going to be in the bedroom. If Sway starts anything, we can break it up in seconds," Fab told him.

"The door at the end of the hall." Arch pointed.

Just then, an older model BMW rolled up the street and turned into the driveway. Sway jumped out and ran up the stairs.

"Sway drives a BMW?" I asked Fab.

"That's Bardy's car," she said with a sniff. "He had a beat-up older model sedan in the driveway but kept the Beemer, his baby, in the garage, and it didn't take long for Sway to get his hands on the keys."

Sway could be heard beating on the door, and it sounded like he was close to kicking it in.

Arch threw open the door. "Damn, dude." He stuck his head outside and took a quick look around.

"What's going on?" Sway threw himself into

one of the two chairs.

"So, the shooting the other night… Cops pulled me over on the way home, as my car matched the description of the one leaving."

Sway stiffened, grinding his teeth. "Yeah, crazy stuff," he muttered, his voice tight. "It's getting rough around here. What did you tell them?"

"That I made a wrong turn. Heard the shots, u-turned, and sped back to the road."

Sway nodded, staring intently. "Did my name come up?"

"They didn't ask about you specifically." Arch eyed him. "I asked you what you knew when we were on the way back to your place and didn't get an answer. I hope you're going to tell me straight now. You were there when the shots were fired — what went down?"

"As you know, I wasn't there long. I barely got a chance to look for my grandfather before shots rang out, and I turned and ran."

"Did you see the shooter? What did they look like?" Arch asked.

"Why all the damn questions?" Sway snapped.

"When they were done questioning me, the cops told me they'd be back. I thought they believed me when I said I didn't shoot anyone, which we both know I didn't, but now I wonder why they'd come back if they did believe me. When pressed, I told them I saw someone driving off but couldn't give a description. What if they want to arrest me?"

"They come back, you tell them that after thinking about it, you still can't remember enough to give a description," Sway snapped, *dumbass* in his tone.

"I'm not risking going to jail for something you and I know that I didn't do. All you need to do is step up and tell them I was in the car the whole time."

"Keep your mouth shut! If you don't..." Sway flipped his jacket back, his shoulder holster on display. "Listen up. If the cops come around again, you don't know anything about me being at that dump motel."

"Didn't know you owned a gun." Wide-eyed, Arch took a step backwards.

"*And* I know how to use it," Sway said menacingly. "There's a lot you don't know, and trust me when I tell you you want to keep it that way." He eyed Arch. "Are we in agreement that if you're questioned again and my name should come up, you don't know anything... in fact, we don't even know one another? If the cops find out you had someone in the car, tell them you gave a ride to a stranger and dumped them on the side of the road."

"They're not going to believe that."

"Your life depends on it," Sway hissed.

"So, not a word about you," Arch promised as he back-stepped to the door and held it open.

"Not if you know what's good for you." Sway stomped out and down the stairs.

Chapter Thirty-Nine

Fab came rushing into the living room. "Take a deep breath," she told Arch. "Sway's dangerous. I'm going to give you some tips on how to stay away from him."

"Signing off," I told Fab. "We're headed to the office."

"Hold up. Does Didier have a key to the truck?"

"If he doesn't, hotwire it or walk." I disconnected before she could go off on me.

Creole laughed. "My money's on Didier telling her that he doesn't have a key and watching while she hotwires it."

"And then the monkey sex."

I showed off my driving skills, taking a couple shortcuts that I was certain wouldn't end us up in mile-high weeds, and got us back to the office in record time.

"So you know, the direct route works for me." Creole smirked.

"That's no fun."

I hopped out of the car, Creole hooked his arm around me like I was going to run off, and we headed into the office. Brad was sitting at the conference table, laughing it up with Casio. Since Lark's car wasn't in the parking lot, it didn't surprise me to see her chair empty.

When I took a seat, Brad leaned over and kissed my cheek. "Happy to see you in one piece."

"Please… didn't set one foot outside the car. Fooled around with…" I pointed to Creole.

"No details." Brad groaned.

"Just a little reminder: there's no reneging on favors owed just because your husband aced me out." Casio eyed the two of us.

"I'm going to let you in on a little secret." I lowered my voice, knowing everyone could still hear. "You're on that special list — you ask and we accommodate."

"Yes." Casio shook his fist overhead in triumph. "Get anything useful on that Sway character?"

"I don't think so." I sighed.

"You're forgetting his gun. With Arch putting Sway at the scene, which he's going to have to do, it's enough for a search warrant," Creole reminded me. "Ballistics will show if the gun was used in the motel shooting."

"However that plays out, unless Sway is in jail, Arch will need to leave town. Sway was convincing — to me, anyway — that he'd make good on his threats." I got up and crossed the room to the refrigerator, in search of caffeine, and found a bottle of tea. Just as I sat back down, Fab and Didier blew through the door and joined us at the table.

"What's our next step?" Fab barked.

"Call your pal Cooper and show him what you've got. It wouldn't surprise me if he gets a search warrant," Creole told her.

"If it turns out that Cooper's a pussy, I've got a guy that can make it happen." Casio grinned.

"One of the ones you've called on before?" I asked. "They didn't call us crazy, but it was clear that's what they thought. Besides, I thought they went off to who knows where."

"I remember those two; they were afraid to share their names," Fab said in disgust.

"It might surprise you, but I've got more than two friends, and this one, you haven't met yet."

"Madison and Fab have a new connection—two, actually—they're supposed to be playing nice with Cooper and Kevin." Creole smirked.

"While you're making calls... have you called your big-butted friend?"

"Really, Madison."

"Don't say I didn't remind you when he blows his fuse." I shot Fab a sneaky smile. "If you're there when he does, get a pic."

Didier leaned over and whispered in Fab's ear, ignoring us all staring at them.

"Let me guess—hubby agrees with me and told you you better get on it and not to drag *your* ass." I returned her flinty stare.

"Fine. I'll be right back." Fab got up and

stomped outside, Didier a step behind her.

"She only gets peeved like that when it's already been on her mind to do it and she doesn't want to," I said.

"Why didn't you tell her to keep her butt in the chair so we can all listen in?" Brad raised his brows.

"If you hung around more often, you'd know that she never puts the big guy on speaker." *So there.* "While we're waiting on Fab, if any of you wants something to drink, go get it yourself." I pointed to the refrigerator. "And bring me back a water."

"That's not friendly," Creole said, a tsk in his tone, as he stood and crossed the room. Brad and Casio yelled out what they wanted, and he came back with his hands full.

"What exactly is it that you and Fab were going to…" I eyed Casio. "Not sure exactly, so what's the latest on the warehouse?"

"We should wait for Fab to get back so she won't get all 'tudey, thinking she got left out."

"Is it something good? Or are you just dragging your feet?" When Casio laughed, I turned to Creole. "Have you found us a renter? Other than pawn shop dude?"

"Thank goodness you're not interested in that kind of business. Talk about trouble," Brad snarked.

"Because everyone's on the up-and-up on this road?"

"Please tell me—"

I cut Brad off. "Before your hair catches fires, Creole and I agreed that we're not interested."

"This is mostly a quiet street, despite what crops up from time to time," Brad reminded us.

Fab and Didier came back in the door, arm in arm, and joined us at the conference table.

"So proud of Fab." Didier grinned. "She updated the man and then told him if he couldn't let it play out to do it himself, that she was out. Guessing he heard that her patience was threadbare. He backed off, and they came to an agreement."

"Once Gunz calmed down, he decided that he wants it resolved so he never hears about it again. He's on board with calling the cops. I talked him into letting me call Cooper and not his guy," Fab told us.

"Surprised that he didn't insist on making Sway disappear—tomorrow," I said.

"Just so happens I was able to decipher his mutterings to mean that he'd mulled it over and decided against it." Fab pasted on a demented smile just for me.

"Which one of you is going to call Cooper?" Didier asked.

Fab and I pointed at each other simultaneously.

"If you need a reminder... Your case. Your client." *So there.*

"Except that Cooper tolerates you more than he does me."

The guys were all eyes and enjoying every minute.

"Not sure if you just made that up or you've had it on the back burner to trot out because you think it sounds good." I picked up my phone and called Cooper. When he answered, I said. "You're on speaker. There's a room full of eavesdroppers, all of which you know, and if you hop on over to the Boardwalk offices, you'll see there's no need for an introduction."

"In the future, no more speaker calls," he grouched.

"Got it. So you won't think I'm wasting your time... The motel shooting—got some information on it, if you're interested."

"My boss would like an arrest in that case ASAP. He's got a relative who works there—you wouldn't know who, would you?" Cooper asked.

"The sheriff has a relation working at that motel?" Dead silence. "If I find out who, I'll pass it along. How's that?"

"We'll be there in under twenty." He disconnected.

"Okay then. Let's put the little bit of time we've got to good use. You're up." I pointed to Casio. "So you know," I told Fab, "when you were outside, I tried to worm information out of him and got nothing." I turned back to Casio. "You can start with who owns the property next door and what you know about them."

"That's being worked on, as it's held by a

corporation and will take some digging. We did make a list of what we're going to need to get law enforcement interested enough to check it out. A copy is in your email." Casio hit some keys on his laptop. "Last night, I decided to check out the security feed and, around midnight, caught a twentyish guy, baseball cap pulled down, climbing the fence from the auto shop side onto your property." Casio jerked his thumb. "He jumped down and headed to the office door. Not sure if he expected to find it unlocked, but when it wasn't, he decided to see if could kick it in. That didn't work either."

"I'll have Cootie check it out—see if it needs to be replaced," Creole said. "When he couldn't get in... what? He left?"

"He prowled every inch of the property. Not sure what he was looking for, since it's empty. The cars caught his attention, and he checked them out. Surprised you haven't already unloaded them." Casio singled me out.

"Takes time to find them a good home." I failed at dialing back the sarcasm.

The guys laughed.

"Back to the trespasser... then what happened?" Fab asked.

"When he was finished prowling, he went back over the fence."

"Wonder what he was looking for," Creole grouched. "More importantly, if he'd gotten inside, then what? The place is empty."

"You've seen a picture of my car thief—was it him?" Fab asked.

"This guy was older by a few years. I downloaded a picture, but don't be grouching when you see it's not the best."

Lark breezed through the door. "The cops are here," she called out. "I let them follow me inside the gate."

"Since I made the call—" I made a face at Fab. "—you get to tell them why they're here."

"Just remember this was Arch's convoluted plan, which he'd set in motion before he called you," Didier reminded her.

"If the need for bail arises, I'm here for you." Brad managed a sympathetic smile before laughing.

"We should know soon," I said as Kevin and Cooper came through the door, both with big smiles for Lark.

She pointed them in the direction of the conference table, and they came over and sat across from us, eyeing the others at the table suspiciously. Lark broke the stare-down by setting sodas in front of them.

"Which one of you has the dead body stashed nearby?" Cooper asked, looking around.

"Thought you got rid of it? Didn't you?" I asked Casio, who grinned. The rest of the guys rolled their eyes.

"Heard that the reason we got called to come here was news about the motel shooting." Not amused, Kevin eyed Casio: *Get to the point.*

"It has to do with my client—Theodore Gunzelman," Fab started.

It wasn't often I heard the man called by his full name.

Kevin groaned. "Have you met him yet?" he asked Cooper, who shook his head. "Yeah, well, you won't be impressed."

"Where was I?" Fab eyed Kevin. "It has to do with a relative of his, Bardy Dowell..." And she launched into a skimmed-over retell, skipping the part where Bardy wasn't actually a relative.

"Had you handed over the plate information, the police would've investigated," Kevin snarked.

"But would Arch have been as charmed by you as he was Fab and called Sway over for a chat?" I asked.

Kevin laughed. After a glance around the table, he said, "Oh, you're serious."

"This Arch fellow is lucky he didn't end up hurt or worse," Cooper said. "Is this all you've got or—"

Casio cut him off. "Fab got enough on tape that if you hustle your ass, you can get a search warrant. Once you recover the gun, forensics will show if it matches the bullets at the scene."

"We'll take a look at what you've got and decide if it's useful or not," Cooper snarked back.

Fab picked up her laptop and changed seats, sitting next to Cooper and sharing the screen.

"Why wouldn't Dowell give a statement to the

cops about everything that went down at his house? He damn near died. Or did he forget that since... what, he's still suffering from amnesia?" Kevin asked, eyeroll in his tone.

"It's not easy when a family member is involved," I said.

"I suppose that other family members are covering for the guy? And they'll what, feign shock when he does it again? Then someone ends up dead. From what I read, if Fab hadn't shown up when she did, that's what would've happened," Kevin grouched. "Do you ever think about calling the police?"

"Kevin..." Cooper motioned him over. The two listened to the replay of Arch's conversation with Sway.

I scooted closer to Creole. "What are we going to do about the intruder on our property?"

My brother, who'd heard, snapped, "*You* aren't going to do a damn thing."

"Keep it down." I crossed my lips with my finger.

Cooper spoke up. "We're going to need a copy."

Fab pulled a USB drive out of her pocket and handed it to him. "Would you let me know if there's an arrest? Because I told Arch he should consider staying with a family or friend in the meantime, and he can't come home until Sway's behind bars."

"What I want in exchange is for you to set up a

meeting with Bardy and for him to answer my questions truthfully, stopping with the amnesia stuff. So you know, the officers that talked to him at the hospital never believed him." Cooper raised his brows, *Deal?*

"What I can do is call his lawyer, Tank, and he can set up a meeting. It'll probably require a return trip." Fab jerked her thumb towards the ceiling.

"To lessen your grumpiness, I'll let Lark know you're both coming, and that means food," I told the two.

We were all quiet until Kevin and Cooper had left the building.

"Back to what we were talking about... I agree with Brad. When those two come back for their meeting, fill them in on what's going on with the warehouse," Didier said.

Before Fab could give her two cents, I cut in. "How about Creole and I issue an edict? 'Our property — we make the decisions. No trespassing to the lot of you.'" There was no controlling my snark.

"What I could do is hire a couple of goons to pay the neighboring business a middle-of-the-night call and shake the stuffing out of whoever's there until they get answers," Creole suggested.

"You're lucky that law enforcement left. Kevin thinks I've always got something illegal up my sleeve, and you'd get added to the list."

"You and I need to—"

I cut Creole off with a quick kiss. "I agree. And later."

"Got a meeting to get to," Casio announced and shoved back his chair. "Tell me once you find out if these two," he said to Fab, pointing at Creole and me, "want us to find out what's going on or mind our own business." With a nod, he left.

"We've compiled a lot of footage showing that your neighbors are up to their ears in illegal—I'm thinking they're running a car theft ring, but there may be more going on." Fab seethed with frustration. "And what? That's 'oh well' now? I have security footage that shows cars coming and leaving by trailer in the middle of the night. Tell me that's not shady."

"The cops were just here, why not say, 'Oh by the way…?'" Brad asked.

"Shady is not evidence of an actual crime, and without it, the cops won't have any choice but to put it on the back burner," Fab hissed at him. "Why are you so worried?"

"I don't want Madison getting hurt, as I know you'll drag her along with you," Brad snapped.

"Calm down. We're going to meet in the morning and decide how to move forward," I said. "It also would be good to talk to our lawyer."

Fab reluctantly agreed.

Chapter Forty

The next day, I contacted Tank and passed along Cooper's request that he arrange a meeting with Bardy.

"Get me a number for Gunz, and I'll call him myself and see how involved he wants to be," Tank told me.

The meeting happened the following day in Tank's office. Fab and I didn't talk about whether Fern was planning to attend, but she clearly wasn't as surprised as I was when the older woman walked into the building with Bardy in tow. We ushered them to the second floor, where Tank, at his desk, stood and waved them to a seat.

"I get to be the one to report back to Gunz," she whispered excitedly. It was meant for me, but everyone heard.

"Got the proofs for you to sign." Tank pushed the paperwork across his desk.

We both stayed standing, as we hadn't been invited to the meeting and weren't planning on crashing the party.

"How about an update?" I asked Tank.

"Didn't surprise me how cooperative the

businesses were, as it was in their best interest," Tank said. "The real estate company removed the listing within an hour. The buyer called to let me know he retracted the offer."

"Is the property still in Sway's name?" Fab asked.

"Sway was a no-show at the court hearing I was able to schedule, and the property was transferred back to Bardy..." Tank nodded at the man, who exuded nervousness. "The judge then referred the case to the district attorney."

"All this bull after Bardy's lived in the house for forty years," Fern spat.

"It's going to be hard to go back there." Bardy shuddered.

Fern patted his back. "No need to worry about that right now."

"Before you make any decisions, we'll go over all your options after the cops are out of here," Tank assured him.

"If referrals are needed to make something happen, no matter how odd you might think the request, call me." I waved.

"You know what would be really fun?" Fern swiveled in her chair.

I was afraid to ask and stayed silent.

Fab poked me in the side.

"How about finding a fun place that caters to old people, where the cost isn't exorbitant?" Excitement lit Fern's eyes. "As long as it's not a sewer hole, I know several folks that would be interested."

I turned to Fab and raised my brow, telegraphing, *Gunz*.

Gunz had buildings where he housed the occasional relative. Maybe he would be in the market for another property.

"It's something to think about." Fab's tone said she'd already forgotten.

Fab and I both heard Kevin and Cooper talking to Clive out in the reception area.

"Keep us in the loop on any updates on Sway," I said to Tank.

Clive stuck his head in the door. "I seated Kevin and Cooper at the conference table, since you're short on room in here."

Tank stood and grabbed his laptop, heading out behind Bardy and Fern, who Clive had corralled and was talking to about beverage options.

Fab jerked her head towards the door, which I deduced to mean, *Let's get out of here,* and I agreed.

"You might want to hear this," Cooper called after us. "In the spirit of cooperation, I thought I'd include you in the update."

Fab and I turned around and made our way back to the conference table. I noted Clive's smirk as we took a seat. He set waters in front of us.

"Reviewed the footage you sent over, questioned Arch, and got a search warrant for

Bardy's house." He nodded to the man. "I know your lawyer has kept you apprised."

"How did it get to this point?" Bardy had covered his face and was mumbling into his hands.

"Find anything fun?" Fab asked.

"You know what we went in looking for, and we found it—a stash of weapons and ammo," Cooper told us.

"When I heard what was discovered, I found it hard to believe and still do," Bardy uttered. "I realize that you found that all in my house, but I'm telling you, they're not mine."

"When questioned, Sway claimed that all he knew was that they belonged to his grandfather, then told us that he didn't know how to find you, that you'd disappeared," Cooper continued.

"So you know, Sway was arrested," Kevin told us. "He'd stopped talking by then, demanding a lawyer, and I heard before we got here that he made bail."

"Surprised my son hasn't called," Bardy said with a shake of his head.

"Bail," I said. "That's not good news."

"You can't go back to the motel," Fab told Bardy. "Before you get worked up, we'll find an alternative and go over it with you before you leave here."

"You mean I will," I grumbled in a low tone. From Kevin's smirk, I guessed he heard me. I turned and went over to Clive's desk. My eyes landed on a small box I knew was a cheap device used for eavesdropping, as we had a couple of them upstairs. "You get caught... better keep the bail dude on speed dial."

"Anyone asks, my story is I haven't figured out how it works yet."

As I sat on the corner of his desk, I was surprised to see Fab and Fern headed our way.

Fern flung herself in a chair. "Sucks I couldn't sit next to my friend and pat his back when he needs it."

I looked at Clive, telegraphing, *Entertain her* with a glance at Fern. Then I took my phone out and walked out into the hallway, Fab following me. I called Mac and put it on speaker. When she answered, I asked, "Is the unit we hold off-market available?"

"You know it," Mac assured me.

I gave her a quick rundown of events. "Since it's Fab's client, if he agrees to the move, she'll be getting back to you."

"Remind the old goat that we've met a few times, and he'll probably be amenable. That said, do we need to be on the lookout for trouble?"

"Don't worry, I'll get it covered," Fab assured her.

We hung up.

"I want to go home." I barely contained my whininess.

"I need a couple minutes to dump all this in Clive's lap, and we're out of here." Fab opened the door and crossed to Clive's desk. While she talked, he nodded.

I watched as Fab unloaded her spiel, and it was clear she had the man onboard by the time she finished.

Chapter Forty-One

Clive called me later that day, full of news. "Bardy was fine with the change of residence. Told him not to feel rushed to figure out what he's doing. Fern also packed her bag. Thinking they're doing you-know-what. Had a couple of damn nosey questions, but thought I'd call in one of my favors, and you could ask."

"Not to be mean, but fat chance. Give it a few days, and check-in with Mac; she'll have your answers."

"Didn't think of that angle."

I rolled my eyes, which he couldn't see. "Anything else?" I left unsaid, *Before I hang up.*

"Ballistics came back, linking Sway's gun to the scene, and he was re-arrested. This time, real estate fraud charges were added on. Hope he enjoys the clink."

"Hopefully, Bardy and his family can put everything behind them." Probably not, but maybe.

"He's hoping the same thing. Gotta go." Clive hung up.

I sent Fab a text and wasn't surprised to get one back that said, *Working a new job.* Was Didier her backup, or was she off on her own? Since she wasn't forthcoming with details, I called the office. When Lark answered, I told her, "Don't let anyone know it's me. If asked, tell them the caller was trying to sell you something."

She laughed. "The guys are in their office and can't hear a word. Even if they were sitting at the conference table, they never listen in."

"Fab there? Didier?"

"Hottie's here. Haven't seen Fab, and just checked the monitor—her car's not in the parking lot either. Since this is the first time you've made this kind of call, what's going on?" Lark asked.

"That's what I'm trying to figure out. When I talked to her last night, she was more vague than usual. I'd like to know what Fab is up to, rather than wonder or wait around for… what, don't know. Well, if you don't have any insight, then I'll figure it out for myself."

"If it looks like trouble, call in your hottie husband."

"Good advice."

"Don't forget to fill me in when you find out."

"Will do." I hung up.

I gathered up my laptop and settled on the couch, kicking my feet up and enjoying the slight breeze coming through the open sliders. I rewound the compound security footage and saw that early this morning, Casio made the trek to Fab's house via the sand, laptop under his arm, and stayed a couple of hours. Now having a good idea of exactly what she was up to, I wondered how long she'd been sneaking around. I rewound the footage even more and found that she'd left shortly after midnight last night in Didier's Mercedes, stopping briefly to pick up Casio.

I brought up the footage for the warehouse. Now that it was ready to be leased out, it would be interesting to see how much interest there'd be in occupying the whole building. We'd delay putting out word of its availability until we knew that whatever was going on next door was entirely legal. We'd thoroughly discussed tipping off law enforcement, but thus far, we only had suspicions, and if nothing came of it, and it was discovered we were involved, retaliation would be a certainty.

The tape showed Didier's Mercedes rolling up to the gate with the headlights off. Fab jumped out of the driver's side, Casio getting out the passenger door. She inserted a key and shoved it open, then jumped back in and drove through the gates, Casio closing them. She, Casio, and Didier then headed over to the corner, where under the only tree, Fab jerked off a tarp covering a couple ladders that hadn't been there the last time I'd been there.

They leaned a ladder up against the fence, and Fab and Casio climbed up a few steps and peered over, but didn't go any farther. That was because the overhead lights on the neighboring property illuminated every inch of their property. Didier went up behind Fab, got an eyeful, and came back down.

Fab and Casio stayed crouched on the ladders for over an hour, Fab with binoculars and Casio with a camera. I fast-forwarded through the footage, as it was boring—two adults peeking over a fence.

Bored, I got up and made myself a cup of coffee, then resettled on the couch.

Fab strolled through the sliders like it was her house instead of mine, which was nothing new. "Thought we'd go to lunch." She peered over my shoulder to get a look at my laptop screen, but I clicked off. She dropped into a chair across from me.

"Hmm... That must mean you're done sneaking around. One would think, being your bestie and all, that I'd know what you're up to, but nopers."

"My guess is that you know exactly what I've been up to." She eyed my laptop as I set it aside. "If I'd asked you to go snooping around the neighboring warehouse in the middle of the night, Creole would have killed you." At my raised eyebrows, she added, "Or me anyway."

"Like that's ever stopped you."

"Good point. But I'm out of the snooping game, at least where your warehouse is concerned. Besides, Didier isn't having it anymore, and I've been banned from going back."

"You've decided that they're running a legit

operation, so no need to be peering over the fence? Or…?"

"Casio thinks we've done enough snooping and doesn't want us to get caught. Besides, he's putting everything we've compiled into a report and handing it off to one of his cop friends."

"If you're involving the cops, that must mean you've got the goods on them."

"If you ask me, yes. But Casio wants to know where that trailer full of vehicles goes when they leave."

"How many cars are inside?"

"Six. When we got the opportunity, I wanted to check out the trailer with Casio, but Didier flipped, and before a disagreement erupted, we left," Fab said with a shake of her head. "On the way back home, Casio said we'd get together in the morning and talk it over. When he showed up, he informed me it was a done deal and handed over the photos. I was kind of relieved, as I knew there wasn't going to be a way around Didier on going back."

"Was Casio in one piece when he showed up?"

"Smug and cocky as usual and didn't want to get into details. Pretty sure that Didier and he came up with the alternate plan… and I've got to say I don't know how it escaped my notice. You can bet I won't let it happen again."

"Why do I get the feeling you're leaving something out?" Based on the stubborn set of Fab's features and the fact that I didn't get an immediate answer, I added, "And don't bother fabricating something."

"It's just frustrating—we do a bunch of snooping and then I'm supposed to just walk away."

"Enough already. It's my property, and I don't want anyone getting hurt. Hand over whatever you've already got to Casio's friend or Cooper and Kevin, and if they think there's a case, they can follow up."

Fab answered her ringing phone. "Why the hell would you go and do that?" she grouched. "If you died, I'd be blamed; you know that, don't you?" After a long pause, she said, "Dude," on an exasperated sigh. She picked up a pen off the table and my notepad. "I'm ready."

I leaned in and saw that she'd scribbled down what looked like a license plate number.

"No need to worry. I'll follow at a distance, and when I find out their destination, I'll call. In the meantime, you call Shirl." She hung up.

"Casio got hurt, didn't he?"

"Bullet grazed his thigh. Damn him." She jumped to her feet. "The hauler is on the move, and I need to follow it. You coming or what?"

"I'll meet you in the driveway." She ran outside and down to the beach. I headed to the bedroom, where I swapped out my dress for crop sweats, a tee, and tennis shoes. I grabbed my purse and was out of the house, getting in the driver's seat and heading to Fab's, where she was just coming out the front door. I hopped out and changed seats. "I'm sending Casio a text: 'If you need anything, don't hesitate to call,'" I read as I typed.

"Casio was at your warehouse, and someone shot at him from over the fence. Lucky him, their aim was off. He'd left his truck a couple businesses down, and as he was about to pull out on the road, the hauler went by."

"Thought they did everything in the middle of the night."

"According to what Casio pieced together, they were waiting on one more car, which arrived in the early morning hours. He figured they'd be pulling out tonight. Instead, another hauler showed up, they switched out the cars, and right before pulling out came the shots."

"Did someone see him hanging his head over the fence?"

"He didn't get into the details." Fab rocketed over to the Overseas and headed north. "They don't have much of a head start, so we should be able to catch up easily."

"Then what?"

"Calm down. When we find out where the hauler ends up, I make a call and head home."

Nothing was ever that simple. "When you call Didier to fill him in, have him update Creole."

Just as she turned onto Highway One, she pointed over the steering wheel. "Think that's the hauler up there."

Chapter Forty-Two

It surprised me that Fab did exactly what she said she'd do — she hung back and followed the hauler. It was possibly the slowest she'd ever driven. When we left the Keys, I really hoped we weren't headed to another state.

"Finally." Fab nodded when the driver turned on his blinker to exit the highway in Miami.

"This area is very familiar," I said as she turned onto a street in a bustling commercial area. The hauler passed several car dealers and continued for about a mile before getting into the turn lane and waiting for a break in traffic.

Fab pulled to the side of the road, and we watched as the hauler turned into Petro's Used Cars and out of sight around the back of the property.

"The best way to check out this property would be at night, but I bet they have security guards." She eased back into traffic and checked out the nearby businesses before making a u-turn and going back for another look at the car lot.

"Your old client Brick is on this road to the north a couple of miles, and I have to say that the areas couldn't be more different, his upscale and Petro's not so much. But I'm betting that Brick could tell you about every business on this street all the way to the state line."

"If he has any kind of association with the business…" Fab made a face. "It could backfire. If he saw something in it for him, he'd tip them off." She turned off the highway and checked for an entrance at the back of the property, finding that there was only one way in, as it backed up to another business and they shared a ten-foot concrete wall.

"If you're insistent about a late-night visit, sneak through the business that backs up to theirs, scale the wall, and say hello to the security guard." I took her snort to mean she didn't like my idea.

"They have to have guards," Fab mused. "When you're running an illegal operation, you have to keep eyes on it at all times."

"This delivery is originating from the warehouse next to mine, and you haven't mentioned seeing anyone there."

"Must've forgot."

"I'm rolling my eyes." That got a faint chuckle out of her.

"Three guys show up every day and go into the warehouse, where they stay all day. I've yet to see a car dropped off. Just guessing, but I'm thinking they're also running a chop business. Big money in that—"

"Just swell."

"I meant to say 'so I've heard.'"

Uh-huh. I chuckled humorlessly. "How are you aware of the tidbit you just shared? And for how long?"

"Remember the cameras I added to the other side of the fence?"

"You're lucky you didn't get caught, but then, you never worry about that. Honestly, all this snooping needs to come to an end."

Without me having to nag her, she made one more trip past the business, then parked on the other side of the busy street, took out her phone, took some pictures, and sent a text.

"I'm hungry, which is my way of saying let's go."

"We're out of here." Fab pocketed her phone. "I could go over, pretend to be interested in buying a car, and snoop around a little…"

"If you're recognized, they might shoot you. At the very least, they'd want to know what you were doing there, and if they didn't like your answer…" I sliced my finger across my throat.

"That's why we're headed back to the Cove." She took another loop around and headed south.

When we were on Highway One, I asked, "Have you and Casio decided when you're going to involve the police?"

"Casio's already filled in his friend, who told him he'd look into it and get back to him. He cautioned that the cops would do their own investigation and not to expect anything to happen overnight and said, in the meantime, no more snooping. Which reminds me…" Fab pulled out her phone and called Casio. When he answered, she told him, "Followed the truck and have an address for you." She held the phone away while he yelled.

I heard him say, "Thought I told you the cops were on it."

"Want the information or not?" Fab barked back. She gave it to him and said, "We're on our way back." She tossed the phone in the cup holder. "That was fun. He did say he'd pass the information along before hanging up on me." She pushed the accelerator to the floor and looked lost in thought as she headed down the road, determination etched on her face.

I knew she wanted to be in the thick of the action but hoped that she would back off and let law enforcement do their job. Happy we were nearing the Cove, I stared out at the water running alongside us and told her, "Lunch is on me; you get to pick the place."

Suddenly, a large pickup truck veered into our lane, its blaring horn drowning out the sound of the other cars. Fab's reflexes kicked in, and she swerved just in time to avoid a collision, her knuckles white as she gripped the steering wheel.

"Who the heck?" I turned in my seat. "This looks deliberate. What do you suppose irked him off?"

"Nothing I did in the last few minutes. Hang on."

I'd been thinking it was over, but it wasn't. After some dangerous maneuvers on the truck driver's part, he came after us, relentless in his pursuit, forcing Fab to cut around traffic, narrowly dodging cars and trucks alike.

She weaved in and out of the two lanes, her focus on the road ahead of her unwavering. As the cat-and-mouse game continued, she said, "Call Casio and put it on speaker."

I grabbed my phone, my fingers dancing across the screen. When he answered, I cut him off before he could say anything. "Fab and I are on speaker."

"I'm on Highway One about ten miles out of town," Fab told him. "I have a testosterone truck on my tail that's made a couple attempts to send me flying into the water."

"Sending the troops," he assured us and hung up.

Fab swerved again as the truck made contact with the corner of the back bumper. She somehow managed to keep the SUV steady. "Hopefully Casio's friends are close by."

I swallowed my squeal as I caught sight of the white truck bearing down again. As he swerved, so did Fab, saving us once again from being bashed into. "Enough of him. How about I blow out his tires? That would slow him down." I pulled my Glock from my thigh holster.

"Not just yet." Fab swerved erratically to shake him off the bumper. "If it looks like I can't hold him off, then you're up." She was relentless, her eyes locked on the truck as she continued to swerve between the lanes, the chase continuing almost to town.

When we caught sight of the flashing lights speeding up the other side of the highway, the truck slowed and chose a lane. Two police cruisers u-turned and cut in front of the driver of the truck, which swerved and nose-dived into the water. Fab pulled over and edged off the road as far as she could get.

"Oh look, familiar faces." I nodded through the windshield as two more cruisers showed up, Kevin and Cooper getting out. The officers in the other cars had beelined to the water. "If the driver of the truck thought that taking a dive was a viable getaway plan, he's going to be disappointed. There's no escape out there."

"I don't want him drowning until we find out what the hell. Let's get out." Fab and I got out, and the two of us met Kevin and Cooper at the bumper.

"Does any of what happened here have to do with you being told to back off what's now a police investigation?" Cooper barked at Fab.

"In case you missed it, the swimmer tried to run me off the road," Fab grouched back, but not as loud.

Kevin motioned me over. I turned to Fab, who

let me know with a look she wasn't going with the whole truth of what we'd been up to.

"Hello, Officer," I said as I approached.

"Don't you get tired of getting into these situations?"

"I was looking forward to going for a swim, but maybe next time."

Kevin snorted. "What happened? Make it concise and truthful."

"Truck tried to run us off the road. And do I know the driver? I didn't get a good enough look to answer that question. What I really wanted to do was hang out the window and shoot out the truck's tires before he killed someone other than himself."

"Surprised you didn't do it, but I'm happy you didn't, as the truck might've taken out other vehicles when it lost control and swerved." Kevin eyed me like a perp ready to go on the run. "Start at the beginning."

"I've got nothing for you. The truck came out of nowhere, intent on running us off the road. Thank goodness it was Fab behind the wheel and not me."

Another cop car rolled up, along with the paramedics and a tow truck.

"Don't go anywhere." Kevin trotted off, meeting up with Cooper, and they had a short conversation.

He hadn't said I couldn't talk to Fab, so when she started back towards the car, I wasn't far behind. She had the lift gate down and had taken a seat, and I sat next to her.

"Do we have permission to talk to each other?" I asked.

"I didn't ask, and since he didn't say anything, it's on him."

"The first two cops that arrived looked like Casio's friends, but I didn't get a good look," I said.

"I recognized them. Lucky us that they were close by."

"What's with the driver of the truck?" I looked out at Blackwater Sound and tried to visualize the map and the options for someone to make it out of the water in one piece.

"Before I came back over here, I heard one of the officers call, 'No sign of the driver.'" Fab blew a frustrated sigh. "What did you tell Kevin?"

"Just that the truck tried to run us off the road. Everything else wasn't relevant... at least, I hope."

"Sounds like what I told Cooper."

"Driver dude doesn't have a lot of options out there in the water." I wanted to stand on the car to get a better look but wasn't about to attempt it. "Once he got out the window, whichever way he turned, it's a long swim. Unless he didn't —"

"Another officer confirmed he made it out of the truck," Fab assured me. "At least he was smart enough to roll down the window before it became an impossibility. Hoping that we don't have to wait until they fish him or his body out of the water."

I slid off the tailgate and walked back to the passenger side. "Calling Creole," I said over my shoulder. I reached in and grabbed my phone, then retrieved two waters and went back to sit next to her, handing off one of the bottles. "Hey, honey," I said when he answered.

He groaned. "Do I want to know?"

"Yes and no. If you haven't hit the speaker button, you should; Didier's already not going to like being the last to know."

"We're all ears, including your bro."

I gave them the same slick version I gave Kevin and reassured them that we were both okay.

"Where are you?"

"Hang on for the human map." I handed my phone to Fab and leaned in to listen.

"Right past the curve, headed north," Fab told them.

"We're on our way."

"Keep in mind that we might be here a while."

Chapter Forty-Three

We were finally able to go home with the same old admonition: "We know where to find you." Fab went with Didier in the truck, and Creole drove the SUV. We stuck close to home for the next couple of days, awaiting whatever happened next in the investigation.

On the third day, we got word that the warehouse in the Cove and the Miami location were both raided in the middle of the night. They arrested five men up north and two at the Cove location. According to Casio's sources, there was over a million dollars in stolen cars. One of the men was more than willing to talk, and the cops arrested the teen carjacker, his mother, and her sister; the husband managed to disappear but was arrested the next day.

Casio arranged to have our warehouse raided too, so hopefully we wouldn't be suspected of tipping off the cops. He also suggested that Fab and I keep a low profile, so Fab and Didier went out of town, while Creole and I spent our time on the sand.

Several days passed, and then Mother called and invited us to a surprise. When I hemmed and hawed, it turned into an order to be ready when our ride showed up. Not believing I would show after my lackluster, "Sounds good," she called Creole and got a "We'll be ready to go" out of him. Fab wasn't the least bit amused that she'd been bypassed in favor of Didier, who assured Mother we'd all be there.

I'd showered and was surveying my closet for something "tropical dressy," as mandated in Mother's follow-up text. Creole was dressed and sitting on the bed, watching me with a smirk. I slapped my hand on my forehead and staggered over to him. "Not sure what came over me, but I can't go anywhere." My almost-laugh didn't help sell my story.

He wrapped his arms around me, pulling me down next to him. "After a few phone calls, I found out that everyone in the family, and then some, has been invited. You're going to want to witness whatever it is your Mother's up to."

"You can bet she's up to something." I got up and crossed back to the closet, reaching in and choosing a sleeveless green tropical midi dress. My first choice of footwear was flip-flops, but I passed them over for a pair of low-heeled slides.

Creole winked.

"We're carpooling with the neighbors?"

"Fab's not driving, and I bet that's a source of contention between her and Didier." Creole hooked his arm around me, and as we started down the hall, the doorbell rang. "We know that's not Fab, because no matter how much bodily harm I threaten, she still uses her lockpick. Every single time when I'm not home, I bet."

"We can't leave whoever is at our door standing there all day." I attempted to step away and was dragged back to his side as he threw open the door.

A man decked out in a black tux smiled. "Mr. and Mrs. Baptiste, your ride is here." He waved to a limo large enough that it could seat half the town.

"Do you get sweat pay?" I asked the man, who appeared confused.

"Would you stop?" Creole whispered in my ear.

"My attempt at humor." I smiled. The man nodded.

We weren't the first to be picked up, as Emerson, Brad, and Casio were already seated inside.

"Where did you ditch the kids?" I asked, sliding onto the bench next to Emerson, Creole next to me, his arm slung around me like I was going to jump out.

Emerson laughed. "The bus came by earlier and picked up the kids, who were excited for another adventure. Crum never disappoints, and he had Clive along, who appeared to be amused, as opposed to having a 'What am I doing here?' look on his face."

"Did your kids make the cut for the bus?" I

asked Casio.

"Crum called and arranged it with Alex. Going to remind him these calls need to come through me, not my kid."

"Sounds like Crum." Creole laughed.

"What's Mother up to?" Brad grouched.

"My answer is the same as when you called — I don't know," I said.

"Calm down." Emerson patted his arm. "You know that whatever Madeline has planned, everyone's going to have a good time."

"Mother being sneaky…" Brad shook his head.

The limo had come to a stop, and the door opened. We craned our heads as Fab and Didier came out the door. Fab advanced on the driver, and whatever she said had Didier laughing and pulling her away.

"You threaten the driver to hand over the keys?" I smirked when she got inside.

Fab shook her head. "This get-together has my father's fingerprints all over it. Wonder if we're flying or boating to the island?"

It didn't take long to get at least one clue, as we soon arrived at the docks where Spoon had his boat parked. We were ready to head down the dock to where Spoon stood waving, a few steps from Caspian's yacht, when the school bus showed up. The kids jumped down the steps and went running to the dock where Spoon was waiting. They all yelled as they got closer and trooped onboard with us behind them. The ride to the island didn't take as long as I thought it would.

We disembarked, the kids running off to explore, and the rest of us hiked up the stairs into the mansion and out to the enormous wraparound patio. None of us showed surprise at seeing Mother seated alongside the Chief and Caspian at the railing, where they could keep an eye on the kids. Caspian flagged us over, and everyone stood, with kisses and handshakes exchanged before we grabbed a seat. A bartender decked out in tropical attire stood ready to take our drink order.

"I'll take a pitcher of martinis, and don't forget a glass full of olives." The way Fab smiled at the man, he'd bring her anything she requested. I didn't miss Didier poking her.

"Make mine a pitcher of margaritas." I waved.

"I'm not going to be left out." Emerson grinned. "Tequila mojito." At the man's raised eyebrows, she said, "Yes, a pitcher."

"You girls better behave," Mother said.

The bartender dude didn't even glance at the guys, as two more came out with a silver cooler filled with an assortment of craft beer and set it on a side table.

Brad chose two, and when the others raised their eyebrows, he said, "I need one for each hand." The rest of us laughed. "Mother," he called down to the other end, "where's my admonition to behave?"

Mother gave him the stink-eye but forgot to cover her grin.

When our drinks arrived, Caspian stood, his glass in hand. "Thank you all for coming, as I thought it would be a great way for us to catch up. As we all know, there's been plenty going on."

"Let's hope everything quiets down," the Chief toasted.

"Have we seen the last of Booker?" I waved my drink, eyeing Caspian the whole time.

"Yeah, have we?" the Chief asked, turning his attention to Caspian.

"If there's a chance he'll turn up..." Creole growled.

"I want to apologize about the first screwup regarding the man." Caspian and the Chief traded raised eyebrows.

"My fault," the Chief told us. "Never thought the man would make bail."

"I put my security team on it, and this Booker fellow has completely disappeared. Odd thing, there's not a single trace of him." Caspian made eye contact with each of us. "As for the Raynes fellow, he also won't be a problem. He knows I have the power to disassemble his business, and he's made it clear he doesn't want any problems."

"If Booker was fed to the wildlife, do you think there's pictures?" I whispered to Fab. Several people heard and tried not to react.

Really, Fab telegraphed.

"Behave. Or try anyway," Creole whispered.

"Any news on the guy that drove his truck into Blackwater Sound?" Didier asked.

All eyes turned to the Chief. "Not a trace." He shrugged.

"That's weird," Fab said. "I wouldn't have bet on him being eaten by anything, but maybe. Would've been nice to know why he wanted to run us off the road."

"I can answer that one," the Chief said. "The truck was stolen, but the driver was ID'd as Roger Dateman, who had a long record of various felonies. He worked for that outfit in Miami. Impressive bust, by the way, and you probably haven't gotten any thanks." He eyed Fab and Casio. "You've got them from me. Without what I'm sure was your relentless poking around, they'd have continued their lucrative business."

Creole stood and turned to me. "I have a surprise for my wife."

"Can't wait. More ashes? Let's not forget about the two bodies that haven't been claimed." A few laughed. "I'll accept your thanks later for not tricking all of you into coming to the group funeral."

"I was one of the guest speakers," Fab said with a grin. Most were skeptical. She stood and repeated her two lines, which had us all laughing.

"I'm putting money on my sister duping you somehow." Brad grinned at Fab.

"You know Madison." She shook her head.

"I admit to being a woman of many talents. Thinking…" I eyed Caspian. "When I'm done orchestrating everything, you can expect to be hearing from me when you least expect it."

"I want in." The Chief waved.

"Hmm…" I tapped my cheek. "That just might work out."

Both men laughed.

"I volunteer to take pictures." Fab laughed.

"What's Creole's surprise?" Mother asked.

He withdrew an envelope from his back pocket and handed it to me. "I snuck around and leased out the warehouse," he announced, proud of himself.

"I was hoping you'd sell," Mother groaned.

"Let me guess, you found some *normal* people?" I opened it, scanned the lease, and laughed. "I like it." I jumped up and threw my arms around his neck.

"It's soon to be a wrestling gym and, in addition, will provide fitness and training for a variety of sports," Creole said.

The men were all in agreement that they liked the idea and thought it would do well in the Cove.

We had an amazing dinner; Caspian's chef outdid himself. Afterward, we moved to chairs at the edge of the deck that faced the water and watched the kids play.

They'd had a cookout on the beach and then ran around until Crum corralled them into the house. They yelled back and forth as they ran up the steps, trying to agree on a movie to watch. It sounded like they'd come to an agreement before they disappeared inside.

As the sun dipped below the horizon, casting a warm, golden hue across the sandy beach, the sound of the waves provided a soothing background. Laughter filled the air as the rest of us shared stories and reminisced about fun times. The evening reminded us all of our bonds of friendship and everything we'd been through together.

~ * ~

About the Author

Deborah Brown is an Amazon bestselling author of the Paradise series. She lives on the Gulf of Mexico, with her ungrateful animals, where Mother Nature takes out her bad attitude in the form of hurricanes.
Hapter

For a free short story, sign up for my newsletter. It will also keep you up-to-date with new releases and special promotions:
www.deborahbrownbooks.com

Follow on FaceBook:
facebook.com/DeborahBrownAuthor

Join private Facebook group:
Deborah Brown's Paradise Fan Club:
facebook.com/groups/1580456012034195

You can contact her at Wildcurls@hotmail.com

Deborah's books are available on Amazon

amazon.com/Deborah-Brown/e/B0059MAIKQ

OTHER TITLES BY DEBORAH BROWN

LAUDERDALE SERIES

In Over Her Head
On The Run
Stealing Hadley
What Happens in Vegas

amzn.to/3Y4w7AL

BISCAYNE BAY SERIES

Hired Killer
Not guilty
Jilted

amazon.com/dp/B09BRFYYYN

PARADISE SERIES

Crazy in Paradise
Deception in Paradise
Trouble in Paradise
Murder in Paradise
Greed in Paradise
Revenge in Paradise
Kidnapped in Paradise
Swindled in Paradise
Executed in Paradise
Hurricane in Paradise
Lottery in Paradise
Ambushed in Paradise
Christmas in Paradise
Blownup in Paradise
Psycho in Paradise
Overdose in Paradise
Initiation in Paradise
Jealous in Paradise
Wronged in Paradise
Vanished in Paradise
Fraud in Paradise
Naïve in Paradise
Bodies in Paradise
Accused in Paradise
Deceit in Paradise
Escaped in Paradise
Fear in Paradise
Theft in Paradise
Retaliation in Paradise
Shark in Paradise
Stolen in Paradise

Available on Amazon
amazon.com/dp/B074CDKKKZ